THE EDGE OF NEVER

Classic and Contemporary Tales
of the Supernatural

THE EDGE OF NEVER

Classic and Contemporary Tales of the Supernatural

Edited by Robert Hoskins

A FAWCETT PREMIER BOOK

Fawcett Publications, Inc., Greenwich, Conn.

THE EDGE OF NEVER: Classic and Contemporary Tales of the Supernatural

A Fawcett Premier Original

Copyright © 1973 by Fawcett Publications, Inc.

Library of Congress Catalog Card Number: 73-76986

Printed in the United States of America
June 1973

The editor and publisher are grateful for permission to reprint the following:

"An Account of Some Strange Disturbances in Aungier Street," by J. Sheridan Le Fanu, originally appeared in *Dublin University Magazine,* Vol. XLII, No. CCLII, December 1853.

"The Rat That Could Speak," by Charles Dickens, originally appeared in *All the Year Around,* Vol. 3, "Nurse's Stories," September 8, 1860.

"An Inhabitant of Carcosa," by Ambrose Bierce, originally appeared in the *San Francisco Examiner,* ca. 1887; first book publication was in *Tales of Soldiers and Civilians,* 1891.

"Lost Hearts," by M. R. James, was first offered as an oral reading by the author, on October 28, 1893. First publication was in *The Pall Mall Magazine,* Vol. VII, No. 32, December 1895.

"The Yellow Sign," by Robert W. Chambers, originally appeared in *The King In Yellow,* 1895.

"The Sealman," by John Masefield, originally appeared in *A Mainsail Haul,* 1905; copyright 1913, 1941 by John Masefield. Reprinted by permission of The Society of Authors, 84 Drayton Gardens, London SW10, England, as literary representatives for the Estate of John Masefield.

"Werewoman," by C. L. Moore, originally appeared in *Leaves,* #2. Reprinted by permission of the author and her agents, Harold Matson Company, Inc.

Contents

THE EDGE OF NEVER

Classic and Contemporary Tales of the Supernatural

The World Beyond

Since the dawn of human intelligence, we have known that man is not alone in the universe. There is too much that we do not, cannot, understand. The universe is a place of great mystery and astonishing marvels, and it seems petty to think that we alone own this great world. There must be other creatures sharing it with us, call them gods, demons, ghosts, fairies—or whatever your imagination can devise.

Imagination, of course, is what separates us from the lower orders; lacking it, our race probably would never have evolved to its present eminence. And imagination can be a very good tool—or a deadly enemy. Imagination can solve the most vexing problems—or send us into paroxysms of terror, if we are facing the hostile unknown. From such latter situations have come the entire body of folklore and myth.

Originally fright was a protective device, a racial instinct intended to keep the too-inquisitive out of potentially dangerous situations. If our imagination peoples the unknown darkness with violent and dangerous creatures, then we are hesitant to venture into a cave where a man-eating tiger may be resting. But as the race evolved, and culture developed to the point where a person could feel relatively safe within his own group, the feeling of terror for the might-be did not wither away. Instead, in many instances, it moved from the survival mechanism of instinct to the area of entertainment. Today the average person may never be placed in a situation where instinct will arouse the ancient feelings—but virtually everyone enjoys the feeling of being scared, whether in the solitary reading of a ghost story or in the company of hundreds of others at a good movie.

The movie is a recent development in the art of story

telling: the story itself is a form that comes down to us from prehistory. The American tradition of supernatural literature first achieved truly wide popularity with the works of Washington Irving (who in turn was borrowing from the folklore of his Dutch forebears). It was not until Edgar Allan Poe that we begin to see in America the creation of a new form of supernatural fiction not deriving primarily from past legends and mythology.

Most of the great nineteenth-century supernaturalists seem to have been English. Outstanding on these shores, after Poe, we can name only Ambrose Bierce and Robert W. Chambers. But with the arrival of the twentieth century, something new was developing in fiction—the pulp magazine that specialized in the fiction of a single genre. The first fantasy magazine in the United States was Street and Smith's *The Thrill Book,* a biweekly venture that lasted only a few months, from 1918 until 1919. It was not until 1923 that a magazine arrived that would last a full thirty years and, in that period, radically change supernatural literature.

The magazine was *Weird Tales;* the first issue was dated March, 1923. From its inception the magazine featured the stories and poetry of a Rhode Island recluse, Howard Phillips Lovecraft, undeniably the greatest influence on the next generation of writers in the field. In love with the sound of words, Lovecraft's prose was so over-written that he seemed interested only with the mood he could create, rather than the story he could tell.

Lovecraft was followed in the pages of *Weird Tales* by such people as August Derleth, Clark Ashton Smith, Seabury Quinn, Robert Bloch, and a myriad more, now nearly forgotten. Many of these writers seized on the mythological world that Lovecraft had created and added to it, embellishing it with characters, legends, and classical allusion to the point that readers began haunting libraries for such nonexistent books as *The Necromanticon.* And in time many of the stories in the magazine reeked of grave mold and crawled with unnamable ancient horrors, until it seemed as though the reader, in simply buying the magazine, had lost his immortal soul.

Edwin Baird was the first editor, succeeded a year later by Farnsworth Wright, who became synonymous with the magazine and the genre. Unfortunately, although the magazine introduced virtually all of the great science-fiction and fantasy writers of the 1920s and 1930s, even bringing fame to such people as Lovecraft, Derleth, and Robert E. Howard, it was never really a commercial success. Rates of payment remained abysmally low, often as little as a quarter of a cent a word. It has been said that Lovecraft never made more than fifteen dollars a week; this is particularly ironic now, when his works have attracted a much broader audience. The royalties now earned by his books in a single year quite possibly exceed his entire lifetime income as a writer.

Weird Tales was sold to the company that published the successful *Short Stories,* an all-genre fiction pulp. Although intended for a male audience, *Short Stories* was edited by a woman, Dorothy McIlwraith, and she took on the additional duties of *Weird Tales.* All through her editorship her name was carried on the masthead as simply D. McIlwraith, an early example of expected male chauvinism.

The change of ownership at first meant little to the readers; Lovecraft and Howard were dead, but most of the other regular contributors kept on working for the new publisher. But changes were coming; gradually the overblown style of writing was changing to a more realistic form. And new writers were coming along, including a youngster named Ray Bradbury, who, for the next half dozen years, would do some of his best work for the magazine. And with the evolution of the entire science-fantasy field, other writers occasionally turned to its pages—writers such as Theodore Sturgeon and Fredric Brown.

The period from 1942 through 1950 may have been the best in the magazine's history.

But a revolution was coming in publishing—spawned in Hollywood, nurtured by the development of the commercially successful paperback book in 1939 and brought to full birth by television. The pulp magazines were dying, and *Weird Tales* was one of the first to go under. At the end there was a brief, desperate attempt to hang on by changing to a digest-sized format, but even that was futile; and it was obvious from the cheapness of the printing in the new size that it could not last. After thirty years the first and greatest of the fantasy magazines was gone. A short time later *Short Stories* too gave up the ghost.

As always in publishing, when a new idea comes along and seems to be commercially successful, a host of imitators is not far behind. There were a number of attempts to cash in on the supernatural bonanza, but most of them lasted no more than a few issues; the economy of the Depression years did not permit the devotee to support more than one magazine, and most of the readers remained loyal to the original. It was not until the Depression was ending that a magazine came along that would meet with a measure of success and at the same time revolutionize fantasy and supernatural literature.

The magazine was *Unknown* (the name was changed to *Unknown Worlds* in 1941 after readers complained of the replies they received from newsdealers when asking for an *Unknown* magazine). The editor was John W. Campbell, Jr. Campbell was already making his mark on science fiction, having just a few months earlier changed the name of his other magazine from *Astounding Stories* to *Astounding Science Fiction*. It has been said that he wanted to drop the adjective altogether, but the publishers were afraid that the public was not yet ready to support a magazine bearing just the simple title of *Science Fiction*. They may have been proven right when a smaller com-

pany brought out just such a title a short time later, only
to have it merged into another, adjectival title a few
issues later.

Unknown printed very few of the *Weird Tales* type of
story—no dripping gore or graveyard denizens. Instead,
the stories presented real people in plausible situations
(granting the fantastic premises on which they were
based). Campbell was the first to use broad humor in his
magazine, but *Unknown* did not neglect the true horror
story. Not at all: Campbell proved that horror is far
more effective when come upon suddenly and unexpectedly, rather than when the entire mood of a story has
been a buildup of terror. The supernatural is most frightening when met in what should be a rational situation.

Many of Campbell's writers turned their hands to *Unknown,* including Theodore Sturgeon, Fritz Leiber, L.
Sprague de Camp, L. Ron Hubbard, and even Robert
Heinlein (whose *They* is one of the most chilling rationali-
zations of paranoia ever written). But though born to
prosperity, it was also born to trouble. It was never as
popular as *Astounding,* and war-time paper rationing killed
the magazine in 1943. At a time when publishers were
selling ninety-eight percent of anything they could grind
out, *Unknown Worlds* was returning copies unsold. After
the war many of the readers begged to have the magazine
revived, but the slow decline of the pulp magazine was
already beginning, and the decision went against it.

Today there are few markets for the supernatural story.
As was the case thirty years earlier, the few magazines
that have appeared invariably have died an early death.
An occasional story appears in the pages of *The Magazine
of Fantasy and Science Fiction,* but there, as in other
markets, the emphasis is on the sister genre.

However, even though the short story form seems to be
in serious trouble, the supernatural novel is making a
strong comeback in popularity. Three of the biggest best-
sellers of the past ten years have been *Rosemary's Baby,*

The Other, and *The Exorcist.* All have already been made into excellent and successful motion pictures. These successes have inspired a search for others in the genre.

Considering the economic vagaries experienced by the two premier magazines in the field, it is probably true that the supernatural field has proven economically successful only in recent years. But even when stories of the genre were difficult to find, there were always those willing to make the effort. As you read through these pages, think a bit: do the ancestral feelings come back to stir your blood, send a chill coursing up and down your spine? Are you willing to spend a night in a haunted house? Or do you whistle your way past the graveyard?

—ROBERT HOSKINS

JOSEPH SHERIDAN Le FANU, (1814–1875), was a Dubliner, a grandnephew of Richard Brinsley Sheridan, the famous eighteenth-century dramatist. Le Fanu first studied for the bar at Trinity College in Dublin, but soon turned to journalism. He was the editor and publisher of several different newspapers and magazines, the most famous of which was the *Dublin University Magazine* (which at that time had no connection with the university). From 1856 to 1869, the period when he was editor, the magazine was one of the leading European periodicals. During his lifetime Le Fanu was a prolific and widely popular author, with fourteen novels to his credit. Of these, *Uncle Silas* is still considered a classic example of the mystery form and is in print today. His greatest fame, however, came as a writer of short stories, including some thirty that explore aspects of the supernatural. No collection of modern supernatural stories can be considered complete without him, and the reader unfamiliar with his other work should seek out his most famous collection, *In a Glass Darkly*.

An Account of Some Strange Disturbances in Aungier Street

J. Sheridan Le Fanu

It is not worth telling, this story of mine—at least, not worth writing. Told, indeed, as I have sometimes been called upon to tell it, to a circle of intelligent and eager faces, lighted up by a good after-dinner fire on a winter's evening, with a cold wind rising and wailing outside, and all snug and cosy within, it has gone off—though I say it, who should not—indifferently well. But it is a venture to do as you would have me. Pen, ink, and paper are cold vehicles for the marvellous, and a "reader" decidedly a more critical animal than a "listener." If, however, you can induce your friends to read it after nightfall, and when the fireside talk has run for a while on thrilling tales of shapeless terror; in short, if you will secure me the *mollia tempora fandi,* I will go to my work, and say my say, with better heart. Well, then, these conditions presupposed, I shall waste no more words, but tell you simply how it all happened.

My cousin (Tom Ludlow) and I studied medicine together. I think he would have succeeded, had he stuck to the profession; but he preferred the church, poor fellow, and died early, a sacrifice to contagion, contracted in the noble discharge of his duties. For my present purpose, I say enough of his character when I mention that he was of a sedate but frank and cheerful nature; very exact in his observance of truth, and not by any means like myself—of an excitable or nervous temperament.

My Uncle Ludlow—Tom's father—while we were attending lectures, purchased three or four old houses in Aungier Street, one of which was unoccupied. *He* resided in the country, and Tom proposed that we should take up our abode in the untenanted house, so long as it should continue unlet; a move which would accomplish the double end of settling us nearer alike to our lecture-rooms and to our amusements, and of relieving us from the weekly charge of rent for our lodgings.

Our furniture was very scant—our whole equipage remarkably modest and primitive; and, in short, our arrangements pretty nearly as simple as those of a bivouac.

Our new plan was, therefore, executed almost as soon as conceived. The front drawing room was our sitting room. I had the bedroom over it, and Tom the back bedroom on the same floor, which nothing could have induced me to occupy.

The house, to begin with, was a very old one. It had been, I believe, newly fronted about fifty years before; but with this exception, it had nothing modern about it. The agent who bought it and looked into the titles for my uncle, told me that it was sold, along with much other forfeited property, at Chichester House, I think, in 1702; and had belonged to Sir Thomas Hacket, who was Lord Mayor of Dublin in James II's time. How old it was *then*, I can't say; but, at all events, it had seen years and changes enough to have contracted all that mysterious and saddened air, at once exciting and depressing, which belongs to most old mansions.

There had been very little done in the way of modernising details; and, perhaps, it was better so; for there was something queer and by-gone in the very walls and ceilings —in the shape of doors and windows—in the odd diagonal site of the chimney-pieces—in the beams and ponderous cornices—not to mention the singular solidity of all the woodwork, from the banisters to the window frames, which hopelessly defied disguise, and would have emphatically proclaimed their antiquity through any conceivable amount of modern finery and varnish.

An effort had, indeed, been made, to the extent of papering the drawing rooms; but somehow, the paper looked raw and out of keeping; and the old woman, who kept a little dirt-pie of a shop in the lane, and whose daughter—a girl of two and fifty—was our solitary handmaid, coming in at sunrise, and chastely receding again as soon as she had made all ready for tea in our state apartment—this woman, I say, remembered it, when old Judge Horrocks (who, having earned the reputation of a particularly "hanging judge," ended by hanging himself, as the coroner's jury found, under an impulse of "temporary insanity," with a child's skipping rope, over the massive old banisters) resided there, entertaining good company, with fine venison and rare old port. In those halcyon days, the drawing rooms were hung with gilded leather, and, I dare say, cut a good figure, for they were really spacious rooms.

The bedrooms were wainscoted, but the front one was not gloomy; and in it the cosiness of antiquity quite overcame its sombre associations. But the back bedroom, with its two queerly placed melancholy windows staring vacantly at the foot of the bed, and with the shadowy recess to be found in most old houses in Dublin, like a large ghostly closet, which, from congeniality of temperament, had amalgamated with the bedchamber, and dissolved the partition. At nighttime, this "alcove"—as our "maid" was wont to call it—had, in my eyes, a specially sinister and suggestive character. Tom's distant and solitary candle glimmered vainly into its darkness. *There* it was always overlooking him—always itself impenetrable. But this was only part of the effect. The whole room was, I can't tell how, repulsive to me. There was, I suppose, in its proportions and features, a latent discord—a certain mysterious and indescribable relation, which jarred indistinctly upon some secret sense of the fitting and the safe, and raised indefinable suspicions and apprehensions of the imagination. On the whole, as I began by saying, nothing could have induced me to pass a night alone in it.

I had never pretended to conceal from poor Tom my superstitious weakness; and he, on the other hand, most unaffectedly ridiculed my tremors. The sceptic was, however, destined to receive a lesson, as you shall hear.

We had not been very long in occupation of our respective dormitories, when I began to complain of uneasy nights and disturbed sleep. I was, I suppose, the more impatient under this annoyance, as I was usually a sound sleeper, and by no means prone to nightmares. It was now, however, my destiny, instead of enjoying my customary repose, every night to "sup full of horrors." After a preliminary course of disagreeable and frightful dreams, my troubles took a definite form, and the same vision, without an appreciable variation in a single detail, visited me at least (on an average) every second night in the week.

Now, this dream, nightmare, or infernal illusion—whichever you please—of which I was the miserable sport, was on this wise:

I saw, or thought I saw, with the most abominable distinctness, although at the time in profound darkness, every article of furniture and accidental arrangement of the chamber in which I lay. This, as you know, is incidental to ordinary nightmare. Well, while in this clairvoyant condition, which seemed but the lighting up of the theatre in which was to be exhibited the monotonous tableau of horror, which made my nights insupportable, my attention invariably became, I know not why, fixed upon the windows opposite the foot of my bed; and, uniformly with the same effect, a sense of dreadful anticipation always took slow but sure possession of me. I became somehow conscious of a sort of horrid but undefined preparation going forward in some unknown quarter, and by some unknown agency, for my torment; and, after an interval, which always seemed to me of the same length, a picture suddenly flew up to the window, where it remained fixed, as if by an electrical attraction, and my discipline of horror then commenced, to last perhaps for hours. The picture thus mysteriously glued to the window-panes, was the portrait of an old man, in a crimson, flowered silk dressing gown, the folds of which I could now describe, with a countenance embodying a strange mixture of intellect, sensuality, and power, but withal sinister and full of malignant omen. His nose was hooked, like the beak of a vulture; his eyes large, grey, and prominent, and lighted up with a more than mortal cruelty and coldness. These features were surmounted by a crimson

velvet cap, the hair that peeped from under which was
white with age, while the eyebrows retained their original
blackness. Well I remember every line, hue, and shadow
of that stony countenance, and well I may! The gaze of
this hellish visage was fixed upon me, and mine returned
it with the inexplicable fascination of nightmare, for what
appeared to me to be hours of agony. At last—

The cock he crew, away then flew

the fiend who had enslaved me through the awful watches
of the night; and, harassed and nervous, I rose to the
duties of the day.

I had—I can't say exactly why, but it may have been
from the exquisite anguish and profound impressions of
unearthly horror, with which this strange phantasmagoria
was associated—an insurmountable antipathy to describing the exact nature of my nightly troubles to my friend
and comrade. Generally, however, I told him that I was
haunted by abominable dreams; and, true to the imputed
materialism of medicine, we put our heads together to
dispel my horrors, not by exorcism, but by a tonic.

I will do this tonic justice, and frankly admit that the
accursed portrait began to intermit its visits under its influence. What of that? Was this singular apparition—as
full of character as of terror—therefore the creature of my
fancy, or the invention of my poor stomach? Was it, in
short, *subjective* (to borrow the technical slang of the
day) and not the palpable aggression and intrusion of an
external agent? That, good friend, as we will both admit,
by no means follows. The evil spirit, who enthralled my
senses in the shape of that portrait, may have been just as
near me, just as energetic, just as malignant, though I saw
him not. What means the whole moral code of revealed
religion regarding the due keeping of our own bodies,
soberness, temperance, etc.? Here is an obvious connection between the material and the invisible; the healthy

tone of the system, and its unimpaired energy, may, for aught we can tell, guard us against influences which would otherwise render life itself terrific. The mesmerist and the electro-biologist will fail upon an average with nine patients out of ten—so may the evil spirit. Special conditions of the corporeal system are indispensable to the production of certain spiritual phenomena. The operation succeeds sometimes—sometimes fails—that is all.

I found afterwards that my would-be sceptical companion had his troubles too. But of these I knew nothing yet. One night, for a wonder, I was sleeping soundly, when I was roused by a step on the lobby outside my room, followed by the loud clang of what turned out to be a large brass candlestick, flung with all his force by poor Tom Ludlow over the banisters, and rattling with a rebound down the second flight of stairs; and almost concurrently with this, Tom burst open my door, and bounced into my room backwards, in a state of extraordinary agitation.

I had jumped out of bed and clutched him by the arm before I had any distinct idea of my own whereabouts. There we were—in our shirts—standing before the open door—staring through the great old banister opposite, at the lobby window, through which the sickly sight of a clouded moon was gleaming.

"What's the matter, Tom? What's the matter with you? What the devil's the matter with you, Tom?" I demanded shaking him with nervous impatience.

He took a long breath before he answered me, and then it was not very coherently.

"It's nothing, nothing at all—did I speak?—what did I say?—where's the candle, Richard? It's dark; I—I had a candle!"

"Yes, dark enough," I said; "but what's the matter?—what *is* it?—why don't you speak, Tom?—have you lost your wits?—what is the matter?"

"The matter?—oh, it is all over. It must have been a

dream—nothing at all but a dream—don't you think so?
It could not be anything more than a dream."

"Of *course,*" said I, feeling uncommonly nervous, "it
was a dream."

"I thought," he said, "there was a man in my room, and
—and I jumped out of bed; and—and—where's the
candle?"

"In your room, most likely," I said, "shall I go and
bring it?"

"No; stay here—don't go; it's no matter—don't, I tell
you; it was all a dream. Bolt the door, Dick; I'll stay here
with you—I feel nervous. So, Dick, like a good fellow,
light your candle and open the window—I am in a
shocking state."

I did as he asked me, and robing himself like Granuaile
in one of my blankets, he seated himself close beside my
bed.

Everybody knows how contagious is fear of all sorts, but
more especially that particular kind of fear under which
poor Tom was at that moment labouring. I would not
have heard, nor I believe would he have recapitulated,
just at that moment, for half the world, the details of the
hideous vision which had so unmanned him.

"Don't mind telling me anything about your nonsensical
dream, Tom," said I, affecting contempt, really in a panic;
"let us talk about something else; but it is quite plain that
this dirty old house disagrees with us both, and hang me
if I stay here any longer, to be pestered with indigestion
and—and—bad nights, so we may as well look out for
lodgings—don't you think so?—at once."

Tom agreed, and, after an interval, said, "I have been
thinking, Richard, that it is a long time since I saw my
father, and I have made up my mind to go down tomorrow
and return in a day or two, and you can take rooms for
us in the meantime."

I fancied that this resolution, obviously the result of the
vision which had so profoundly scared him, would prob-

ably vanish next morning with the damps and shadows of night. But I was mistaken. Off went Tom at peep of day to the country, having agreed that so soon as I had secured suitable lodgings, I was to recall him by letter from his visit to my Uncle Ludlow.

Now, anxious as I was to change my quarters, it so happened, owing to a series of petty procrastinations and accidents, that nearly a week elapsed before my bargain was made and my letter of recall on the wing to Tom; and, in the meantime, a trifling adventure or two had occurred to your humble servant, which, absurd as they now appear, diminished by distance, did certainly at the time serve to whet my appetite for change considerably.

A night or two after the departure of my comrade, I was sitting by my bedroom fire, the door locked, and the ingredients of a tumbler of hot whisky-punch upon the crazy spider table; for, as the best mode of keeping the

> Black spirits and white,
> Blue spirits and grey,

with which I was environed, at bay, I had adopted the practice recommended by the wisdom of my ancestors, and "kept my spirits up by pouring spirits down." I had thrown aside my volume of anatomy, and was treating myself by way of a tonic, preparatory to my punch and bed, to half-a-dozen pages of the *Spectator,* when I heard a step on the flight of stairs descending from the attic. It was two o'clock, and the streets were as silent as a churchyard—the sounds were, therefore, perfectly distinct. There was a slow, heavy tread, characterised by the emphasis and deliberation of age, descending by the narrow staircase from above; and, what made the sound more singular, it was plain that the feet which produced it were perfectly bare, measuring the descent with something between a pound and a flop, very ugly to hear.

I knew quite well that my attendant had gone away

many hours before, and that nobody but myself had any business in the house. It was quite plain also that the person who was coming downstairs had no intention whatever of concealing his movements; but, on the contrary, appeared disposed to make even more noise, and proceed more deliberately, than was at all necessary. When the step reached the foot of the stairs outside my room, it seemed to stop; and I expected every moment to see my door open spontaneously, and give admission to the original of my detested portrait. I was, however, relieved in a few seconds by hearing the descent renewed, just in the same manner, upon the staircase leading down to the drawing rooms, and thence, after another pause, down the next flight, and so on to the hall, whence I heard no more.

Now, by the time the sound had ceased, I was wound up, as they say, to a very unpleasant pitch of excitement. I listened, but there was not a stir. I screwed up my courage to a decisive experiment—opened my door, and in a stentorian voice bawled over the banisters, "Who's there?" There was no answer but the ringing of my own voice through the empty old house—no renewal of the movement; nothing, in short, to give my unpleasant sensations a definite direction. There is, I think, something most disagreeably disenchanting in the sound of one's own voice under such circumstances, exerted in solitude, and in vain. It redoubled my sense of isolation, and my misgivings increased on perceiving that the door, which I certainly thought I had left open, was closed behind me; in a vague alarm, lest my retreat should be cut off, I got again into my room as quickly as I could, where I remained in a state of imaginary blockade, and very uncomfortable indeed, till morning.

Next night brought no return of my barefooted fellow lodger; but the night following, being in my bed, and in the dark—somewhere, I suppose, about the same hour as before, I distinctly heard the old fellow again descending from the garrets.

This time I had had my punch, and the *morale* of the garrison was consequently excellent. I jumped out of bed, clutched the poker as I passed the expiring fire, and in a moment was upon the lobby. The sound had ceased by this time—the dark and chill were discouraging; and, guess my horror, when I saw, or thought I saw, a black monster, whether in the shape of a man or a bear I could not say, standing, with its back to the wall, on the lobby, facing me, with a pair of great greenish eyes shining dimly out. Now, I must be frank, and confess that the cupboard which displayed our plates and cups stood just there, though at the moment I did not recollect it. At the same time I must honestly say, that making every allowance for an excited imagination, I never could satisfy myself that I was made the dupe of my own fancy in this matter; for this apparition, after one or two shiftings of shape, as if in the act of incipient transformation, began, as it seemed on second thoughts, to advance upon me in its original form. From an instinct of terror rather than of courage, I hurled the poker, with all my force, at its head; and to the music of a horrid crash made my way into my room, and double-locked the door. Then, in a minute more, I heard the horrid bare feet walk down the stairs, till the sound ceased in the hall, as on the former occasion.

If the apparition of the night before was an ocular delusion of my fancy sporting with the dark outlines of our cupboard, and if its horrid eyes were nothing but a pair of inverted teacups, I had, at all events, the satisfaction of having launched the poker with admirable effect, and in true "fancy" phrase, "knocked its two daylights into one," as the commingled fragments of my tea service testified. I did my best to gather comfort and courage from these evidences; but it would not do. And then what could I say of those horrid bare feet, and the regular tramp, tramp, tramp, which measured the distance of the entire staircase through the solitude of my haunted dwelling, and at an hour when no good influence was stirring? Confound it!—the whole affair was abominable. I was out of spirits, and dreaded the approach of night.

It came, ushered ominously in with a thunder storm and dull torrents of depressing rain. Earlier than usual the streets grew silent; and by twelve o'clock nothing but the comfortless pattering of the rain was to be heard.

I made myself as snug as I could. I lighted *two* candles instead of one. I forswore bed, and held myself in readiness for a sally, candle in hand; for, *coûte qui coûte,* I was resolved to *see* the being, if visible at all, who troubled the nightly stillness of my mansion. I was fidgety and nervous and tried in vain to interest myself with my books. I walked up and down my room, whistling in turn martial and hilarious music, and listening ever and anon for the dreaded noise. I sat down and stared at the square label on the solemn and reserved-looking black bottle, until "FLANAGAN & CO'S BEST OLD MALT WHISKY" grew into a sort of subdued accompaniment to all the fantastic and horrible speculations which chased one another through my brain.

Silence, meanwhile, grew more silent, and darkness darker. I listened in vain for the rumble of a vehicle, or the dull clamour of a distant row. There was nothing but the sound of a rising wind, which had succeeded the thunder storm that had travelled over the Dublin mountains quite out of hearing. In the middle of this great city I began to feel myself alone with nature, and Heaven knows what beside. My courage was ebbing. Punch, however, which makes beasts of so many, made a man of me again—just in time to hear with tolerable nerve and firmness the lumpy, flabby, naked feet deliberately descending the stairs again.

I took a candle, not without a tremour. As I crossed the floor I tried to extemporise a prayer, but stopped short to listen, and never finished it. The steps continued. I confess

I hesitated for some seconds at the door before I took heart of grace and opened it. When I peeped out the lobby was perfectly empty—there was no monster standing on the staircase; and as the detested sound ceased, I was reassured enough to venture forward nearly to the banisters. Horror of horrors! within a stair or two beneath the spot where I stood the unearthly tread smote the floor. My eye caught something in motion; it was about the size of Goliath's foot—it was grey, heavy, and flapped with a dead weight from one step to another. As I am alive, it was the most monstrous grey rat I ever beheld or imagined.

Shakespeare says—"Some men there are cannot abide a gaping pig, and some that are mad if they behold a cat." I went well-nigh out of my wits when I beheld this *rat;* for, laugh at me as you may, it fixed upon me, I thought, a perfectly human expression of malice; and, as it shuffled about and looked up into my face almost from between my feet, I saw, I could swear it—I felt it then, and know it now, the infernal gaze and the accursed countenance of my old friend in the portrait, transfused into the visage of the bloated vermin before me.

I bounced into my room again with a feeling of loathing and horror I cannot describe, and locked and bolted my door as if a lion had been at the other side. Damn him or *it;* curse the portrait and its original! I felt in my soul that the rat—yes, the *rat,* the RAT I had just seen—was that evil being in masquerade, and rambling through the house upon some infernal night lark.

Next morning I was early trudging through the miry streets; and, among other transactions, posted a peremptory note recalling Tom. On my return, however, I found a note from my absent "chum," announcing his intended return next day. I was doubly rejoiced at this, because I had succeeded in getting rooms; and because the change of scene and return of my comrade were rendered specially pleasant by the last night's half-ridiculous, half-horrible adventure.

I slept extemporaneously in my new quarters in Digges' Street that night, and next morning returned for breakfast to the haunted mansion, where I was certain Tom would call immediately on his arrival.

I was quite right—he came; and almost his first question referred to the primary object of our change of residence.

"Thank God," he said with genuine fervour, on hearing that all was arranged. "On *your* account I am delighted. As to myself, I assure you that no earthly consideration could have induced me ever again to pass a night in this disastrous old house."

"Confound the house!" I ejaculated, with a genuine mixture of fear and detestation. "We have not had a pleasant hour since we came to live here"; and so I went on, and related incidentally my adventure with the plethoric old rat.

"Well, if that were *all,*" said my cousin, affecting to make light of the matter, "I don't think I should have minded it very much."

"Ay, but its eye—its countenance, my dear Tom," urged I; "if you had seen *that,* you would have felt it might be *anything* but what it seemed."

"I incline to think the best conjurer in such a case would be an able-bodied rat," he said, with a provoking chuckle.

"But let us hear your own adventure," I said tartly.

At this challenge he looked uneasily round him. I had poked up a very unpleasant recollection.

"You shall hear it, Dick; I'll tell it to you," he said. "Begad, sir, I should feel quite queer, though, telling it *here,* though we are too strong a body for ghosts to meddle with just now."

Though he spoke this like a joke, I think it was serious calculation. Our Hebe was in a corner of the room, packing our cracked delft tea and dinner service in a basket. She soon suspended operations, and with mouth and eyes wide open became an absorbed listener. Tom's experiences were told nearly in these words:

"I saw it three times, Dick—three distinct times; and I am perfectly certain it meant me some infernal harm. I was, I say, in danger—in *extreme* danger; for, if nothing else had happened, my reason would most certainly have failed me, unless I had escaped so soon. Thank God, I *did* escape.

"The first night of this hateful disturbance, I was lying in the attitude of sleep, in that lumbering old bed. I hate to think of it. I was really wide awake, though I had put out my candle, and was lying as quietly as if I had been asleep; and although accidentally restless, my thoughts were running in a cheerful and agreeable channel.

"I think it must have been two o'clock at least when I thought I heard a sound in that—that odious dark recess at the far end of the bedroom. It was as if someone was drawing a piece of cord slowly along the floor, lifting it up, and dropping it softly down again in coils. I sat up once or twice in my bed, but I could see nothing, so I concluded it must be mice in the wainscot. I felt no emotion graver than curiosity, and after a few minutes ceased to observe it.

"While lying in this state, strange to say; without at first a suspicion of anything supernatural, on a sudden I saw an old man, rather stout and square, in a sort of roan-red dressing gown, and with a black cap on his head, moving stiffly and slowly in a diagonal direction, from the recess, across the floor of the bedroom, passing my bed at the foot, and entering the lumber closet at the left. He had something under his arm; his head hung a little at one side; and, merciful God! when I saw his face."

Tom stopped for a while, and then said—

"That awful countenance, which living or dying I never can forget, disclosed what he was. Without turning to the right or left, he passed beside me, and entered the closet by the bed's head.

"While this fearful and indescribable type of death and guilt was passing, I felt that I had no more power to speak or stir than if I had been myself a corpse. For hours after it had disappeared, I was too terrified and weak to move. As soon as daylight came, I took courage, and examined the room, and especially the course which the frightful intruder had seemed to take, but there was not a vestige to indicate anybody's having passed there; no sign of any disturbing agency visible among the lumber that strewed the floor of the closet.

"I now began to recover a little. I was fagged and exhausted, and at last, overpowered by a feverish sleep. I came down late; and finding you out of spirits, on account of your dreams about the portrait, whose *original* I am now certain disclosed himself to me, I did not care to talk about the infernal vision. In fact, I was trying to persuade myself that the whole thing was an illusion, and I did not like to revive in their intensity the hated impressions of the past night—or to risk the constancy of my scepticism, by recounting the tale of my sufferings.

"It required some nerve, I can tell you, to go to my haunted chamber next night, and lie down quietly in the same bed," continued Tom. "I did so with a degree of trepidation, which, I am not ashamed to say, a very little matter would have sufficed to stimulate to downright panic. This night, however, passed off quietly enough, as also the next; and so too did two or three more. I grew more confident, and began to fancy that I believed in the theories of spectral illusions, with which I had at first vainly tried to impose upon my convictions.

"The apparition had been, indeed, altogether anomalous. It had crossed the room without any recognition of my presence: I had not disturbed *it*, and *it* had no mission to *me*. What, then, was the imaginable use of its crossing the room in a visible shape at all? Of course, it might have *been* in the closet instead of *going* there, as easily as it introduced itself into the recess without entering the chamber in a shape discernible by the senses. Besides, how the deuce *had* I seen it? It was a dark night; I had no candle; there was no fire; and yet I saw it as distinctly, in colouring and outline, as ever I beheld human form! A cataleptic dream would explain it all; and I was determined that a dream it should be.

"One of the most remarkable phenomena connected with the practice of mendacity is the vast number of deliberate lies we tell ourselves, whom, of all persons, we can least expect to deceive. In all this, I need hardly tell you, Dick, I was simply lying to myself, and did not believe one word of the wretched humbug. Yet I went on, as men will do, like persevering charlatans and impostors, who tire people into credulity by the mere force of reiteration; so I hoped to win myself over at last to a comfortable scepticism about the ghost.

"He had not appeared a second time—that certainly was a comfort; and what, after all, did I care for him, and his queer old toggery and strange looks? Not a fig! I was nothing the worse for having seen him, and a good story the better. So I tumbled into bed, put out my candle, and, cheered by a loud drunken quarrel in the back lane, went fast asleep.

"From this deep slumber I awoke with a start. I knew I had had a horrible dream; but what it was I could not remember. My heart was thumping furiously; I felt bewildered and feverish; I sat up in the bed and looked about the room. A broad flood of moonlight came in through the curtainless window; everything was as I had last seen it; and though the domestic squabble in the back lane was, unhappily for me, allayed, I yet could hear a pleasant fellow singing, on his way home, the popular comic ditty called, 'Murphy Delany.' Taking advantage of this diversion I lay down again, with my face towards the fireplace, and closing my eyes, did my best to think of nothing else but the song, which was every moment growing fainter in the distance:

> 'Twas Murphy Delany, so funny and frisky,
>   Stept into a shebeen shop to get his skin full;
> He reeled out again pretty well lined with whiskey,
>   As fresh as a shamrock, as blind as a bull.

"The singer, whose condition I dare say resembled that of his hero, was soon too far off to regale my ears any more; and as his music died away, I myself sank into a doze, neither sound nor refreshing. Somehow the song had got into my head, and I went meandering on through the adventures of my respectable fellow countryman, who, on emerging from the 'shebeen shop,' fell into a river, from which he was fished up to be 'sat upon' by a coroner's jury, who having learned from a 'horse doctor' that he was 'dead as a door nail, so there was an end,' returned their verdict accordingly, just as he returned to his senses, when an angry altercation and a pitched battle between the body and the coroner winds up the lay with due spirit and pleasantry.

"Through this ballad I continued with a weary monotony to plod, down to the very last line, and then *da capo,* and so on, in my uncomfortable half-sleep, for how long, I can't conjecture. I found myelf at last, however, muttering, *'dead* as a door nail, so there was an end'; and something like another voice within me, seemed to say, very faintly, but sharply, 'Dead! dead! *dead!* and may the Lord have mercy on your soul!' And instantaneously I was wide awake, and staring right before me from the pillow.

"Now—will you believe it, Dick?—I saw the same accursed figure standing full front, and gazing at me with its stony and fiendish countenance, not two yards from the bedside."

Tom stopped here, and wiped the perspiration from his face. I felt very queer. The girl was as pale as Tom; and, assembled as we were in the very scene of these adventures, we were all, I dare say, equally grateful for the clear daylight and the resuming bustle out of doors.

"For about three seconds only I saw it plainly; then it grew indistinct; but, for a long time, there was something like a column of dark vapour where it had been standing, between me and the wall; and I felt sure that he was still there. After a good while, this appearance went too. I took my clothes downstairs to the hall, and dressed there, with the door half open; then went out into the street, and walked about the town till morning, when I came back, in a miserable state of nervousness and exhaustion. I was such a fool, Dick, as to be ashamed to tell you how I came to be so upset. I thought you would laugh at me; especially as I had always talked philosophy, and treated *your* ghosts with contempt. I concluded you would give me no quarter; and so kept my tale of horror to myself.

"Now, Dick, you will hardly believe me, when I assure you, that for many nights after this last experience, I did not go to my room at all. I used to sit up for a while in the drawing room after you had gone up to your bed; and then steal down softly to the hall-door, let myself out, and sit in the Robin Hood tavern until the last guest went off; and then I got through the night like a sentry, pacing the streets till morning.

"For more than a week I never slept in a bed. I sometimes had a snooze on a form in the Robin Hood, and sometimes a nap in a chair during the day; but regular sleep I had absolutely none.

"I was quite resolved that we should get into another house; but I could not bring myself to tell you the reason, and I somehow put it off from day to day, although my life was, during every hour of this procrastination, rendered as miserable as that of a felon with the constables on his track. I was growing absolutely ill from this wretched mode of life.

"One afternoon I determined to enjoy an hour's sleep upon your bed. I hated mine; so that I had never, except in a stealthy visit every day to unmake it, lest Martha should discover the secret of my nightly absence, entered the ill-omened chamber.

"As ill-luck would have it, you had locked your bedroom, and taken away the key. I went into my own to unsettle the bedclothes, as usual, and give the bed the appearance of having been slept in. Now, a variety of circumstances concurred to bring about the dreadful scene through which I was that night to pass. In the first place, I was literally overpowered with fatigue, and longing for sleep; in the next place, the effect of this extreme exhaustion upon my nerves resembled that of a narcotic, and rendered me less susceptible than, perhaps, I should in any other condition have been, of the exciting fears which had become habitual to me. Then again, a little bit of the window was open, a pleasant freshness pervaded the room, and, to crown all, the cheerful sun of day was making the room quite pleasant. What was to prevent my enjoying an hour's nap *here?* The whole air was resonant with the cheerful hum of life, and the broad matter-of-fact light of day filled every corner of the room.

"I yielded—stifling my qualms—to the almost overpowering temptation; and merely throwing off my coat, and loosening my cravat, I lay down, limiting myself to *half*-an-hour's doze in the unwonted enjoyment of a feather bed, a coverlet, and a bolster.

"It was horribly insidious; and the demon, no doubt, marked my infatuated preparations. Dolt that I was, I fancied, with mind and body worn out for want of sleep, and an arrear of a full week's rest to my credit, that such measure as *half*-an-hour's sleep, in such a situation, was possible. My sleep was deathlike, long, and dreamless.

"Without a start or fearful sensation of any kind, I waked gently, but completely. It was, as you have good reason to remember, long past midnight—I believe, about two o'clock. When sleep has been deep and long enough to satisfy nature thoroughly, one often wakens in this way, suddenly, tranquilly, and completely.

"There was a figure seated in that lumbering, old sofa chair, near the fireplace. Its back was rather towards me, but I could not be mistaken; it turned slowly round, and, merciful heavens! There was the stony face, with its infernal lineaments of malignity and despair, gloating on me. There was now no doubt as to its consciousness of my presence, and the hellish malice with which it was animated, for it arose, and drew closer to the bedside. There was a rope about its neck, and the other end, coiled up, it held stiffly in its hand.

"My good angel nerved me for this horrible crisis. I remained for some seconds transfixed by the gaze of this tremendous phantom. He came close to the bed, and appeared on the point of mounting upon it. The next instant I was upon the floor at the far side, and in a moment more was, I don't know how, in the lobby.

"But the spell was not yet broken; the valley of the shadow of death was not yet traversed. The abhorred phantom was before me there; it was standing near the banisters, stooping a little, and with one end of the rope round its own neck, was poising a noose at the other, as if to throw over mine; and while engaged in this baleful pantomime, it wore a smile so sensual, so unspeakably dreadful, that my senses were nearly overpowered. I saw and remember nothing more, until I found myself in your room.

"I had a wonderful escape, Dick—there is no disputing *that*—an escape for which, while I live, I shall bless the mercy of heaven. No one can conceive or imagine what it is for flesh and blood to stand in the presence of such a thing, but one who has had the terrific experience. Dick, Dick, a shadow has passed over me—a chill has crossed my blood and marrow, and I will never be the same again —never, Dick—never!"

Our handmaid, a mature girl of two and fifty, as I have

said, stayed her hand, as Tom's story proceeded, and by little and little drew near to us, with open mouth, and her brows contracted over her little, beady black eyes, till stealing a glance over her shoulder now and then, she established herself close behind us. During the relation, she made various earnest comments, in an undertone; but these and her ejaculations, for the sake of brevity and simplicity, I have omitted in my narration.

"It's often I heard tell of it," she now said, "but I never believed it rightly till now—though, indeed, why should not I? Does not my mother, down there in the lane, know quare stories, God bless us, beyant telling about it? But you ought not to have slept in the back bedroom. She was loath to let me be going in and out of that room even in the day time, let alone for any Christian to spend the night in it; for sure she says it was his own bedroom."

"Whose own bedroom?" we asked, in a breath.

"Why, *his*—the ould Judge's—Judge Horrock's, to be sure. God rest his sowl"; and she looked fearfully round.

"Amen!" I muttered. "But did he die there?"

"Die there! No, not quite *there,"* she said. "Shure, was not it over the banisters he hung himself, the ould sinner, God be merciful to us all? And was not it in the alcove they found the handles of the skipping rope cut off, and the knife where he was settling the cord, God bless us, to hang himself with? It was his housekeeper's daughter owned the rope, my mother often told me, and the child never throve after, and used to be starting up out of her sleep, and screeching in the night time, wid dhrames and frights that cum an her; and they said how it was the speerit of the ould Judge that was tormentin' her; and she used to be roaring and yelling out to hould back the big ould fellow with the crooked neck; and then she'd screech 'Oh, the master! the master! he's stampin' at me, and beckoning to me! Mother, darling, don't let me go!' And so the poor crathure died at last, and the docthers said it was wather on the brain, for it was all they could say."

"How long ago was all this?" I asked.

"Oh, then, how would I know?" she answered. "But it must be a wondherful long time ago, for the housekeeper was an ould woman, with a pipe in her mouth, and not a tooth left, and better nor eighty years ould when my mother was first married; and they said she was a rale buxom, fine-dressed woman when the ould Judge come to his end; an', indeed, my mother's not far from eighty years ould herself this day; and what made it worse for the unnatural ould villain, God rest his soul, to frighten the little girl out of the world the way he did, was what was mostly thought and believed by every one. My mother says how the poor little crathure was his own child; for he was by all accounts an ould villain every way, an' the hangin'est judge that ever was known in Ireland's ground."

"From what you said about the danger of sleeping in that bedroom," said I, "I suppose there were stories about the ghost having appeared there to others."

"Well, there *was* things said—quare things, surely," she answered, as it seemed, with some reluctance. "And why would not there? Sure was it not up in that same room he slept for more than twenty years? And was it not in the *alcove* he got the rope ready that done his own business at last, the way he done many a betther man's in his lifetime?—and was not the body lying in the same bed after death, and put in the coffin there, too, and carried out to his grave from it in Pether's churchyard, after the coroner was done? But there was quare stories— my mother has them all—about how one Nicholas Spaight got into trouble on the head of it."

"And what did they say of this Nicholas Spaight?" I asked.

"Oh, for that matter, it's soon told," she answered.

And she certainly did relate a very strange story, which so piqued my curiosity, that I took occasion to visit the ancient lady, her mother, from whom I learned many very curious particulars. Indeed, I am tempted to tell the tale, but my fingers are weary, and I must defer it. But if you wish to hear it another time, I shall do my best.

When we had heard the strange tale I have *not* told you, we put one or two further questions to her about the alleged spectral visitations, to which the house had, ever since the death of the wicked old Judge, been subjected.

"No one ever had luck in it," she told us. "There was always cross accidents, sudden deaths, and short times in it. The first that tuck it was a family—I forget their name —but at any rate there was two young ladies and their papa. He was about sixty, and a stout healthy gentleman as you'd wish to see at that age. Well, he slept in that unlucky back bedroom; and—God between us an' harm! —sure enough he was found dead one morning, half out of the bed, with his head as black as a sloe, and swelled like a puddin', hanging down near the floor. It was a fit, they said. He was as dead as a mackerel, and so *he* could not say what it was; but the ould people was all sure that it was nothing at all but the ould Judge—God bless us!— that frightened him out of his senses and his life together.

"Some time after there was a rich old maiden lady took the house. I don't know which room *she* slept in, but she lived alone; and at any rate, one morning, the servants going down early to their work, found her sitting on the passage stairs, shivering and talkin' to herself, quite mad; and never a word more could any of *them* or her friends get from her afterwards but, 'Don't ask me to go, for I promised to wait for him.' They never made out from her who it was she meant by *him*, but, of course, those that knew all about the ould house were at no loss for the meaning of all that happened to her.

"Then afterwards, when the house was let out in lodgings, there was Micky Byrne that took the same room, with his wife and three little children; and sure I heard Mrs. Byrne myself telling how the children used to be lifted up in the bed at night, she could not see by what mains; and how they were starting and screeching every hour, just all as one as the housekeeper's little girl that died, till at last one night poor Micky had a dhrop in him, the way he used now and again; and what do you think? In the middle of the night he thought he heard a noise on the stairs, and being in liquor, nothing less id do him but out he must go himself to see what was wrong. Well, after that, all she ever heard of him was himself sayin', 'Oh, God!' and a rumble that shook the very house; and there, sure enough, he was lying on the lower stairs, under the lobby, with his neck smashed double undher him, where he was flung over the banisters."

Then the handmaiden added:

"I'll go down to the lane, and send up Joe Gavvey to pack up the rest of the taythings, and bring all the things across to your new lodgings."

And so we all sallied out together, each of us breathing more freely, I have no doubt, as we crossed that ill-omened threshold for the last time.

Now, I may add thus much, in compliance with the immemorial usage of the realm of fiction, which sees the hero not only through his adventures, but fairly out of the world. You must have perceived that what the flesh, blood, and bone hero of romance proper is to the regular compounder of fiction, this old house of brick, wood, and mortar is to the humble recorder of this true tale. I, therefore, relate, as in duty bound, the catastrophe which ultimately befell it, which was simply this—that about two years subsequently to my story it was taken by a quack doctor, who called himself Baron Duhlstoerf, and filled the parlour windows with bottles of indescribable horrors preserved in brandy, and the newspapers with the usual grandiloquent and mendacious advertisements. This gentleman among his virtues did not reckon sobriety, and one night, being overcome with much wine, he set fire to his bed curtains, partially burned himself, and totally consumed the house. It was afterwards rebuilt, and for a time an undertaker established himself in the premises.

I have now told you my own and Tom's adventures, together with some valuable collateral particulars; and having acquitted myself of my engagement, I wish you a very good night, and pleasant dreams.

CHARLES DICKENS, (1812–1870), was very much at
home in the world of the supernatural, visiting there most
frequently in his Christmas stories (including *A Christmas
Carol)*. Many of his allegories fall into the supernatural
area. Less well-known to the general reader are a number
of his shorter pieces, the distillation of stories told to him
by his nurse half a century earlier. These appeared in his
own magazine, *All the Year Round,* starting in 1860, and
have been collected as Chapter XV, "Nurse's Stories," of
Volume XXIX of the standard *Works of Charles Dickens*.
Dickens said, ". . . I suspect we should find our nurses
responsible for most of the dark corners we are forced to
go back to, against our wills." It is interesting to note that
the legend transcribed in the following story is also mentioned in passing in the M. R. James story, which appears
later in this collection.

The Rat That Could Speak

Charles Dickens

There was once a shipwright, and he wrought in a Government Yard, and his name was Chips. And his father's
name before him was Chips, and *his* father's name before

him was Chips, and they were all Chipses. And Chips the father had sold himself to the Devil for an iron pot and a bushel of tenpenny nails and half a ton of copper and a rat that could speak; and Chips the grandfather had sold himself to the Devil for an iron pot and a bushel of tenpenny nails and a half a ton of copper and a rat that could speak; and Chips the great-grandfather had disposed of himself in the same direction on the same terms; and the bargain had run in the family for a long long time. So, one day, when young Chips was at work in the dock slip all alone, down in the dark hold of an old Seventy-four that was hauled up for repairs, the Devil presented himself, and remarked:

A Lemon has pips,
And a Yard has ships,
And *I*'ll have Chips!

Chips looked up when he heard the words, and there he saw the Devil with saucer eyes that squinted. And whenever he winked his eyes, showers of blue sparks came out, and his eyelashes made a clattering like flints and steels striking lights. And hanging over one of his arms by the handle was an iron pot, and under that arm was a bushel of tenpenny nails, and under his other arm was half a ton of copper, and sitting on one of his shoulders was a rat that could speak. So, the Devil said again:

A Lemon has pips,
And a Yard has ships,
And *I*'ll have Chips!

So, Chips answered never a word, but went on with his work. "What are you doing, Chips?" said the rat that could speak. "I am putting in new planks where you and your gang have eaten old away," said Chips. "But we'll eat them too," said the rat that could speak; "and we'll let in the water and drown the crew, and we'll eat them too." Chips, being only a shipwright, and not a man-of-war's man, said, "You are welcome to it." But he couldn't keep his eyes off the half a ton of copper or the bushel of tenpenny nails; for nails and copper are a shipwright's sweethearts, and shipwrights will run away with them whenever they can. So, the Devil said, "I see what you are looking at, Chips. You had better strike the bargain. You know the terms. Your father before you was well acquainted with them, and so were your grandfather and great-grandfather before him." Says Chips, "I like the copper, and I like the nails, and I don't mind the pot, but I don't like the rat." Says the Devil, fiercely, "You can't have the metal without him—and *he's* a curiosity. I'm going." Chips, afraid of losing the half a ton of copper and the bushel of nails, then said, "Give us hold!" So, he got the copper and the nails and the pot and the rat that could speak, and the Devil vanished. Chips sold the copper, and he sold the nails, and he would have sold the pot; but whenever he offered it for sale, the rat was in it, and the dealers dropped it, and would have nothing to say to the bargain. So, Chips resolved to kill the rat, and, being at work in the Yard one day with a great kettle of hot pitch on one side of him and the iron pot with the rat in it on the other he turned the scalding pitch into the pot, and filled it full. Then he kept his eye upon it till it cooled and hardened, and then he let it stand for twenty days, and then he heated the pitch again and turned it back into the kettle, and then he sank the pot in water for twenty days more, and then he got the smelters to put it in the furnace for twenty days more, and then they gave it him out, red hot, and looking like red-hot glass instead of iron—yet there was the rat in it, just the same as ever! And it said with a jeer:

> A Lemon has pips,
> And a Yard has ships,
> And *I'*ll have Chips!

Now, as the rat leaped out of the pot when it had spoken, and made off, Chips began to hope that it wouldn't keep its word. But, a terrible thing happened next day. For, when dinner time came, and the dock bell rang to strike work, he put his rule into the long pocket at the side of his trousers, and there he found a rat—not that rat, but another rat. And in his hat, he found another; and in his pocket handkerchief, another. And from that time he found himself so frightfully intimate with all the rats in the Yard, that they climbed up his legs when he was at work, and sat on his tools while he used them. And they could all speak to one another, and he understood what they said. And they got into his lodging, and into his bed, and into his teapot, and into his beer, and into his boots. And he was going to be married to a corn chandler's daughter; and when he gave her a workbox he had himself made for her, a rat jumped out of it; and when he put his arm round her waist, a rat clung about her; so the marriage was broken off, though the banns were already twice put up—which the parish clerk well remembers, for, as he handed the book to the clergyman for the second time of asking, a large fat rat ran over the leaf.

You may believe that all this was very terrible for Chips; but even all this was not the worst. He knew besides, what the rats were doing, wherever they were. So, sometimes he would cry aloud, when he was at his club at night, "Oh! Keep the rats out of the convicts' burying ground! Don't let them do that!" Or, "There's one of them at the cheese downstairs!" Or, "There's two of them smelling at the baby in the garret!" Or, other things of that sort. At last, he was voted mad, and lost his work in the Yard, and could get no other work. But, King George wanted men, so before very long he got pressed for a sailor. And so he was taken off in a boat one evening to his ship, lying at Spithead, ready to sail. And so the first thing he made out in her as he got near her, was the figure-head of the old Seventy-four, where he had seen the Devil. She was called the *Argonaut,* and they rowed right under the bowsprit where the figurehead of the *Argonaut,* with a sheepskin in his hand and a blue gown on, was looking out to sea; and sitting staring on his forehead was the rat who could speak, and his exact words were these: "Chips ahoy! Old boy! We've pretty well eaten them too, and we'll drown the crew, and will eat them too!"

The ship was bound for the Indies; and if you don't know where that is, you ought to, and angels will never love you. The ship set sail that very night, and she sailed, and sailed, and sailed. Chips's feelings were dreadful. Nothing ever equalled his terrors. No wonder. At last, one day he asked leave to speak to the Admiral. The Admiral giv' leave. Chips went down on his knees in the Great State Cabin. "Your Honour, unless your Honour, without a moment's loss of time, makes sail for the nearest shore, this is a doomed ship, and her name is the Coffin!" "Young man, your words are a madman's words." "Your Honour, no; they are nibbling us away." "They?" "Your Honour, them dreadful rats. Dust and hollowness where solid oak ought to be! Rats nibbling a grave for every man on board! Oh! Does your Honour love your lady and your pretty children?" "Yes, my man, to be sure." "Then, for God's sake, make for the nearest shore, for at this present moment the rats are all stopping in their work, and are all looking straight towards you with bare teeth, and are all saying to one another that you shall never, never, never, never, see your lady and your children more." "My poor fellow, you are a case for the doctor. Sentry, take this man!"

So, he was bled and he was blistered, and he was this and that, for six whole days and nights. So, then he again asked leave to speak to the Admiral. The Admiral giv' leave. He went down on his knees in the Great State Cabin. "Now, Admiral, you must die! You took no warning; you must die! The rats are never wrong in their calculations, and they make out that they'll be through, at twelve tonight. So, you must die!—With me and all the rest!" And so at twelve o'clock there was a great leak reported in the ship, and a torrent of water rushed in and nothing could stop it, and they all went down, every living soul. And what the rats—being water rats—left of Chips, at last floated to shore, and sitting on him was an immense overgrown rat, laughing, that dived when the corpse touched the beach and never came up. And there was a deal of seaweed on the remains. And if you get thirteen bits of seaweed, and dry them and burn them in the fire, they will go off like in these thirteen words as plain as plain can be:

> A Lemon has pips,
> And a Yard has ships,
> And *I*'ve got Chips!

AMBROSE GWINNET BIERCE, (1842–1914), wrote a total of ninety-three short stories between 1870 and 1896; forty-four of these are classified as horror tales, and most of them are studies of some aspect of the supernatural. Although a popular writer of his day and one who made his living from writing for half a century, Bierce never wrote to please the popular taste but only to satisfy himself. His *Devil's Dictionary* is considered a classic of modern English literature and is still in print in several editions. A fierce iconoclast, Bierce disappeared into Mexico during the revolution of 1914; it was rumored that he was offering himself as a mercenary to the forces of Pancho Villa. Presumably he died there, although neither the date nor the place of his passing is known.

An Inhabitant of Carcosa

Ambrose Bierce

For there be divers sorts of death—some wherein the body remaineth; and in some it vanisheth quite away with the spirit. This commonly occurreth only in solitude

(such is God's will) and, none seeing the end, we say
the man is lost, or gone on a long journey—which indeed
he hath; but sometimes it hath happened in sight of
many, as abundant testimony showeth. In one kind of
death the spirit also dieth, and this it hath been known
to do while yet the body was in vigor for many years.
Sometimes, as is veritably attested, it dieth with the body,
but after a season is raised up again in that place where
the body did decay.

Pondering these words of Hali (whom God rest) and
questioning their full meaning, as one who, having an
intimation, yet doubts if there be not something behind,
other than that which he has discerned, I noted not whither
I had strayed until a sudden chill wind striking my face
revived in me a sense of my surroundings. I observed with
astonishment that everything seemed unfamiliar. On every
side of me stretched a bleak and desolate expanse of plain,
covered with a tall overgrowth of sere grass, which rustled
and whistled in the autumn wind with heaven knows what
mysterious and disquieting suggestion. Protruded at long
intervals above it, stood strangely shaped and somber-
colored rocks, which seemed to have an understanding
with one another and to exchange looks of uncomfortable
significance, as if they had reared their heads to watch
the issue of some foreseen event. A few blasted trees here
and there appeared as leaders in this malevolent conspir-
acy of silent expectation.

The day, I thought, must be far advanced, though the
sun was invisible; and although sensible that the air was
raw and chill my consciousness of that fact was rather
mental than physical—I had no feeling of discomfort.
Over all the dismal landscape a canopy of low, lead-col-
ored clouds hung like a visible curse. In all this there were
a menace and a portent—a hint of evil, an intimation of
doom. Bird, beast, or insect there was none. The wind
sighed in the bare branches of the dead trees and the gray
grass bent to whisper its dread secret to the earth; but no

other sound nor motion broke the awful repose of that dismal place.

I observed in the herbage a number of weather-worn stones, evidently shaped with tools. They were broken, covered with moss and half sunken in the earth. Some lay prostrate, some leaned at various angles, none was vertical. They were obviously headstones of graves, though the graves themselves no longer existed as either mounds or depressions; the years had leveled all. Scattered here and there, more massive blocks showed where some pompous tomb or ambitious monument had once flung its feeble defiance at oblivion. So old seemed these relics, these vestiges of vanity and memorials of affection and piety, so battered and worn and stained—so neglected, deserted, forgotten the place, that I could not help thinking myself the discoverer of the burial ground of a prehistoric race of men whose very name was long extinct.

Filled with these reflections, I was for some time heedless of the sequence of my own experiences, but soon I thought, "How came I hither?" A moment's reflection seemed to make this all clear and explain at the same time, though in a disquieting way, the singular character with which my fancy had invested all that I saw or heard. I was ill. I remembered now that I had been prostrated by a sudden fever, and that my family had told me that in my periods of delirium I had constantly cried out for liberty and air, and had been held in bed to prevent my escape out of doors. Now I had eluded the vigilance of my attendants and had wandered hither to—to where? I could not conjecture. Clearly I was at a considerable distance from the city where I dwelt—the ancient and famous city of Carcosa.

No signs of human life were anywhere visible nor audible; no rising smoke, no watchdog's bark, no lowing of cattle, no shouts of children at play—nothing but that dismal burial place, with its air of mystery and dread, due to my own disordered brain. Was I not becoming

again delirious, there beyond human aid? Was it not indeed *all* an illusion of my madness? I called aloud the
names of my wives and sons, reaching out my hands in
search of theirs, even as I walked among the crumbling
stones and in the withered grass.

A noise behind me caused me to turn about. A wild
animal—a lynx—was approaching. The thought came to
me: If I break down here in the desert—if the fever
return and I fail, this beast will be at my throat. I sprang
toward it, shouting. It trotted tranquilly by within a hand's
breadth of me and disappeared behind a rock.

A moment later a man's head appeared to rise out of
the ground a short distance away. He was ascending the
farther slope of a low hill whose crest was hardly to be
distinguished from the general level. His whole figure soon
came into view against the background of gray clouds.
He was half-naked, half-clad in skins. His hair was un-
kempt, his beard long and ragged. In one hand he carried
a bow and arrow; the other held a blazing torch with a
long trail of black smoke. He walked slowly and with
caution, as if he feared falling into some open grave concealed by the tall grass. This strange apparition surprised
but did not alarm, and taking such a course as to inter-
cept him I met him almost face to face, accosting him
with the familiar salutation, "God keep you."

He gave no heed, nor did he arrest his pace.

"Good stranger," I continued, "I am ill and lost. Direct
me, I beseech you, to Carcosa."

The man broke into a barbarous chant in an unknown
tongue, passing on and away.

An owl on the branch of a decayed tree hooted dismally and was answered by another in the distance. Looking upward, I saw through a sudden rift in the clouds
Aldebaran and the Hyades! In all this there was a hint of
night—the lynx, the man with the torch, the owl. Yet I
saw—I saw even the stars in absence of the darkness. I

saw, but was apparently not seen nor heard. Under what awful spell did I exist?

I seated myself at the root of a great tree, seriously to consider what it were best to do. That I was mad I could no longer doubt, yet recognized a ground of doubt in the conviction. Of fever I had no trace. I had, withal, a sense of exhilaration and vigor altogether unknown to me—a feeling of mental and physical exaltation. My senses seemed all alert; I could feel the air as a ponderous substance; I could hear the silence.

A great root of the giant tree against whose trunk I leaned as I sat held enclosed in its grasp a slab of stone, a part of which protruded into a recess formed by another root. The stone was thus partly protected from the weather, though greatly decomposed. Its edges were worn round, its corners eaten away, its surface deeply furrowed and scaled. Glittering particles of mica were visible in the earth about it—vestiges of its decomposition. This stone had apparently marked the grave out of which the tree had sprung ages ago. The tree's exacting roots had robbed the grave and made the stone a prisoner.

A sudden wind pushed some dry leaves and twigs from the uppermost face of the stone; I saw the low-relief letters of an inscription and bent to read it. God in Heaven! *My* name in full!—The date of *my* birth!—The date of *my* death!

The level shaft of light illuminated the whole side of the tree as I sprang to my feet in terror. The sun was rising in the rosy east. I stood between the tree and his broad red disk—no shadow darkened the trunk!

A chorus of howling wolves saluted the dawn. I saw them sitting on their haunches, singly and in groups, on the summits of irregular mounds and tumuli filling a half of my desert prospect and extending to the horizon. And then I knew that these trees were ruins of the ancient and famous city of Carcosa.

Such are the facts imparted to the medium Bayrolles by the spirit Hoseib Alar Robardin.

MONTAGUE RHODES JAMES, (1862–1936), was considered, during his career, to be the world's greatest authority on medieval manuscripts. His entire life was spent in scholarly research, and his monumental series of manuscript catalogs was undoubtedly what he considered the culmination of his career. But there was another, lighter (or darker, considering the focus of his interests) side to James: he was an authority on supernatural fiction of all ages. As a lark, in 1893 he started writing ghost stories, which he read aloud at meetings of the Chitchat Club, at his rooms in Cambridge. The first two stories were "Lost Hearts," included here, and "Canon Alberic's Scrap-Book." The reading thereafter became a yearly event on Christmas Eve. James was finally persuaded, in 1904, to write an entire book of ghost stories. Writing for relaxation rather than as a vocation, he produced only four such volumes over the next twenty years. James himself considered J. Sheridan Le Fanu the best writer of supernatural stories of all times and his own most important influence.

Lost Hearts

M. R. James

It was, as far as I can ascertain, in September of the year 1811 that a post-chaise drew up before the door of Aswarby Hall, in the heart of Lincolnshire. The little boy

who was the only passenger in the chaise, and who jumped
out as soon as it had stopped, looked about him with the
keenest curiosity during the short interval that elapsed
between the ringing of the bell and the opening of the hall
door. He saw a tall, square, red-brick house, built in the
reign of Anne; a stone-pillared porch had been added in
the purer classical style of 1790; the windows of the
house were many, tall and narrow, with small panes and
thick white woodwork. A pediment, pierced with a round
window, crowned the front. There were wings to right and
left, connected by curious glazed galleries, supported by
colonnades, with the central block. These wings plainly
contained the stables and offices of the house. Each was
surmounted by an ornamental cupola with a gilded vane.

An evening light shone on the building, making the
window panes glow like so many fires. Away from the
Hall in front stretched a flat park studded with oaks and
fringed with firs, which stood out against the sky. The
clock in the church tower, buried in trees on the edge of
the park, only its golden weather cock catching the light,
was striking six, and the sound came gently beating down
the wind. It was altogether a pleasant impression, though
tinged with the sort of melancholy appropriate to an evening in early autumn, that was conveyed to the mind of
the boy who was standing on the porch, waiting for the
door to open to him.

The post-chaise had brought him from Warwickshire,
where, some six months before, he had been left an orphan. Now, owing to the generous offer of his elderly
cousin, Mr. Abney, he had come to live at Aswarby. The
offer was unexpected, because all who knew anything of
Mr. Abney looked upon him as a somewhat austere recluse, into whose steady-going household the advent of a
small boy would import a new and, it seemed, incongruous
element. The truth is that very little was known of Mr.
Abney's pursuits or temper. The professor of Greek at
Cambridge had been heard to say that no one knew more

of the religious beliefs of the later pagans than did the owner of Aswarby. Certainly his library contained all of the then available books bearing on the Mysteries, the Orphic poems, the worship of Mithras, and the neo-Platonists. In the marble-paved hall stood a fine group of Mithras slaying a bull, which had been imported from the Levant at great expense by the owner. He had contributed a description of it to the *Gentleman's Magazine,* and he had written a remarkable series of articles in the *Critical Museum* on the superstitions of the Romans of the Lower Empire. He was looked upon, in fine, as a man wrapped up in his books, and it was a matter of great surprise among his neighbours that he should ever have heard of his orphan cousin, Stephen Elliott, much more that he should have volunteered to make him an inmate of Aswarby Hall.

Whatever may have been expected by his neighbours, it is certain that Mr. Abney—the tall, the thin, the austere—seemed inclined to give his young cousin a kindly reception. The moment the front door was opened he darted out of his study, rubbing his hands with delight.

"How are you, my boy? How are you? How old are you?" said he. "That is, you are not too much tired, I hope, by your journey to eat your supper?"

"No, thank you, sir," said Master Elliott. "I am pretty well."

"That's a good lad," said Mr. Abney. "And how old are you, my boy?"

It seemed a little odd that he should have asked the question twice in the first two minutes of their acquaintance.

"I'm twelve years old next birthday, sir," said Stephen.

"And when is your birthday, my dear boy? Eleventh of September, eh? That's well—that's very well. Nearly a year hence, isn't it? I like—ha, ha!—I like to get these things down in my book. Sure it's twelve? Certain?"

"Yes, quite sure, sir."

"Well, well! Take him to Mrs. Bunch's room, Parkes, and let him have his tea—supper—whatever it is."

"Yes, sir," answered the staid Mr. Parkes; and conducted Stephen to the lower regions.

Mrs. Bunch was the most comfortable and human person whom Stephen had as yet met in Aswarby. She made him completely at home; they were great friends in a quarter of an hour: and great friends they remained. Mrs. Bunch had been born in the neighbourhood some fifty-five years before the date of Stephen's arrival, and her residence at the Hall was of twenty years' standing. Consequently, if anyone knew the ins and outs of the house and the district, Mrs. Bunch knew them; and she was by no means disinclined to communicate her information.

Certainly there were plenty of things about the Hall and the Hall gardens which Stephen, who was of an adventurous and inquiring turn, was anxious to have explained to him. "Who built the temple at the end of the laurel walk? Who was the old man whose picture hung on the staircase, sitting at a table, with a skull under his hand?" These and many similar points were cleared up by the resources of Mrs. Bunch's powerful intellect. There were others, however, of which the explanations furnished were less satisfactory.

One November evening Stephen was sitting by the fire in the housekeeper's room reflecting on his surroundings.

"Is Mr. Abney a good man, and will he go to heaven?" he suddenly asked, with the peculiar confidence which children possess in the ability of their elders to settle these questions, the decision of which is believed to be reserved for other tribunals.

"Good? Bless the child!" said Mrs. Bunch. "Master's as kind a soul as ever I see! Didn't I never tell you of the little boy as he took in out of the street, as you may say, this seven years back? And the little girl, two years after I first come here?"

"No. Do tell me all about them, Mrs. Bunch—now this minute!"

"Well," said Mrs. Bunch, "the little girl I don't seem to recollect so much about. I know master brought her back with him from his walk one day, and give orders to Mrs. Ellis, as was housekeeper then, as she should be took every care with. And the pore child hadn't no one belonging to her—she telled me so her own self—and here she lived with us a matter of three weeks it might be; and then, whether she were somethink of a gypsy in her blood or what not, but one morning she was out of her bed afore any of us had opened a eye, and neither track nor trace of her have I set eyes on since. Master was wonderful put about, and had all the ponds dragged; but it's my belief she was had away by them gypsies, for there was singing round the house for as much as an hour the night she went, and Parkes, he declare as he heard them a-calling in the woods all that afternoon. Dear, dear! A hodd child she was, so silent in her ways and all, but I was wonderful taken up with her, so domesticated she was—surprising."

"And what about the little boy?" said Stephen.

"Ah, that pore boy!" sighed Mrs. Bunch. "He were a foreigner—Jevanny he called hisself—and he come a-tweaking his 'urdy-gurdy round and about the drive one winter day, and master 'ad him in that minute, and ast all about where he came from, and how old he was, and how he made his way, and where was his relatives, and all as kind as heart could wish. But it went the same way with him. They're a hunruly lot, them foreign nations, I do suppose, and he was off one fine morning just the same as the girl. Why he went and what he done was our question for as much as a year after; for he never took his 'urdy-gurdy, and there it lays on the shelf."

The remainder of the evening was spent by Stephen in miscellaneous cross-examination of Mrs. Bunch and in efforts to extract a tune from the hurdy-gurdy.

That night he had a curious dream. At the end of the passage at the top of the house, in which his bedroom was situated, there was an old disused bathroom. It was kept locked, but the upper half of the door was glazed, and, since the muslin curtains which used to hang there had long been gone, you could look in and see the lead-lined bath affixed to the wall on the right hand, with its head towards the window.

On the night of which I am speaking, Stephen Elliott found himself, as he thought, looking through the glazed door. The moon was shining through the window, and he was gazing at a figure which lay in the bath.

His description of what he saw reminds me of what I once beheld myself in the famous vaults of St. Michan's Church in Dublin, which possesses the horrid property of preserving corpses from decay for centuries. A figure inexpressibly thin and pathetic, of a dusty leaden colour, enveloped in a shroudlike garment, the thin lips crooked into a faint and dreadful smile, the hands pressed tightly over the region of the heart.

As he looked upon it, a distant, almost inaudible moan seemed to issue from its lips, and the arms began to stir. The terror of the sight forced Stephen backwards and he awoke to the fact that he was indeed standing on the cold boarded floor of the passage in the full light of the moon. With a courage which I do not think can be common among boys of his age, he went to the door of the bathroom to ascertain if the figure of his dream were really there. It was not, and he went back to bed.

Mrs. Bunch was much impressed next morning by his story, and went so far as to replace the muslin curtain over the glazed door of the bathroom. Mr. Abney, moreover, to whom he confided his experiences at breakfast, was greatly interested, and made notes of the matter in what he called "his book."

The spring equinox was approaching, as Mr. Abney frequently reminded his cousin, adding that this had been always considered by the ancients to be a critical time for the young: that Stephen would do well to take care of himself, and to shut his bedroom window at night; and that Censorinus had some valuable remarks on the subject. Two incidents that occurred about this time made an impression upon Stephen's mind.

The first was after an unusually uneasy and oppressed night that he had passed—though he could not recall any particular dream that he had had.

The following evening Mrs. Bunch was occupying herself in mending his nightgown.

"Gracious me, Master Stephen!" she broke forth rather irritably, "how do you manage to tear your nightdress all to flinders this way? Look here, sir, what trouble you do give to poor servants that have to darn and mend after you!"

There was indeed a most destructive and apparently wanton series of slits or scorings in the garment, which would undoubtedly require a skilful needle to make good. They were confined to the left side of the chest—long, parallel slits, about six inches in length, some of them not quite piercing the texture of the linen. Stephen could only express his entire ignorance of their origin: he was sure they were not there the night before.

"But," he said, "Mrs. Bunch, they are just the same as the scratches on the outside of my bedroom door: and I'm sure I never had anything to do with making *them*."

Mrs. Bunch gazed at him open-mouthed, then snatched up a candle, departed hastily from the room, and was heard making her way upstairs. In a few minutes she came down.

"Well," she said, "Master Stephen, it's a funny thing to me how them marks and scratches can 'a' come there—too high up for any cat or dog to 'ave made 'em, much less a rat: for all the world like a Chinaman's fingernails, as my uncle in the tea trade used to tell us of when we was girls together. I wouldn't say nothing to master, not if

I was you, Master Stephen, my dear; and just turn the key of the door when you go to your bed."

"I always do, Mrs. Bunch, as soon as I've said my prayers."

"Ah, that's a good child: always say your prayers, and then no one can't hurt you."

Herewith Mrs. Bunch addressed herself to mending the injured nightgown, with intervals of meditation, until bedtime. This was on a Friday night in March, 1812.

On the following evening the usual duet of Stephen and Mrs. Bunch was augmented by the sudden arrival of Mr. Parkes, the butler, who as a rule kept himself rather to himself in his own pantry. He did not see that Stephen was there: he was, moreover, flustered and less slow of speech than was his wont.

"Master may get up his own wine, if he likes, of an evening," was his first remark. "Either I do it in the daytime or not at all, Mrs. Bunch. I don't know what it may be: very likely it's the rats, or the wind got into the cellars; but I'm not so young as I was, and I can't go through with it as I have done."

"Well, Mr. Parkes, you know it is a surprising place for the rats, is the Hall."

"I'm not denying that, Mrs. Bunch; and, to be sure, many a time I've heard the tale from the men in the shipyards about the rat that could speak. I never laid no confidence in that before; but tonight, if I'd demeaned myself to lay my ear to the door of the further bin, I could pretty much have heard what they was saying."

"Oh, there, Mr. Parkes, I've no patience with your fancies! Rats talking in the wine cellar indeed!"

"Well, Mrs. Bunch, I've no wish to argue with you: all I say is, if you choose to go to the far bin, and lay your ear to the door, you may prove my words this minute."

"What nonsense you do talk, Mr. Parkes—not fit for children to listen to! Why, you'll be frightening Master Stephen there out of his wits."

"What! Master Stephen?" said Parkes, awaking to the consciousness of the boy's presence. "Master Stephen knows well enough when I'm a-playing a joke with you, Mrs. Bunch."

In fact, Master Stephen knew much too well to suppose that Mr. Parkes had in the first instance intended a joke. He was interested, not altogether pleasantly, in the situation; but all his questions were unsuccessful in inducing the butler to give any more detailed account of his experiences in the wine cellar.

We have now arrived at March 24, 1812. It was a day of curious experiences for Stephen: a windy, noisy day, which filled the house and the gardens with a restless impression. As Stephen stood by the fence of the grounds, and looked out into the park, he felt as if an endless procession of unseen people were sweeping past him on the wind, borne on resistlessly and aimlessly, vainly striving to stop themselves, to catch at something that might arrest their flight and bring them once again into contact with the living world of which they had formed a part. After luncheon that day Mr. Abney said:

"Stephen, my boy, do you think you could manage to come to me tonight as late as eleven o'clock in my study? I shall be busy until that time, and I wish to show you something connected with your future life which it is most important that you should know. You are not to mention this matter to Mrs. Bunch nor to anyone else in the house; and you had better go to your room at the usual time."

Here was a new excitement added to life: Stephen eagerly grasped at the opportunity of sitting up till eleven o'clock. He looked in at the library door on his way upstairs that evening, and saw a brazier, which he had often noticed in the corner of the room, moved out before the fire; an old silver-gilt cup stood on the table, filled with red wine, and some written sheets of paper lay near it. Mr. Abney was sprinkling some incense on the brazier from a round silver box as Stephen passed, but did not seem to notice his step.

The wind had fallen, and there was a still night and a full moon. At about ten o'clock Stephen was standing at the open window of his bedroom, looking out over the country. Still as the night was, the mysterious population of the distant moon-lit woods was not yet laid to rest. From time to time strange cries as of lost and despairing wanderers sounded from across the mere. They might be the notes of owls or water birds, yet they did not quite resemble either sound. Were not they coming nearer? Now they sounded from the nearer side of the water, and in a few moments they seemed to be floating about among the shrubberies. Then they ceased; but just as Stephen was thinking of shutting the window and resuming his reading of *Robinson Crusoe,* he caught sight of two figures standing on the gravelled terrace that ran along the garden side of the Hall—the figures of a boy and girl, as it seemed; they stood side by side, looking up at the windows. Something in the form of the girl recalled irresistibly his dream of the figure in the bath. The boy inspired him with more acute fear.

Whilst the girl stood still, half smiling, with her hands clasped over her heart, the boy, a thin shape, with black hair and ragged clothing, raised his arms in the air with an appearance of menace and of unappeasable hunger and longing. The moon shone upon his almost transparent hands, and Stephen saw that the nails were fearfully long and that the light shone through them. As he stood with his arms thus raised, he disclosed a terrifying spectacle. On the left side of his chest there opened a black and gaping rent; and there fell upon Stephen's brain, rather than upon his ear, the impression of one of those hungry and desolate cries that he had heard resounding over the woods of Aswarby all that evening. In another moment this dreadful pair had moved swiftly and noiselessly over the dry gravel, and he saw them no more.

Inexpressibly frightened as he was, he determined to take his candle and go down to Mr. Abney's study, for the hour appointed for their meeting was near at hand. The study or library opened out of the front hall on one side, and Stephen, urged on by his terrors, did not take long in getting there. To effect an entrance was not so easy. It was not locked, he felt sure, for the key was on the outside of the door as usual. His repeated knocks produced no answer. Mr. Abney was engaged: he was speaking. What! Why did he try to cry out? And why was the cry choked in his throat? Had he, too, seen the mysterious children? But now everything was quiet, and the door yielded to Stepen's terrified and frantic pushing.

On the table in Mr. Abney's study certain papers were found which explained the situation to Stephen Elliott when he was of an age to understand them. The most important sentences were as follows:

"It was a belief very strongly and generally held by the ancients—of whose wisdom in these matters I have had such experiences as induces me to place confidence in their assertions—that by enacting certain processes, which to us moderns have something of a barbaric complexion, a very remarkable enlightenment of the spiritual faculties in man may be attained: that, for example, by absorbing the personalities of a certain number of his fellow creatures, an individual may gain a complete ascendancy over those orders of spiritual beings which control the elemental forces of our universe.

"It is recorded of Simon Magus that he was able to fly in the air, to become invisible, or to assume any form he pleased, by the agency of the soul of a boy whom, to use the libellous phrase employed by the author of the *Clementine Recognitions,* he had 'murdered.' I find it set down, moreover, with considerable detail in the writings of Hermes Trismegistus, that similarly happy results may be produced by the absorption of the hearts of not less than three human beings below the age of twenty-one years. To the testing of the truth of this receipt I have devoted the greater part of the last twenty years, selecting as the *copora vilia* of my experiment such persons as could conveniently be removed without occasioning a sensible gap in society. The first step I effected by the removal of one Phoebe Stanley, a girl of gypsy extraction, on March 24, 1792. The second, by the removal of a wandering Italian lad, named Giovanni Paoli, on the night of March 23, 1805. The final 'victim'—to employ a word repugnant in the highest degree to my feelings—must be my cousin, Stephen Elliott. His day must be this March 24, 1812.

"The best means of effecting the required absorption is to remove the heart from the *living* subject, to reduce it to ashes, and to mingle them with about a pint of some red wine, preferably port. The remains of the first two subjects, at least, it will be well to conceal: a disused bathroom or wine cellar will be found convenient for such a purpose. Some annoyance may be experienced from the psychic portion of the subjects, which popular language dignifies with the name of ghosts. But the man of philosophic temperament—to whom alone the experiment is appropriate—will be little prone to attach importance to the feeble efforts of these beings to wreak their vengeance on him. I contemplate with the liveliest satisfaction the enlarged and emancipated existence which the experiment, if successful, will confer on me; not only placing me beyond the reach of human justice (so-called), but eliminating to a great extent the prospect of death itself."

Mr. Abney was found in his chair, his head thrown back, his face stamped with an expression of rage, fright, and mortal pain. In his left side was a terrible lacerated wound, exposing the heart. There was no blood on his hands, and a long knife that lay on the table was perfectly clean. A savage wildcat might have inflicted the injuries. The window of the study was open, and it was the opinion of the coroner that Mr. Abney had met his death by the agency of some wild creature. But Stephen Elliott's study of the papers I have quoted led him to a very different conclusion.

ROBERT WILLIAM CHAMBERS, (1865–1933), was the author of more than seventy popular novels and countless short stories, articles, and verse. A contemporary and close friend of Charles Dana Gibson, Chambers studied with him at the New York Art Students League and later roomed with him for a time. Chambers was one of the most commercially successful writers of his time, always following the trend of the market in aiming his novels at the widest possible audience. For this reason, the great majority of his work is little more than drivel and better forgotten. There are two exceptions, however: an early collection of stories and a later character. The collection, *The King in Yellow,* appeared in 1895 and has been nominated by some as the most important American work in the genre since Poe. The character appeared in the 1906 novel, *The Tracer of Lost Persons,* and virtually everyone over the age of thirty will remember the long-running radio series and the early television series featuring Mr. Keene.

The Yellow Sign

Robert W. Chambers

Along the shore the cloud waves break,
The twin suns sink behind the lake,
The shadows lengthen
                In Carcosa.

Strange is the night where black stars rise,
And strange moons circle through the skies,
But stranger still is
                    Lost Carcosa.

Songs that the Hyades shall sing,
Where flap the tatters of the King,
Must die unheard in
                    Dim Carcosa.

Song of my soul, my voice is dead,
Die thou, unsung, as tears unshed
Shall dry and die in
                    Lost Carcosa.

Cassilda's Song in *The King in Yellow*.
                    ACT 1. SCENE 2.

I. Being the Contents of an Unsigned Letter Sent to the Author

There are so many things which are impossible to explain! Why should certain chords in music make me think of the brown and golden tints of autumn foliage? Why should the Mass of Sainte Cécile send my thoughts wandering among caverns whose walls blaze with ragged masses of virgin silver? What was it in the roar and turmoil of Broadway at six o'clock that flashed before my eyes the picture of a still Breton forest where sunlight filtered through spring foliage and Sylvia bent, half curiously, half tenderly, over a small green lizard, murmuring: "To think that this also is a little ward of God!"

When I first saw the watchman his back was toward me. I looked at him indifferently until he went into the church. I paid no more attention to him than I had to any other man who lounged through Washington Square that

morning, and when I shut my window and turned back
into my studio I had forgotten him. Late in the afternoon,
the day being warm, I raised the window again and leaned
out to get a sniff of air. A man was standing in the court-
yard of the church, and I noticed him again with as little
interest as I had that morning. I looked across the square
to where the fountain was playing and then, with my mind
filled with vague impressions of trees, asphalt drives, and
the moving groups of nursemaids and holiday makers, I
started to walk back to my easel. As I turned, my listless
glance included the man below in the churchyard. His face
was toward me now, and with a perfectly involuntary
movement I bent to see it. At the same moment he raised
his head and looked at me. Instantly I thought of a coffin
worm. Whatever it was about the man that repelled me I
did not know, but the impression of a plump white grave
worm was so intense and nauseating that I must have
shown it in my expression, for he turned his puffy face
away with a movement which made me think of a disturbed grub in a chestnut.

I went back to my easel and motioned the model to
resume her pose. After working awhile I was satisfied that
I was spoiling what I had done as rapidly as possible, and
I took up a palette knife and scraped the color out again.
The flesh tones were sallow and unhealthy, and I did not
understand how I could have painted such sickly color into
a study which before that had glowed with healthy tones.

I looked at Tessie. She had not changed, and the clear
flush of health dyed her neck and cheeks as I frowned.

"Is it something I've done," she said.

"No, I've made a mess of this arm, and for the life of
me I can't see how I came to paint such mud as that into
the canvas," I replied.

"Don't I pose well?" she insisted.

"Of course, perfectly."

"Then it's not my fault?"

"No. It's my own."

"I'm very sorry," she said.

I told her she could rest while I applied rag and turpentine to the plague spot on my canvas, and she went off to smoke a cigarette and look over the illustrations in the *Courier Français*.

I did not know whether it was something in the turpentine or a defect in the canvas, but the more I scrubbed the more that gangrene seemed to spread. I worked like a beaver to get it out, and yet the disease appeared to creep from limb to limb of the study before me. Alarmed I strove to arrest it, but now the color on the breast changed and the whole figure seemed to absorb the infection as a sponge soaks up water. Vigorously I plied palette knife, turpentine, and scraper, thinking all the time what a séance I should hold with Duval who had sold me the canvas; but soon I noticed that it was not the canvas which was defective nor yet the colors of Edward. "It must be the turpentine," I thought angrily, "or else my eyes have become so blurred and confused by the afternoon light that I can't see straight." I called Tessie, the model. She came and leaned over my chair blowing rings of smoke into the air.

"What *have* you been doing to it?" she exclaimed.

"Nothing," I growled, "it must be this turpentine!"

"What a horrible color it is now," she continued. "Do you think my flesh resembles green cheese?"

"No, I don't," I said angrily, "did you ever know me to paint like that before?"

"No, indeed!"

"Well, then!"

"It must be the turpentine, or something," she admitted.

She slipped on a Japanese robe and walked to the window. I scraped and rubbed until I was tired and finally picked up my brushes and hurled them through the canvas with a forcible expression, the tone alone of which reached Tessie's ears.

Nevertheless she promptly began: "That's it! Swear and act silly and ruin your brushes! You have been three weeks on that study, and now look! What's the good of ripping the canvas? What creatures artists are!"

I felt about as much ashamed as I usually did after such an outbreak, and I turned the ruined canvas to the wall. Tessie helped me clean my brushes, and then danced away to dress. From the screen she regaled me with bits of advice concerning whole or partial loss of temper, until, thinking, perhaps, I had been tormented sufficiently, she came out to implore me to button her waist where she could not reach it on the shoulder.

"Everything went wrong from the time you came back from the window and talked about that horrid-looking man you saw in the churchyard," she announced.

"Yes, he probably bewitched the picture," I said, yawning. I looked at my watch.

"It's after six, I know," said Tessie, adjusting her hat before the mirror.

"Yes," I replied, "I didn't mean to keep you so long." I leaned out of the window but recoiled with disgust, for the young man with the pasty face stood below in the churchyard. Tessie saw my gesture of disapproval and leaned from the window.

"Is that the man you don't like?" she whispered.

I nodded.

"I can't see his face, but he does look fat and soft. Someway or other," she continued, turning to look at me, "he reminds me of a dream—an awful dream I once had. Or," she mused, looking down at her shapely shoes, "was it a dream after all?"

"How should I know?" I smiled.

Tessie smiled in reply.

"You were in it," she said, "so perhaps you might know something about it."

"Tessie! Tessie!" I protested, "don't you dare flatter by saying you dream about me!"

"But I did," she insisted. "Shall I tell you about it?"

"Go ahead," I replied, lighting a cigarette.

Tessie leaned back on the open window sill and began very seriously.

"One night last winter I was lying in bed thinking about nothing at all in particular. I had been posing for you and I was tired out, yet it seemed impossible for me to sleep. I heard the bells in the city ring ten, eleven, and midnight. I must have fallen asleep about midnight because I don't remember hearing the bells after that. It seemed to me that I had scarcely closed my eyes when I dreamed that something impelled me to go to the window. I rose, and raising the sash, leaned out. Twenty-fifth Street was deserted as far as I could see. I began to be afraid; everything outside seemed so—so black and uncomfortable. Then the sound of wheels in the distance came to my ears, and it seemed to me as though that was what I must wait for. Very slowly the wheels approached, and, finally, I could make out a vehicle moving along the street. It came nearer and nearer, and when it passed beneath my window I saw it was a hearse. Then, as I trembled with fear, the driver turned and looked straight at me. When I awoke I was standing by the open window shivering with cold, but the black-plumed hearse and the driver were gone. I dreamed this dream again in March last, and again awoke beside the open window. Last night the dream came again. You remember how it was raining; when I awoke, standing at the open window, my night dress was soaked."

"But where did I come into the dream?" I asked.

"You—you were in the coffin; but you were not dead."

"In the coffin?"

"Yes."

"How did you know? Could you see me?"

"No; I only knew you were there."

"Had you been eating Welsh rarebits, or lobster salad?"

I began laughing, but the girl interrupted me with a frightened cry.

"Hello! What's up?" I said, as she shrank into the embrasure by the window.

"The—the man below in the churchyard—he drove the hearse."

"Nonsense," I said, but Tessie's eyes were wide with terror. I went to the window and looked out. The man was gone. "Come, Tessie," I urged, "don't be foolish. You have posed too long; you are nervous."

"Do you think I could forget that face?" she murmured. "Three times I saw the hearse pass below my window, and every time the driver turned and looked up at me. Oh, his face was so white and—and soft? It looked dead—it looked as if it had been dead a long time."

I induced the girl to sit down and swallow a glass of Marsala. Then I sat down beside her, and tried to give her some advice.

"Look here, Tessie," I said, "you go to the country for a week or two, and you'll have no more dreams about hearses. You pose all day, and when night comes your nerves are upset. You can't keep this up. Then again, instead of going to bed when your day's work is done, you run off to picnics at Sulzer's Park, or go to the Eldorado or Coney Island, and when you come down here next morning you are fagged out. There was no real hearse. That was a soft-shell crab dream."

She smiled faintly.

"What about the man in the churchyard?"

"Oh, he's only an ordinary, unhealthy, everyday creature."

"As true as my name is Tessie Reardon, I swear to you, Mr. Scott, that the face of the man below in the churchyard is the face of the man who drove the hearse!"

"What of it?" I said. "It's an honest trade."

"Then you think I *did* see the hearse?"

"Oh," I said, diplomatically, "if you really did, it might not be unlikely that the man below drove it. There is nothing in that."

Tessie rose, unrolled her scented handkerchief, and taking a bit of gum from a knot in the hem, placed it in her mouth. Then drawing on her gloves she offered me her hand, with a frank, "Good night, Mr. Scott," and walked out.

II

The next morning, Thomas, the bellboy, brought me the *Herald* and a bit of news. The church next door had been sold. I thanked Heaven for it, not that being a Catholic I had any repugnance for the congregation next door, but because my nerves were shattered by a blatant exhorter, whose every word echoed through the aisle of the church as if it had been my own rooms, and who insisted on his *r*s with a nasal persistence which revolted my every instinct. Then, too, there was a fiend in human shape, an organist, who reeled off some of the grand old hymns with an interpretation of his own, and I longed for the blood of a creature who could play the doxology with an amendment of minor chords which one hears only in a quartet of very young undergraduates. I believe the minister was a good man, but when he bellowed: "And the Lorrrrd said unto Moses, the Lorrrd is a man of war; the Lorrrd is his name. My wrath shall wax hot and I will kill you with the sworrrd!" I wondered how many centuries of purgatory it would take to atone for such a sin.

"Who bought the property?" I asked Thomas.

"Nobody that I knows, sir. They do say the gent wot owns this 'ere 'Amilton flats was lookin' at it. 'E might be a-bildin' more studios."

I walked to the window. The young man with the unhealthy face stood by the churchyard gate, and at the mere sight of him the same overwhelming repugnance took possession of me.

"By the way, Thomas," I said, "who is that fellow down there?"

Thomas sniffed. "That there worm, sir? 'E's night watchman of the church, sir. 'E makes me tired a-sittin' out all night on them steps and lookin' at you insultin' like. I'd a punched 'is 'ed, sir—beg pardon, sir—"

"Go on, Thomas."

"One night a-comin' 'ome with 'Arry, the other English boy, I sees 'im a sittin' there on them steps. We 'ad Molly and Jen with us, sir, the two girls on the tray service, an' 'e looks so insultin' at us that I up and sez: 'Wat you looking hat, you fat slug?'—beg pardon, sir, but that's 'ow I sez, sir. Then 'e don't say nothin' and I sez: 'Come out and I'll punch that puddin' 'ed.' Then I hopens the gate an' goes in, but 'e don't say nothin', only looks insultin' like. Then I 'its 'im one, but, ugh! 'Is 'ed was that cold and mushy it ud sicken you to touch 'im."

"What did he do, then?" I asked, curiously.

" 'Im? Nawthin'."

"And you, Thomas?"

The young fellow flushed with embarrassment and smiled uneasily.

"Mr. Scott, sir, I ain't no coward an' I can't make it out at all why I run. I was in the Fifth Lawncers, sir, bugler at Tel-el-Kebir, an' was shot by the wells."

"You don't mean to say you ran away?"

"Yes, sir; I run."

"Why?"

"That's just what I want to know, sir. I grabbed Molly an' run, an' the rest was as frightened as I."

"But what were they frightened at?"

Thomas refused to answer for a while, but now my

curiosity was aroused about the repulsive young man below and I pressed him. Three years' sojourn in America had not only modified Thomas' Cockney dialect but had given him the American's fear of ridicule.

"You won't believe me, Mr. Scott, sir?"

"Yes, I will."

"You will lawf at me, sir?"

"Nonsense!"

He hesitated. "Well, sir, it's God's truth that when I 'it 'im 'e grabbed me wrists, sir, and when I twisted 'is soft, mushy fist one of 'is fingers come off in me 'and."

The utter loathing and horror of Thomas' face must have been reflected in my own for he added:

"It's orful, an' now when I see 'im I just go away. 'E maikes me hill."

When Thomas had gone I went to the window. The man stood beside the church railing with both hands on the gate, but I hastily retreated to my easel again, sickened and horrified, for I saw that the middle finger of his right hand was missing.

At nine o'clock Tessie appeared and vanished behind the screen with a merry "Good-morning, Mr. Scott." When she had reappeared and taken her pose upon the model stand I started a new canvas much to her delight. She remained silent as long as I was on the drawing, but as soon as the scrape of the charcoal ceased and I took up my fixative she began to chatter.

"Oh, I had such a lovely time last night. We went to Tony Pastor's."

"Who are 'we'?" I demanded.

"Oh, Maggie, you know, Mr. Whyte's model, and Pinkie McCormick—we call her Pinkie because she's got that beautiful red hair you artists like so much—and Lizzie Burke."

I sent a shower of spray from the fixative over the canvas, and said: "Well, go on."

"We saw Kelly and Baby Barnes the skirt dancer and —and all the rest. I made a mash."

"Then you have gone back on me, Tessie?"

She laughed and shook her head.

"He's Lizzie Burke's brother, Ed. He's a perfect gen'l'-man."

I felt constrained to give her some parental advice concerning mashing, which she took with a bright smile.

"Oh, I can take care of a strange mash," she said, examining her chewing gum, "but Ed is different. Lizzie is my best friend."

Then she related how Ed had come back from the stocking mill in Lowell, Massachusetts, to find her and Lizzie grown up, and what an accomplished young man he was, and how he thought nothing of squandering half a dollar for ice-cream and oysters to celebrate his entry as clerk into the woollen department of Macy's. Before she finished I began to paint, and she resumed the pose, smiling and chattering like a sparrow. By noon I had the study fairly well rubbed in and Tessie came to look at it.

"That's better," she said.

I thought so too, and ate my lunch with a satisfied feeling that all was going well. Tessie spread her lunch on a drawing table opposite me and we drank our claret from the same bottle and lighted our cigarettes from the same match. I was very much attached to Tessie. I had watched her shoot up into a slender but exquisitely formed woman from a frail, awkward child. She had posed for me during the last three years, and among all my models she was my favorite. It would have troubled me very much indeed had she become "tough" or "fly," as the phrase goes, but I never noticed any deterioration of her manner, and felt at heart that she was all right. She and I never discussed morals at all, and I had no intention of doing so, partly because I had none myself, and partly because I knew she would do what she liked in spite of me. Still I did hope she would steer clear of complications, because I wished her well, and then also I had a selfish desire to retain the best model I had. I knew that mashing, as she termed it, had no significance with girls like Tessie, and that such things in America did not resemble in the least the same things in Paris. Yet, having lived with my eyes open, I also knew that somebody would take Tessie away some day, in one manner or another, and though I professed to myself that marriage was nonsense, I sincerely hoped that, in this case, there would be a priest at the end of the vista. I am a Catholic. When I listen to high mass, when I sign myself, I feel that everything, including myself, is more cheerful, and when I confess, it does me good. A man who lives as much alone as I do, must confess to somebody. Then, again, Sylvia was Catholic, and it was reason enough for me. But I was speaking of Tessie, which is very different. Tessie was also Catholic and much more devout than I, so, taking it all in all, I had little fear for my pretty model until she should fall in love. But *then* I knew that fate alone would decide her future for her, and I prayed inwardly that fate would keep her away from men like me and throw into her path nothing but Ed Burkes and Jimmy McCormicks, bless her sweet face!

Tessie sat blowing rings of smoke up to the ceiling and tinkling the ice in her tumbler.

"Do you know, Kid, that I also had a dream last night?" I observed. I sometimes called her "the Kid."

"Not about that man," she laughed.

"Exactly. A dream similar to yours, only much worse."

It was foolish and thoughtless of me to say this, but you know how little tact the average painter has.

"I must have fallen asleep about ten o'clock," I continued, "and after awhile I dreamt that I awoke. So plainly did I hear the midnight bells, the wind in the tree branches, and the whistle of steamers from the bay, that even now I can scarcely believe I was not awake. I seemed to be lying in a box which had a glass cover. Dimly I saw the street lamps as I passed, for I must tell you, Tessie, the box in which I reclined appeared to lie in a cushioned wagon which jolted me over a stony pavement. After a while I became impatient and tried to move but the box was too narrow. My hands were crossed on my breast so I could not raise them to help myself. I listened and then tried to call. My voice was gone. I could hear the trample of the horses attached to the wagon and even the breathing of the driver. Then another sound broke upon my ears like the raising of a window sash. I managed to turn my head a little, and found I could look, not only through the glass cover of my box, but also through the glass panes in the side of the covered vehicle. I saw houses, empty and silent, with neither light nor life about any of them excepting one. In that house a window was open on the first floor and a figure all in white stood looking down into the street. It was you."

Tessie had turned her face away from me and leaned on the table with her elbow.

"I could see your face," I resumed, "and it seemed to me to be very sorrowful. Then we passed on and turned into a narrow black lane. Presently the horses stopped. I waited and waited, closing my eyes with fear and impatience, but all was silent as the grave. After what seemed to me hours, I began to feel uncomfortable. A sense that somebody was close to me made me unclose my eyes. Then I saw the white face of the hearse driver looking at me through the coffin lid—"

A sob from Tessie interrupted me. She was trembling like a leaf. I saw I had made an ass of myself and attempted to repair the damage.

"Why, Tess," I said, "I only told you this to show you what influence your story might have on another person's dreams. You don't suppose I really lay in a coffin, do you? What are you trembling for? Don't you see that your dream and my unreasonable dislike for that inoffensive watchman of the church simply set my brain working as soon as I fell asleep?"

She laid her head between her arms and sobbed as if her heart would break. What a precious triple donkey I had made of myself! But I was about to break my record. I went over and put my arm about her.

"Tessie dear, forgive me," I said; "I had no business to frighten you with such nonsense. You are too sensible a girl, too good a Catholic to believe in dreams."

Her hand tightened on mine and her head fell back upon my shoulder, but she still trembled and I petted her and comforted her.

"Come, Tess, open your eyes and smile."

Her eyes opened with a slow languid movement and met mine, but their expression was so queer that I hastened to reassure her again.

"It's all humbug, Tessie, you surely are not afraid that any harm will come to you because of that."

"No," she said, but her scarlet lips quivered.

"Then what's the matter? Are you afraid?"

"Yes. Not for myself."

"For me, then?" I demanded gayly.

"For you," she murmured in a voice almost inaudible, "I—I care for you."

At first I started to laugh, but when I understood her, a shock passed through me and I sat like one turned to stone. This was the crowning bit of idiocy I had committed. During the moment which elapsed between her reply and my answer I thought of a thousand responses to that innocent confession. I could pass it by with a laugh, I could misunderstand her and reassure her as to my health, I could simply point out that it was impossible she could love me. But my reply was quicker than my thoughts, and I might think and think now when it was too late, for I had kissed her on the mouth.

That evening I took my usual walk in Washington Park, pondering over the occurrences of the day. I was thoroughly committed. There was no back out now, and I stared the future straight in the face. I was not good, not even scrupulous, but I had no idea of deceiving either myself or Tessie. The one passion of my life lay buried in the sunlit forests of Brittany. Was it buried forever? Hope cried "No!" For three years I had been listening to the voice of Hope, and for three years I had waited for a footstep on my threshold. Had Sylvia forgotten? "No!" cried Hope.

I said that I was not good. That is true, but still I was not exactly a comic opera villain. I had led an easy-going, reckless life, taking what invited me of pleasure, deploring and sometimes bitterly regretting consequences. In one thing alone, except my painting, was I serious, and that was something which lay hidden, if not lost, in the Breton forests.

It was too late now for me to regret what had occurred during the day. Whatever it had been, pity, a sudden tenderness for sorrow, or the more brutal instinct of gratified vanity, it was all the same now, and unless I wished to bruise an innocent heart my path lay marked before me. The fire and strength, the depth of passion of a love which I had never even suspected, with all my imagined experience in the world, left me no alternative but to respond or send her away. Whether because I am so cowardly about giving pain to others, or whether it was that I have little of the gloomy Puritan in me, I do not know, but I shrank from disclaiming responsibility for that thoughtless kiss, and in fact had no time to do so before the gates of her heart opened and the flood poured forth. Others who habitually do their duty and find a sullen satisfaction in making themselves and everybody else unhappy, might have withstood it. I did not. I dared not. After the storm had abated I did tell her that she might better have loved Ed Burke and worn a plain gold ring,

but she would not hear of it, and I thought perhaps that
as long as she had decided to love somebody she could
not marry, it had better be me. I, at least, could treat her
with an intelligent affection, and whenever she became
tired of her infatuation she could go none the worse for it.
For I was decided on that point although I knew how
hard it would be. I remembered the usual termination of
Platonic liaisons and thought how disgusted I had been
whenever I heard of one. I knew I was undertaking a
great deal for so unscrupulous a man as I was, and I
dreaded the future, but never for one moment did I doubt
that she was safe with me. Had it been anybody but Tessie
I should not have bothered my head about scruples. For it
did not occur to me to sacrifice Tessie as I would have
sacrificed a woman of the world. I looked the future
squarely in the face and saw the several probable endings
to the affair. She would either tire of the whole thing, or
become so unhappy that I should have either to marry her
or go away. If I married her we would be unhappy. I with
a wife unsuited to me, and she with a husband unsuitable
for any woman. For my past life could scarcely entitle me
to marry. If I went away she might either fall ill, recover,
and marry some Eddie Burke, or she might recklessly or
deliberately go and do something foolish. On the other
hand if she tired of me, then her whole life would be
before her with beautiful vistas of Eddie Burkes and
marriage rings and twins and Harlem flats and Heaven
knows what. As I strolled along through the trees by the
Washington Arch, I decided that she should find a sub-
stantial friend in me anyway and the future could take
care of itself. Then I went into the house and put on my
evening dress, for the little faintly perfumed note on my
dresser said, "Have a cab at the stage door at eleven,"
and the note was signed, "Edith Carmichel, Metropolitan
Theater, June 19th, 189—."

I took supper that night, or rather we took supper, Miss

Carmichel and I, at Solari's and the dawn was just beginning to gild the cross on the Memorial Church as I entered Washington Square after leaving Edith at the Brunswick. There was not a soul in the park as I passed among the trees and took the walk which leads from the Garibaldi statue to the Hamilton Apartment House, but as I passed the churchyard I saw a figure sitting on the stone steps. In spite of myself a chill crept over me at the sight of the white puffy face, and I hastened to pass. Then he said something which might have been addressed to me or might merely have been a mutter to himself, but a sudden furious anger flamed up within me that such a creature should address me. For an instant I felt like wheeling about and smashing my stick over his head, but I walked on, and entering the Hamilton, went to my apartment. For some time I tossed about the bed trying to get the sound of his voice out of my ears, but could not. It filled my head, that muttering sound, like thick oily smoke from a fat-rendering vat or an odor of noisome decay. And as I lay and tossed about, the voice in my ears seemed more distinct, and I began to understand the words he had muttered. They came to me slowly as if I had forgotten them, and at last I could make some sense out of the sounds. It was this:

Have you found the Yellow Sign?
Have you found the Yellow Sign?
Have you found the Yellow Sign?

I was furious. What did he mean by that? Then with a curse upon him and his I rolled over and went to sleep, but when I awoke later I looked pale and haggard, for I had dreamed the dream of the night before and it troubled me more than I cared to think.

I dressed and went down into my studio. Tessie sat by the window, but as I came in she rose and put both arms around my neck for an innocent kiss. She looked so sweet and dainty that I kissed her again and then sat down before the easel.

"Hello! Where's the study I began yesterday?" I asked.

Tessie looked conscious, but did not answer. I began to hunt among the piles of canvases, saying, "Hurry up, Tess, and get ready; we must take advantage of the morning light."

When at last I gave up the search among the other canvases and turned to look around the room for the missing study I noticed Tessie standing by the screen with her clothes still on.

"What's the matter," I asked, "don't you feel well?"

"Yes."

"Then hurry."

"Do you want me to pose as—as I have always posed?"

Then I understood. Here was a new complication. I had lost, of course, the best nude model I had ever seen. I looked at Tessie. Her face was scarlet. Alas! Alas! We had eaten of the tree of knowledge, and Eden and native innocence were dreams of the past—I mean for her.

I suppose she noticed the disappointment on my face, for she said: "I will pose if you wish. The study is behind the screen here where I put it."

"No," I said, "we will begin something new;" and I went into my wardrobe and picked out a Moorish costume which fairly blazed with tinsel. It was a genuine costume, and Tessie retired to the screen with it, enchanted. When she came forth again I was astonished. Her long black hair was bound above her forehead with a circlet of turquoises, and the ends curled about her glittering girdle. Her feet were encased in the embroidered pointed slippers and the skirt of her costume, curiously wrought with arabesques in silver, fell to her ankles. The deep metallic blue vest embroidered with silver and the short Mauresque jacket spangled and sewn with turquoises became her wonderfully. She came up to me and held up her face smiling. I slipped my hand into my pocket and drawing out a gold chain with a cross attached, dropped it over her head.

"It's yours, Tessie."

"Mine?" she faltered.

"Yours. Now go and pose." Then with a radiant smile she ran behind the screen and presently reappeared with a little box on which was written my name.

"I had intended to give it to you when I went home tonight," she said, "but I can't wait now."

I opened the box. On the pink cotton inside lay a clasp of black onyx, on which was inlaid a curious symbol or letter in gold. It was neither Arabic nor Chinese, nor as I found afterwards did it belong to any human script.

"It's all I had to give you for a keepsake," she said, timidly.

I was annoyed, but I told her how much I should prize it, and promised to wear it always. She fastened it on my coat beneath the lapel.

"How foolish, Tess, to go and buy me such a beautiful thing as this," I said.

"I did not buy it," she laughed.

"Where did you get it?"

Then she told me how she had found it one day while coming from the Aquarium in the Battery, how she had advertised it and watched the papers, but at last gave up all hopes of finding the owner.

"That was last winter," she said, "the very day I had the first horrid dream about the hearse."

I remembered my dream of the previous night but said nothing, and presently my charcoal was flying over a new canvas, and Tessie stood motionless on the model stand.

III

The day following was a disastrous one for me. While moving a framed canvas from one easel to another my foot slipped on the polished floor and I fell heavily on both wrists. They were so badly sprained that it was useless to attempt to hold a brush, and I was obliged to wander about the studio, glaring at unfinished drawings and sketches until despair seized me and I sat down to smoke and twiddle my thumbs with rage. The rain blew against the windows and rattled on the roof of the church, driving me into a nervous fit with its interminable patter. Tessie sat sewing by the window, and every now and then raised her head and looked at me with such innocent compassion that I began to feel ashamed of my irritation and looked about for something to occupy me. I had read all the papers and all the books in the library, but for the sake of something to do I went to the bookcases and shoved them open with my elbow. I knew every volume by its color and examined them all, passing slowly around the library and whistling to keep up my spirits. I was turning to go into the dining room when my eye fell upon a book bound in yellow, standing in a corner of the top shelf of the last bookcase. I did not remember it and from the floor could not decipher the pale lettering on the back, so I went to the smoking room and called Tessie. She came in from the studio and climbed up to reach the book.

"What is it?" I asked.

"The King in Yellow."

I was dumbfounded. Who had placed it there? How came it in my rooms? I had long ago decided that I should never open that book, and nothing on earth could have persuaded me to buy it. Fearful lest curiosity might tempt me to open it, I had never even looked at it in book stores. If I ever had had any curiosity to read it, the awful tragedy of young Castaigne, whom I knew, prevented me from exploring its wicked pages. I had always refused to listen to any description of it, and indeed, nobody ever ventured to discuss the second part aloud, so I had absolutely no knowledge of what those leaves might reveal. I stared at the poisonous yellow bindings as I would at a snake.

"Don't touch it, Tessie," I said. "Come down."

Of course my admonition was enough to arouse her curiosity, and before I could prevent it she took the book and, laughing, danced away into the studio with it. I called to her but she slipped away with a tormenting smile at my helpless hands, and I followed her with some impatience.

"Tessie!" I cried, entering the library. "Listen, I am serious. Put that book away. I do not wish you to open it!" The library was empty. I went into both drawing rooms, then into the bedrooms, laundry, kitchen, and finally returned to the library and began a systematic search. She had hidden herself so well that it was half an hour later when I discovered her crouching white and silent by the latticed window in the storeroom above. At the first glance I saw she had been punished for her foolishness. *The King in Yellow* lay at her feet, but the book was open at the second part. I looked at Tessie and saw it was too late. She had opened *The King in Yellow*. Then I took her by the hand and led her into the studio. She seemed dazed, and when I told her to lie down on the sofa she obeyed me without a word. After a while she closed her eyes and her breathing became regular and deep, but I could not determine whether or not she slept. For a long while I sat silently beside her, but she neither stirred nor spoke, and at last I rose and, entering the unused storeroom, took the yellow book in my least injured hand. It seemed heavy as lead, but I carried it into the studio again, and sitting down on the rug beside the sofa, opened it and read it through from beginning to end.

When, faint with the excess of my emotions, I dropped the volume and leaned wearily back against the sofa, Tessie opened her eyes and looked at me.

We had been speaking for some time in a dull monotonous strain before I realized that we were discussing *The King in Yellow*. Oh the sin of writing such words—words which are clear as crystal, limpid and musical as bubbling springs, words which sparkle and glow like the poisoned diamonds of the Medicis! Oh the wickedness, the hopeless damnation of a soul who could fascinate and paralyze human creatures with such words—words understood by the ignorant and wise alike, words which are more precious than jewels, more soothing than Heavenly music, more awful than death itself.

We talked on, unmindful of the gathering shadows, and she was begging me to throw away the clasp of black onyx quaintly inlaid with what we now knew to be the Yellow Sign. I never shall know why I refused, though even at this hour, here in my bedroom as I write this confession, I should be glad to know *what* it was that prevented me from tearing the Yellow Sign from my breast and casting it into the fire. I am sure I wished to do so, but Tessie pleaded with me in vain. Night fell and the hours dragged on, but still we murmured to each other of the King and the Pallid Mask, and midnight sounded from the misty spires in the fog-wrapped city. We spoke of Hastur and of Cassilda, while outside the fog rolled against the blank window panes as the cloud waves roll and break on the shores of Hali.

The house was very silent now and not a sound from the misty streets broke the silence. Tessie lay among the cushions, her face a gray blot in the gloom, but her hands were clasped in mine and I knew that she knew and read my thoughts as I read hers, for we had understood the mystery of the Hyades and the Phantom of Truth was laid.

Then as we answered each other, swiftly, silently, thought on thought, the shadows stirred in the gloom about us, and far in the distant streets we heard a sound. Nearer and nearer it came, the dull crunching of wheels, nearer and yet nearer, and now, outside before the door it ceased, and I dragged myself to the window and saw a black-plumed hearse. The gate below opened and shut, and I crept shaking to my door and bolted it, but I knew no bolts, no locks, could keep that creature out who was coming for the Yellow Sign. And now I heard him moving very softly along the hall. Now he was at the door, and the bolts rotted at his touch. Now he had entered. With eyes starting from my head I peered into the darkness, but when he came into the room I did not see him. It was only when I felt him envelop me in his cold, soft grasp that I cried out and struggled with deadly fury, but my hands were useless and he tore the onyx clasp from my coat and struck me full in the face. Then, as I fell, I heard Tessie's soft cry and her spirit fled to God, and even while falling I longed to follow her, for I knew that the King in Yellow had opened his tattered mantle and there was only Christ to cry to now.

I could tell more, but I cannot see what help it will be to the world. As for me I am past help or hope. As I lie here, writing, careless even whether or not I die before I finish, I can see the doctor gathering up his powders and phials with a vague gesture to the good priest beside me, which I understand.

They will be very curious to know the tragedy—they of the outside world who write books and print millions of newspapers, but I shall write no more, and the father confessor will seal my last words with the seal of sanctity when his holy office is done. They of the outside world may send their creatures into wrecked homes and death-smitten firesides, and their newspapers will batten on blood and tears, but with me their spies must halt before the confessional. They know that Tessie is dead and that

I am dying. They know how the people in the house, aroused by an infernal scream, rushed into my room and found one living and two dead, but they do not know what I shall tell them now; they do not know that the doctor said as he pointed to a horrible decomposed heap on the floor—the livid corpse of the watchman from the church: "I have no theory, no explanation. That man must have been dead for months!"

I think I am dying. I wish the priest would—

JOHN MASEFIELD, (1878–1967), first wanted to go to sea, and after two years of training he was apprenticed at fifteen to a windjammer, in which he sailed around Cape Horn. On the voyage he became seriously ill and was forced to return home by steamer. Recovering, he was appointed to the White Star Line's *Adriatic,* but before he reached his new post, he changed his mind and instead spent the next three years in New York working at a variety of minor jobs. He returned to England in 1897, determined to become a writer. His first book of poetry, *Salt-Water Ballads,* was published in 1902; it included his most famous poem of all, "Sea Fever." He soon established himself as poet, playwright, and novelist, and wrote a great many stories of action and adventure for boys. He was named poet laureate of England in 1930, the highest honor his government could bestow upon him.

The Sealman

John Masefield

"The seals is pretty when they do be playing," said the old woman. "Ah, I seen them frisking their tails till you'd think it was rocks with the seas beating on them, the time the storm's on. I seen the merrows of the sea sitting yonder on the dark stone, and they had crowns on them, and they were laughing. The merrows is not good; it's not good to see too many of them. They are beautiful like young men in their shirts playing hurley. They're as beautiful as anything you would be seeing in Amerikey or Australeyey, or any place. The seals is beautiful too, going through the water in the young of the day; but they're not so beautiful as them. The seals is no good either. It's a great curse keeps them the way they are, not able to live either in the sea or on the land." She shook her head saldy.

"One time there was a man of the O'Donnells came here, and he was a bad man. A saint in Heaven would have been bothered to find good in him. He died of the fever that came before the Famine. I was a girl then; and if you'd seen the people in them times; there wasn't enough to bury them. The pigs used to eat them in the loanings. And their mouths would be all green where they'd eaten grass from want of food. If you'd seen the houses there was then, indeed, you'd think the place bewitched. But the cabins is all fell in, like yonder, and there's no dancing or fiddling, or anything at all, and all of my friends is gone to Amerikey or Australeyey; I've no one at all to bury me, unless it's that humpy one who comes here, and she's as proud as a Jew. She's no cause to be proud, with a hump on her; her father was just a poor man, the same as any.

"This O'Donnell I was telling you. My father was at his wake. And they'd the candles lit, and they were drinking putcheen. My father was nearest the door, and a fear took him, and he got up, with his glass in his hand, and he cried out: 'There's something here is not good.' And another of them said: 'There's something wants to get out.' And another said: 'It's himself wants to go out into the dark night.' And another said: 'For the love of God, open the door.' So my father flung the door open; and, outside, the moon shone down to the sea. And the corpse of the O'Donnell was all blue, and it got up with the sheet knotted on it, and walked out without leaving a track. So they followed it, saying their prayers to Almighty God, and it walked on down to the sea. And when it came to the edge of the sea, the sea was like a flame before it. And it bowed there, three times; and each time it rose up it screamed. And all the seals, and all the merrows, and all them that's under the tides, they came up to welcome it. They called out to the corpse and laughed; and the corpse laughed back, and fell on to the sand. My father and the other men saw the wraith pass from it, into the water, as it fell.

"It was like a little black boy, laughing; with great long arms on him. It was all bald and black; and its hands moved like he was tickling.

"And after that the priest had him buried, like they buried the Old Ones; but the wraith passed into a bull seal. You would be feared to see the like of the bull seal. There was a man of the O'Kanes fired a blessed shilling at him, and the seal roared up at him and tore his arm across. There was marks like black stars on him after till he died. And the bull seal walked like a man at the change of the moon, like a big, tall, handsome man stepping the roads. You'd be feared, sir, if you saw the like. He set his eyes on young Norah O'Hara. Lovely she was. She'd little ways, sir, would draw the heart out of an old bachelor. Wasn't it a great curse he should take her when there was old hags the like of Mary that has no more beauty than a withered broom that you wouldn't be bothered to mend, or a done-out old gather-up of a duck that a hungry dog would blush to be biting? Still, he took Norah.

"She had a little son, and the little son was a sealman; the priest wouldn't sign him with the cross. When Norah died he used always to be going to the sea; he would always be swimming. He'd little soft brown hair, like a seal's, the prettiest you would be seeing. He used to talk to the seals. My father was coming home one night from Carnmore, and he saw the little sealman in the sea; and the seals were playing with him, singing songs. But my father was feared to hear; he ran away. They stoned the sealman, whiles, after that; but whiles they didn't stone it. They had a kindness for it, although it had no holy water on it. It was a very young thing to be walking the world, and it was a beautiful wee thing, with its eyes so pretty; so it grew up to be a man.

"Them that live in the water, they have ways of calling people. Them who passed this sealman, they felt the call in their hearts. Indeed, if you passed the sealman, stepping the roads, you would get a queer twist from the way he looked at you.

"And he set his love on a young girl of the O'Keefes, a little young girl with no more in her than the flower on its stalk. You would see them in the loanings coming home, or in the bright of the day going. There was a strong love was on them two young things; it was like the love of the Old Ones that took nine deaths to kill. They would be telling Kate it was not right she should set her love on one who wasn't like ourselves; but there's few indeed as the young'll listen. They are all for pleasure, all for pleasure, before they are withered hags. And at last they shut her up at home, to keep her from seeing him. And he came by her cabin to the west of the road, calling. There was a strong love came up to her at that, and she put down her sewing on the table, and 'Mother,' she says, 'there's no lock, and no key, and no bolt, and no door. There's no iron, nor no stone, nor anything at all will keep me this night from the man I love.' And she went out into the moonlight to him, there by the bush where the flowers is pretty, beyond the river. And he says to her: 'You are all of the beauty of the world, will you come where I go, over the waves of the sea?' And she says to him: 'My treasure and strength,' she says, 'I would follow you on the frozen hills, my feet bleeding.'

"Then they went down into the sea together, and the moon made a track upon the sea, and they walked down it; it was like a flame before them. There was no fear at all on her, only a great love like the love of the Old Ones, that was stronger than the touch of the fool. She had a little white throat, and little cheeks like flowers, and she went down into the sea with her man, who wasn't a man at all. She was drowned, of course. It's like he never thought that she wouldn't bear the sea like himself.

"When it come light they saw the sealman sitting yonder on the rock, and she lying by him dead, with her face as white as a flower. He was crying and beating her hands to bring life to her. It would have drawn pity from a priest to hear him though he wasn't a Christian. And at last, when he saw that she was drowned, he took her in his arms and slipped into the sea like a seal. And he swam, carrying her, with his head up, laughing and laughing and laughing, and no one ever saw him again at all."

CLARK ASHTON SMITH, (1893–1961), had only five years of formal school education. He began writing early, and by the age of seventeen he was selling regularly to *The Black Cat, The Overland Monthly,* and other popular magazines of the day. His first book of verse was published when he was nineteen. Always steeped in the supernatural tradition, Smith did not begin to make a name for himself in fiction until he began writing for *Weird Tales* in 1928. There he was influenced most heavily, as were virtually all of the contributors to the magazine during that time, by the works of H. P. Lovecraft. Smith started out to create his own mythological world, Hypoborea, elements of which were adopted by Lovecraft. During the 1930s, Smith, Lovecraft, and Robert E. Howard were the three most popular writers appearing in the magazine. The following story is typical of the magazine during its first twenty years, in its concentration on mood and evocation of dark images, rather than on story line.

A Night in Malnéant

Clark Ashton Smith

My sojourn in the city of Malnéant occurred during a period of my life no less dim and dubious than that city itself and the misty regions lying thereabout. I have no

precise recollection of its locality, nor can I remember
exactly when and how I came to visit it. But I had heard
vaguely that such a place was situated along my route;
and when I came to the fog-enfolded river that flows beside its walls, and heard beyond the river the mortuary
tolling of many bells, I surmised that I was approaching
Malnéant.

On reaching the gray, colossal bridge that crosses the
river, I could have continued at will on other roads leading to remoter cities: but it seemed to me that I might as
well enter Malnéant as any other place. And so it was
that I set foot on the bridge of shadowy arches, under
which the black waters flowed in stealthy division and were
joined again in a silence as of Styx and Acheron.

That period of my life, I have said, was dim and dubious: all the more so, mayhap, because of my need for
forgetfulness, my persistent and at times partially re-
warded search for oblivion. And that which I needed to
forget above all was the death of the lady Mariel, and the
fact that I myself had slain her as surely as if I had done
the deed with my own hand. For she had loved me with
an affection deeper and purer and more stable than mine;
and my changeable temper, my fits of cruel indifference or
ferocious irritability, had broken her gentle heart. So it
was that she had sought the anodyne of a lethal poison;
and after she was laid to rest in the somber vaults of her
ancestors, I had become a wanderer, followed and forever
tortured by a belated remorse. For months, or years, I
am uncertain which, I roamed from old-world city to city,
heeding little where I went if only wine and the other
agents of oblivion were available. . . . And thus I came,
somewhile in my indefinite journeying, to the dim en-
virons of Malnéant.

The sun (if ever there was a sun above this region)
had been lost for I knew not how long in a sky of leaden
vapors; the day was drear and sullen at best. But now, by
the thickening of the shadows and the mist, I felt that

evening must be near; and the bells I had heard, however heavy and sepulchral their tolling, gave at least the assurance of prospective shelter for the night. So I crossed the long bridge and entered the grimly yawning gate with a quickening of my footsteps even if with no alacrity of spirit.

The dusk had gathered behind the gray walls, but there were few lights in the city. Few people were abroad, and these went upon their way with a sort of solemn haste, as if on some funereal errand that would admit of no delay. The streets were narrow, the houses high, with overhanging balconies and heavily curtained or shuttered windows. All was very silent, except for the bells, which tolled recurrently, sometimes faint and far off, and sometimes with a loud and startling clangor that seemed to come almost from overhead.

As I plunged among the shadowy mansions, along the streets from which a visible twilight issued to envelop me, it seemed that I was going farther and farther away from my memories at every step. For this reason I did not at once inquire my way to a tavern but was content to lose myself more and more in the gray labyrinth of buildings, which grew vaguer and vaguer amid the ever-mounting darkness and fog, as if they were about to dissolve in oblivion.

I think that my soul would have been almost at peace with itself, if it had not been for the reiterant ringing of the bells, which were like all bells that toll for the repose of the dead, and therefore set me to remembering those that had rung for Mariel. But whenever they ceased, my thoughts would drift back with an indolent ease, a recovered security, to the all-surrounding vagueness. . . .

I have no idea how far I had gone in Malnéant, nor how long I had roamed among those houses that hardly seemed as if they could be peopled by any but the sleeping or the dead. At last, however, I became aware that I was very tired, and bethought me of food and wine and a lodging for the night. But nowhere in my wanderings had I noticed the sign board of an inn; so I resolved to ask the next passerby for the desired direction.

As I have said before, there were few people abroad. Now, when I made up my mind to address one of them, it appeared that there was no one at all; and I walked onward through street after street in my futile search for a living face.

At length I met two women, clothed in gray that was cold and dim as the folds of the fog, and veiled withal, who were hurrying along with the same funereal intentness I had perceived in all other denizens of that city. I made bold to accost them, asking if they could direct me to an inn.

Scarcely pausing or even turning their heads, they answered: "We cannot tell you. We are shroud weavers, and we have been busy making a shroud for the lady Mariel."

Now, at that name, which of all names in the world was the one I should least have expected or cared to hear, an unspeakable chill invaded my heart, and a dreadful dismay smote me like the breath of the tomb. It was indeed strange that in this dim city, so far in time and space from all I had fled to escape, a woman should have recently died who was also named Mariel. The coincidence appeared so sinister, that an odd fear of the streets through which I had wandered was born suddenly in my soul. The name had evoked, with a more irrevocable fatality than the tolling of the bells, all that I had vainly wished to forget; and my memories were like living coals in my heart.

As I went onward, with paces that had become more hurried, more feverish than those of the people of Malnéant, I met two men, who were likewise dressed from head to foot in gray; and I asked of them the same question I had asked of the shroud weavers.

"We cannot tell you," they replied. "We are coffin makers, and we have been busy making a coffin for the lady Mariel."

As they spoke, and hastened on, the bells rang out again, this time very near at hand, with a more dismal and sepulchral menace in their leaden tolling. And everything about me, the tall and misty houses, the dark, indefinite streets, the rare and wraithlike figures, became as if part of the obscure confusion and fear and bafflement of a nightmare. Moment by moment, the coincidence on which I had stumbled appeared all too bizarre for belief, and I was troubled now by the monstrous and absurd idea that the Mariel I knew had only just died, and that this fantastic city was in some unsurmisable manner connected with her death. But this, of course, my reason rejected summarily, and I kept repeating to myself: "The Mariel of whom they speak is another Mariel." And it irritated me beyond all measure that a thought so enormous and ludicrous should return when my logic had dismissed it.

I met no more people of whom to inquire my way. But at length, as I fought with my shadowy perplexity and my burning memories, I found that I had paused beneath the weather-beaten sign of an inn, on which the lettering had been half-effaced by time and the brown lichens. The building was obviously very old, like all the houses in Malnéant; its upper stories were lost in the swirling fog, except for a few furtive lights that glowed obscurely down; and a vague and musty odor of antiquity came forth to greet me as I mounted the steps and tried to open the ponderous door. But the door had been locked or bolted; so I began to pound upon it with my fists to attract the attention of those within.

After much delay, the door was opened slowly and grudgingly, and a cadaverous-looking individual peered forth, frowning with portentous gravity as he saw me.

"What do you desire?" he queried, in tones that were both brusk and solemn.

"A room for the night, and wine," I requested.

"We cannot accommodate you. All the rooms are occupied by people who have come to attend the obsequies of the lady Mariel; and all the wine in the house has been requisitioned for their use. You will have to go elsewhere."

He closed the door quickly upon me with the last words.

I turned to resume my wanderings, and all that had troubled me before was now intensified a hundredfold. The gray mists and the grayer houses were full of the menace of memory: they were like traitorous tombs from which the cadavers of dead hours poured forth to assail me with envenomed fangs and talons. I cursed the hour when I had entered Malnéant, for it seemed to me now that in so doing I had merely completed a funereal, sinister circle through time, and had returned to the day of Mariel's death. And certainly, all my recollections of Mariel, of her final agony and her entombment, had assumed the frightful vitality of present things. But my reason still maintained, of course, that the Mariel who lay dead somewhere in Malnéant, and for whom all these obsequial preparations were being made, was not the lady whom I had loved, but another.

After threading streets that were even darker and narrower than those before traversed, I found a second inn, bearing a similar weather-beaten sign, and in all other respects very much like the first. The door was barred, and I knocked thereon with trepidation and was in no manner surprised when a second individual with a cadaverous face informed me in tones of sepulchral solemnity:

"We cannot accommodate you. All the rooms have been taken by the musicians and mourners who will serve at the obsequies of the lady Mariel; and all the wine has been reserved for their use."

Now I began to dread the city about me with a manifold fear: for apparently the whole business of the people in Malnéant consisted of preparations for the funeral of this lady Mariel. And it began to be obvious that I must walk the streets of the city all night because of these same preparations. All at once, an overwhelming weariness was mingled with my nightmare terror and perplexity.

I had not long continued my peregrinations, after leaving the second inn, when the bells were tolled once more. For the first time, I found it possible to identify their source: they were in the spires of a great cathedral which loomed immediately before me through the fog. Some people were entering the cathedral, and a curiosity, which I knew to be both morbid and perilous, prompted me to follow them. Here, I somehow felt, I should be able to learn more regarding the mystery that tormented me.

All was dim within, and the light of many tapers scarcely served to illumine the vast nave and altar. Masses were being said by priests in black whose faces I could not see distinctly; and to me, their chanting was like words in a dream; and I could hear nothing, and nothing was plainly visible in all the place, except a bier of opulent fabrics on which there lay a motionless form in white. Flowers of many hues had been strewn upon the bier, and their fragrance filled the air with a drowsy languor, with an anodyne that seemed to drug my heart and brain. Such flowers had been cast on the bier of Mariel; and even thus, at her funeral, I had been overcome by a momentary dulling of the senses because of their perfume.

Dimly I became aware that someone was at my elbow. With eyes still intent on the bier, I asked:

"Who is it that lies yonder, for whom these masses are being said and these bells are rung?" And a slow, sepulchral voice replied:

"It is the lady Mariel, who died yesterday and who will be interred tomorrow in the vaults of her ancestors. If you wish, you may go forward and gaze upon her."

So I went down the cathedral aisle, even to the side of the bier, whose opulent fabrics trailed on the cold flags. And the face of her who lay thereon, with a tranquil smile upon the lips, and tender shadows upon the shut eyelids, was the face of the Mariel I had loved and of none other. The tides of time were frozen in their flowing; and all that was or had been or could be, all of the world that existed aside from her, became as fading shadows; and even as once before (was it eons or instants ago?) my soul was locked in the marble hell of its supreme grief and regret. I could not move, I could not cry out nor even weep, for my very tears were turned to ice. And now I knew with a terrible certitude that this one event, the death of the lady Mariel, had drawn apart from all other happenings, had broken away from the sequences of time and had found for itself a setting of appropriate gloom and solemnity; or perhaps had even built around itself the whole enormous maze of that spectral city, in which to abide my destined return among the mists of a deceptive oblivion.

At length, with an awful effort of will, I turned my eyes away; and leaving the cathedral with steps that were both hurried and leaden, I sought to find an egress from the dismal labyrinth of Malnéant to the gate by which I had entered. But this was by no means easy, and I must have roamed for hours in alleys blind and stifling as tombs, and along the tortuous, self-reverting thoroughfares, ere I came to a familiar street and was able henceforward to direct my paces with something of surety. And a dull and sunless daylight was dawning behind the mists when I crossed the bridge and came again to the road that would lead me away from that fatal city.

Since then, I have wandered long and in many places. But never again have I cared to revisit those old-world realms of fog and mist, for fear that I should come once more to Malnéant, and find that its people are still busied with their preparations for the obsequies of the lady Mariel.

CATHERINE LUCILLE MOORE, (b. 1911), in Indianapolis, burst into prominence and immediate popularity with the publication of her first story, "Shambleau," in *Weird Tales*. The first of a series of adventures of Northwest Smith, the story was science fiction, rather than fantasy. But it had been rejected by all of the science-fiction markets of the day because of its dark atmosphere —something in which *Weird Tales* specialized. The story that follows also features Northwest Smith, but is pure fantasy. It originally appeared in the second issue of an amateur magazine that had a total circulation of only sixty copies, but is a perfect example of the *Weird Tales* subclass of the fantasy genre. After she married fellow author Henry Kuttner in June, 1940, the C. L. Moore byline rarely appeared. But she had not entered retirement; rather, for the next eighteen years, from their marriage until his untimely death of a heart attack, virtually every story to appear under the Kuttner name or any of his multitudinous bylines was a team effort. An occasional story, however, still showed the Moore trademark, as in the most famous story of all to come from the team, *Vintage Season* (published under the pseudonym of Lawrence O'Donnell and frequently anthologized).

Werewoman

C. L. Moore

With the noise of battle fading behind him down the wind, Northwest Smith staggered into the west and the twilight, stumbling as he went. Blood spattered brightly behind him on the rocks, leaving a clear trail to track him by, but he knew he would not be followed far. He was headed into the salt wastelands to the westward, and they would not follow him there.

He urged his reluctant feet faster, for he knew that he must be out of sight in the gray waste before the first of the scavengers came to loot the dead. They would follow —that trail of blood and staggering footsteps would draw them like wolves on his track, hot in the hope of further spoils—but they would not come far. He grinned a little wryly at the thought, for he was going into no safety here, though he left certain death behind. He was stumbling, slow step by step, into almost as certain a death, of fever and thirst and hunger in the wastelands, if no worse death caught him first. They told tales of this gray salt desert . . .

He had never before come even this far into the cold waste during all the weeks of their encampment. He was too old an adventurer not to know that when people shun a place completely and talk of it in whispers and tell little half-finished, fearful stories of it over campfires, that place is better left alone. Some might have been spurred by that very reticence into investigation, but Northwest Smith had seen too many strange things in his checkered career to doubt the basis of fact behind folk-tales or care to rush in heedlessly where others had learned by experience not to tread.

The sound of battle had dwindled to a faint murmur on the evening breeze. He lifted his head painfully and stared into the gathering dark ahead with narrowed eyes the no-color of pale steel. The wind touched his keen, scarred face with a breath of utter loneliness and desolation. No man-smell of smoke or byre or farmstead tainted it, blowing clear across miles beyond miles of wastelands. Smith's nostrils quivered to that scent of unhumanity. He saw the grayness stretching before him, flat and featureless, melting into the dark. There was a sparse grass growing, and low shrub and a few stunted trees, and brackish water in deep, still pools dotted the place at far intervals. He found himself listening . . .

Once in very long-ago ages, so campfire whispers had told him, a forgotten city stood here. Who dwelt in it, or what, no man knew. It was a great city spreading over miles of land, rich and powerful enough to wake enmity, for a mighty foe had come at last out of the lowlands and in a series of tremendous battles razed it to the ground. What grievance they had against the dwellers in the city no one will ever know now, but it must have been dreadful, for when the last tower was laid to earth and the last stone toppled from its foundation, they had sown the land with salt, so that for generations no living thing grew in all the miles of desolation. And not content with this, they had laid a curse upon the very earth wherein the city had its roots, so that even today men shun the place without understanding why.

It was very long past, that battle, and history forgot the very name of the city, and victor and vanquished alike sank together into the limbo of the forgotten. In time the salt-sown lands gained a measure of life again and the sparse vegetation that now clothed it struggled up through the barren soil. But men still shunned the place.

They said, in whispers, that there were dwellers yet in the saltlands. Wolves came out by night sometimes and carried off children straying late; sometimes a new-made grave was found open and empty in the morning, and people breathed of ghouls . . . late travellers had heard voices wailing from the wastes by night, and those daring hunters who ventured in search of the wild game that ran through the underbrush spoke fearfully of naked werewomen that howled in the distance. No one knew what became of the adventurous souls who traveled too far alone into the desolation of the place. It was accursed for human feet to travel, and those who dwelt there, said the legends, must be less than human.

Smith discounted much of this when he turned from the
bloody shambles of that battle into the wastelands beyond.
Legends grow, he knew. But a basis for the tales he did
not doubt, and he glanced ruefully down at the empty
holsters hanging low on his legs. He was completely unarmed, perhaps for the first time in more years than he
liked to remember; for his path had run for the most part
well outside the law, and such men do not go unarmed
anywhere—even to bed.

Well, no help for it now. He shrugged a little, and then
grimaced and caught his breath painfully, for that slash in
the shoulder was deep, and blood still dripped to the
ground, though not so freely as before. The wound was
closing. He had lost much blood—the whole side of his
leather garment was stiff with it, and the bright stain
spattering behind him told of still greater losses. The pain
of his shoulder stabbed at him yet, but it was being swallowed up now in a vast, heaving grayness . . .

He drove his feet on stubbornly over the uneven
ground, though the whole dimming landscape was wavering before him like a sea—swelling monstrously—receding
into the vague distances . . . The ground floated up to
meet him with surprising gentleness.

He opened his eyes presently to a gray twilight, and
after a while staggered up and went on. No more blood
flowed, but the shoulder was stiff and throbbing, and the
wasteland heaved still like a rolling sea about him. The
singing in his ears grew loud, and he was not sure whether
the faint echoes of sound he heard came over gray distances or rang in his own head—long, faint howls, like
wolves wailing their hunger to the stars. When he fell the
second time he did not know it, and was surprised to
open his eyes upon full dark with stars looking down on
him and the grass tickling his cheek.

He went on. There was no great need of it now—he
was well beyond pursuit, but the dim urge to keep moving
dinned in his weary brain. He was sure now that the long

howls were coming to him over the waste stretches; coming nearer. By instinct his hand dropped to clutch futilely at the empty holster.

There were queer little voices going by overhead in the wind. Thin, shrill. With immense effort he slanted a glance upward and thought he could see, with the clarity of exhaustion, the long, clean lines of the wind streaming across the sky. He saw no more than that, but the small voices shrilled thinly in his ears.

Presently he was aware of motion beside him—life of some nebulous sort moving parallel to his course, invisible in the starlight. He was aware of it through the thrill of evil that prickled at the roots of his hair, pulsing from the dimness at his side—though he could see nothing. But with that clarity of inner vision he felt the vast and shadowy shape lurching formlessly through the grass at his side. He did not turn his head again, but the hackles of his neck bristled. The howls were nearing, too. He set his teeth and drove on, unevenly.

He fell for the third time by a clump of stunted trees, and lay for a while breathing heavily while long, slow waves of oblivion washed over him and receded like waves over sand. In the intervals of lucidity he knew that those howls were coming closer over the grayness of salt-lands.

He went on. The illusion of that formless walker-in-the-dark still haunted him through the grass, but he was scarcely heeding it now. The howls had changed to short, sharp yaps, crisp in the starlight, and he knew that the wolves had struck his trail. Again, instinctively, his hand flashed downward toward his gun, and a spasm of pain crossed his face. Death he did not mind—he had kept pace with it too many years to fear that familiar visage—but death under fangs, unarmed . . . He staggered on a little faster, and the breath whistled through his clenched teeth.

Dark forms were circling his, slipping shadowily through

the grass. They were wary, these beasts of the outlands. They did not draw near enough for him to see them save as shadows gliding among the shadows, patient and watching. He cursed them futilely with his failing breath, for he knew now that he dared not fall again. The gray waves washed upward, and he shouted something hoarse in his throat and called upon a last reservoir of strength to bear him up. The dark forms started at his voice.

So he went on, wading through oblivion that rose waist-high, shoulder-high, chin-high—and receded again before the indomitable onward drive that dared not let him rest. Something was wrong with his eyes now—the pale-steel eyes that had never failed him before—for among the dark forms he was thinking he saw white ones, slipping and gliding wraithlike in the shadow . . .

For an endless while he stumbled on under the chilly stars while the earth heaved gently beneath his feet and the grayness was a sea that rose and fell in blind waves, and white figures weaved about through the hollow dark.

Quite suddenly he knew that the end of his strength had come. He knew it surely, and in the last moment of lucidity left to him he saw a low tree outlined against the stars and staggered to it—setting his broad back against the trunk, fronting the dark watchers with lowered head and pale eyes that glared defiance. For that one moment he faced them resolutely—then the tree trunk was sliding upward past him—the ground was rising—he gripped the sparse grass with both hands, and swore as he fell.

When he opened his eyes again he stared into a face straight out of hell. A woman's face, twisted into a diabolical smile, stooped over him—glare-eyed in the dark. White fangs slavered as she bent to his throat.

Smith choked back a strangled sound that was half oath, half prayer, and struggled to his feet. She started back with a soundless leap that set her wild hair flying, and stood staring him in the face with wide slant eyes that glared greenly from the pallor of her face. Through dark hair, her body was white as a sickle moon, half-veiled in the long, wild hair.

She glared with hungry fangs a-drip. Beyond her he sensed other forms, dark and white, circling restlessly through the shadows—and he began to understand dimly, and knew that there was no hope in life for him, but he spread his long legs wide and gave back glare for glare, pale-eyed and savage.

The pack circled him, dim blurs in the dark, the green glare of eyes shining alike from white shapes and black. And to his dizzied eyes it seemed that the forms were not stable; shifting from dark to light and back again with only the green-glowing eyes holding the same glare through all the changing. They were closing in now, the soft snarls rising and sharp yaps impatiently breaking through the guttural undernotes, and he saw the gleam of teeth, white under the stars.

He had no weapon, and the wasteland reeled about him and the earth heaved underfoot, but he squared his shoulders savagely and fronted them in hopeless defiance, waiting for the wave of darkness and hunger to come breaking over him in an overwhelming tide. He met the green desire of the woman's wild eyes as she stepped forward, gathering herself for the lunge, and suddenly something about the fierceness of her struck a savage chord within him, and —facing death as he was—he barked a short, wild laugh at her, and yelled into the rising wind. "Come on, werewoman! Call your pack!"

She stared for the briefest instant, half-poised for leaping—while something like a spark seemed to flash between them, savageness calling to savageness across the barriers of everything alive—and suddenly she flung up her arms, the black hair whirling, and tossed back her head and bayed to the stars; a wild, long ululating yell and tossed it from voice to voice across the saltlands until the very stars shivered at the wild, exultant baying.

And as the long yell trembled into silence something

inexplicable happened to Smith. Something quivered in answer within him, agonizingly, the gray oblivion he had been fighting so long swallowed him up at a gulp—and then he leaped within himself in a sudden, ecstatic rush; and while one part of him slumped to its knees and then to its face in the grass, the living vital being that was Smith sprang free into the cold air that stung like sharp wine.

The wolf-pack rushed clamorously about him, the wild, high yells shivered delightfully along every nerve of his suddenly awakened body. And it was as if a muffling darkness had lifted from his senses, for the night opened up in all directions to his new eyes, and his nostrils caught fresh, exciting odor on the streaming wind and in his ears a thousand tiny sounds took on sudden new clarity and meaning.

The pack that had surged so clamorously about him was a swirl of dark bodies for an instant—then in a blur and a flash they were dark no longer—rose on hind legs and cast off the darkness as they rose—and slim, white, naked werewomen swirled around him in a tangle of flashing limbs and streaming hair.

He stood half-dazed at the transition, for even the wide salt moor was no longer dark and empty, but pale gray under the stars and peopled with nebulous, unstable beings that wavered away from the white wolf-pack which ringed him, and above the clamour of wild voices that thin, shrill chattering went streaming down the wind overhead.

Out of the circling pack a white figure broke suddenly, and he felt cold arms about his neck and a cold, thin body pressing his. Then the white whirl parted violently and another figure thrust through—the fierce-eyed woman who had called him across the barriers of flesh into this half-land of her own. Her green-glaring eyes stabbed at the sister-wolf whose arms twined Smith's neck, and the growl that broke from her lips was a wolf's guttural. The woman fell away from Smith's embrace, crouching at bay, as the other, with a toss of wild hair, bared her fangs and launched herself straight at the throat of the interloper. They went down in a tangle of white and tossing dark, and the pack fell still so that the only sound was the heavy breathing of the fighters and the low, choked snarls that rippled from their throats. Then over the struggle of white and black burst a sudden torrent of scarlet. Smith's nostrils flared to the odor that had a new, fascinating sweetness now—and the werewoman rose, bloody-mouthed, from the body of her rival. The green-glowing eyes met his, and a savage exultation flowing from them met as savage a delight wakening in his, and her keen, moon-white face broke into a smile of hellish joy.

She flung up her head again and bayed a long, triumphant cry to the stars, and the pack about her took up the yell, and Smith found his own face turned to the sky and his own throat shouting a fierce challenge to the dark.

Then they were running—jostling one another in savage play, flying over the coarse grass on feet that scarcely brushed the ground. It was like the rush of the wind, that effortless racing, as the earth flowed backward under their spurning feet and the wind streamed in their nostrils with a thousand tingling odors. The white werewoman raced at his side, her long hair flying behind her like a banner, her shoulder brushing his.

They ran through strange places. The trees and the grass had taken on new shapes and meanings, and in a vague, half-realized way he was aware of curious forms looming round him—buildings, towers, walls, high turrets shining in the starlight, yet so nebulous that they did not impede their flight. He could see these shadows of a city very clearly sometimes—sometimes he ran down marble streets, and it seemed to him that his feet rang in golden sandals on the pavement and rich garments whipped behind him in the wind of his speed, and a sword clanked at his side. He thought the woman beside him fled in bright-colored sandals too, and her long skirts rippled away from her

flying limbs and the streaming hair was twined with jewels
—yet he knew he ran naked beside a moon-bare wolfwoman over coarse grass that rustled to his tread.

And sometimes, too, it seemed to him that he fled on
four legs, not two—fleetly as the wind, thrusting a pointed
muzzle into the breeze and lolling a red tongue over dripping fangs . . .

Dim shapes fled from their sweeping onward rush—
great, blurred, formless things; dark beings with eyes; thin
wraiths wavering backward from their path. The great
moor teemed with these half-seen monstrosities; fierce-
eyed, some of them, breathing out menace, and evil, angry
shapes that gave way reluctantly before the werepack's
sweep. But they gave way. There were terrible things in
that wasteland, but the most terrible of all were the werewomen, and all the dreadful, unreal beings made way at
the bay of those savage voices. All this he knew intuitively.
Only the thin chattering that streamed down the wind did
not hush when the werevoices howled.

There were many odors on the wind that night, sharp
and sweet and acrid, wild odors of wild, desolate lands
and the dwellers therein. And then, quite suddenly on a
vagrant breeze, lashing their nostrils like a whip—the
harsh, rich, blood-tingling scent of man. Smith flung up
his head to the cold stars and bayed long and shudder-
ingly, and the wild wolf-yell rang from throat to throat
through the pack until the whole band of them was shaking the very air to that savage chorus. They loped down
the wind stream, nostrils flaring to that full, rich scent.

Smith ran at the forefront, shoulder to shoulder with
the wild white creature who had fought for him. The man-
smell was sweet in his nostrils, and hunger wrenched at
him as the smell grew stronger and faint atavistic stirrings
of anticipation rose in his memory . . . Then they saw
them.

A little band of hunters was crossing the moorland,
crashing through the underbrush, guns on their shoulders.

Blindly they walked, stumbling over hummocks that were clear to Smith's new eyes. And all about them the vague denizens of the place were gathering unseen. Great, nebulous, cloudy shapes dogged their footsteps through the grass, lurching along formlessly. Dark things with eyes flitted by, turning a hungry glare unseen upon the hunters. White shapes wavered from their path and closed in behind. The men did not see them. They must have sensed the presence of inimical beings, for now and then one would glance over his shoulder nervously, or hitch a gun forward as if he had almost seen—then lower it sheepishly and go on.

The very sight of them fired that strange hunger in Smith's new being, and again he flung back his head and yelled fiercely the long wolf-cry toward the frosty stars. At the sound of it a ripple of alarm went through the unclean, nebulous crowd that dogged the hunters' footsteps. Eyes turned toward the approaching pack, glaring angrily from bodies as unreal as smoke. But as they drew nearer the press began to melt away, the misty shapes wavering off reluctantly into the pallor of the night before the sweep of the wolves.

They skimmed over the grass, flying feet spurning the ground, and with a rush and a shout they swooped down around the hunters, yelling their hunger. The men had huddled into a little knot, backs together and guns bristling outward as the werepack eddied round them. Three or four men fired at random into the circling pack, the flash and sound of it sending a wavering shudder through the pale things that had drawn back to a safe distance, watching. But the wolfwomen paid no heed.

Then the leader—a tall man in a white fur cap— shouted suddenly in a voice of panic terror. "No use to fire! No use—don't you see? These aren't real wolves . . ."

Smith had a fleeting realization that to human eyes they must, then, seem wolf-formed, though all about him in the pale night he saw clearly only white, naked women with flying hair circling the hunters and baying hungrily with wolf-voices as they ran.

The dark hunger was ravaging him as he paced the narrowing circle with short, nervous steps—the human bodies so near, smelling so richly of blood and flesh. Vaguely memories of that blood running sweetly eddied through his mind, and the feel of teeth meeting solidly to flesh; and beyond that a deeper hunger, inexplicably, for something he could not name. Only he felt he would never have peace again until he had sunk his teeth into the throat of that man in the white fur cap; felt blood gushing over his face . . .

"Look!" shouted the man, pointing as his eyes met Smith's ravenous glare. "See—the big one with white eyes, running with the she-wolf . . ." He fumbled for something inside his coat. "The Devil himself—all the rest are green-eyed, but—white eyes—see!"

Something in the sound of his voice lashed that hunger in Smith to the breaking point. It was unbearable. A snarl choked up in his throat and he gathered himself to spring. The man must have seen the flare of it in the pale eyes meeting his, for he shouted, "God in Heaven!" and clawed desperately at his collar. And just as Smith's feet left the ground in a great, steel-muscled spring straight for that tempting throat, the man ripped out what he had been groping for and the starlight caught the glint of it exposed —a silver cross dangling from a broken chain.

Something blinding exploded in Smith's innermost brain. Something compounded of thunder and lightning smote him in midair. An agonized howl ripped itself from his throat as he fell back, blinded and deafened and dazed, while his brain rocked to its foundations and long shivers of dazzling force shuddered through the air about him.

Dimly, from a great distance, he heard the agonized howls of the werewomen, the shouts of men, the trample of shod feet on the ground. Behind his closed eyes he could still see that cross upheld, a blinding symbol from which streamers of forked lightning blazed away and the air crackled all around.

When the tumult had faded in his ears and the blaze died away and the shocked air shuddered into stillness again, he felt the touch of cold, gentle hands upon him and opened his eyes to the green glare of other eyes bending over him. He pushed her away and struggled to his feet, swaying a little as he stared round the plain. All the white werewomen were gone, save the one at his side. The huntsmen were gone. Even the misty denizens of the place were gone. Empty in the gray dimness the wasteland stretched away. Even the thin piping overhead had fallen into shocked silence. All about them the plain lay still, shuddering a little and gathering its forces again after the ordeal.

The werewoman had trotted off a little way and was beckoning to him impatiently over her shoulder. He followed, instinctively anxious to leave the spot of the disaster. Presently they were running again, shoulder to shoulder across the grass, the plain spinning away under their flying feet. The scene of that conflict fell behind them, and strength was flowing again through Smith's light-footed body, and overhead, faintly, the thin, shrill chattering began anew.

With renewed strength the old hunger flooded again through him, compellingly. He tossed up his head to test the wind, and a little whimper of eagerness rippled from his throat. An answering whine from the running woman replied to it. She tossed back her hair and sniffed the wind, hunger flaming in her eyes. So they ran through the pale night, hunter and huntress, while dim shapes wavered from their path and the earth reeled backward under their spurning feet.

It was pleasant to run so, in perfect unison, striding effortlessly with the speed of the wind, arrogantly in the knowledge of their strength, as the dreadful dwellers of the aeon-cursed moor fled from their approach and the very air shuddered when they bayed.

Again the illusion of misty towers and walls wavered in the dimness before Smith's eyes. He seemed to run down marble-paved streets, and felt again the clank of a belted sword and the ripple of rich garments, and saw the skirts of the woman beside him moulded to her limbs as she fled along with streaming, jewel-twined hair. He thought that the buildings rising so nebulously all around were growing higher as they advanced. He caught vague glimpses of arches and columns and great domed temples, and began, somehow uneasily, to sense presences in the streets, unseen but thronging.

Then simultaneously his feet seemed to strike a yielding resistance, as if he had plunged at a stride knee-deep into heavy water, and the woman beside him threw up her arms wildly in a swirl of hair and tossed back her head and screamed hideously, humanly, despairingly—the first human sound he had heard from her lips—and stumbled to her knees on the grass that was somehow a marble pavement.

Smith bent to catch her as she fell, plunging his arms into unseen resistance as he did so. He felt it suck at her as he wrenched the limp body out of those amazing, invisible wavelets that were lapping higher and higher up his legs with incredible swiftness. He swung her up clear of them, feeling the uncontrollable terror that rippled out from her body course in unbroken wavelets through his own, so he shook with nameless panic, not understanding why. The thick tide had risen mufflingly about his thighs when he turned back the way he had come and began to fight his way out of the clinging horror he could not see, the woman a weight of terror in his arms.

It seemed to be a sort of thickness in the air, indescribable, flowing about him in deepening waves that lapped up and up as if some half-solidified jelly were swiftly and relentlessly engulfing him. Yet he could see nothing but the grass underfoot, the dim, dreamlike marble pavement, the night about, the cold stars overhead. He struggled forward through the invisible thickness. It was worse than trying to run through water, with the retarded motion of nightmares. It sucked at him, draggingly, as he struggled forward through the deeps of it, stumbling, not daring to fall, the woman a dead weight in his arms.

And very slowly he won free. Very slowly he forced his way out of the clinging horror. The little lapping waves of it ceased to mount. He felt the thickness receding downward, past his knees, down about his ankles, until only his feet sucked and stumbled in invisibility, the nameless mass shuddering and quaking. And at long last he broke again, and as his feet touched the clear ground, he leaped forward wildly, like an arrow from a bow, into the delightful freedom of the open air. It felt like pure flying after that dreadful struggle through the unseen. Muscles exulting at the release, he fled over the grass like a winged thing while the dim building reeled away behind him and the woman stirred a little in his arms, an inconsidered weight in the joy of freedom.

Presently she whimpered a little, and he paused by a stunted tree to set her down again. She glanced round wildly. He saw from the look on her bone-white face that the danger was not yet past, and glanced round himself, seeing nothing but the dim moor with wraith-like figures wavering here and there and the stars shining down coldly. Overhead the thin shrilling went by changelessly in the wind. All this was familiar. Yet the werewoman stood poised for instant flight, seeming unsure in just what direction danger lay, and her eyes glared panic into the dimness. He knew then that dreadful though the werepack was, a more terrible thing haunted the wasteland—invisibly, frightfully indeed to wake in the wolfwoman's eyes that staring horror. Then something touched his foot.

He leaped like the wild thing he was, for he knew that feel—even in so short a time he knew that feel. It was flowing round his foot, sucking at his ankle even as he poised for flight. He seized the woman's wrist and twisted round, wrenching his foot from the invisible grip, leaping forward arrow-swift into the pale darkness. He heard her catch her breath in a sobbing gasp, eloquent of terror, as she fell into stride beside him.

So they fled, invisibility ravening at their heels. He knew, somehow, that it followed. The thick, clutching waves of it were lapping faster and faster just short of his flying feet, and he strained to the utmost, skimming over the grass like something winged and terror-stricken, the sobbing breath of the woman keeping time to his stride. What he fled he could not even guess. It had no-form in any image he could conjure up. Yet he felt dimly that it was nothing alien, but rather something too horribly akin to him . . . and the deadly danger he did not understand spurred on his flying feet.

The plain whirled by blurrily in their speed. Dim things with eyes fluttered away in panic as they neared, clearing a terror-stricken way for the dreadful werepeople who fled in such blind horror of something more dreadful yet.

For eternities they ran. Misty towers and walls fell away behind them. In his terror-dimmed mind it seemed to him in flashes that he was the other runner clad in rich garments and belted with the sword, running beside that other fleeing woman from another horror whose nature he did not know. He scarcely felt the ground underfoot. He ran blindly, knowing only that he must run and run until he dropped, that something far more dreadful than any death he could die was lapping hungrily at his heels, threatening him with an unnameable, incomprehensible horror—that he must run and run and run . . .

And so, very slowly, the panic cleared. Very gradually sanity returned to him. He ran still, not daring to stop, for he knew the invisible hunger lapped yet not far behind —knew it surely without understanding how—but his mind had cleared enough for him to think, and his thoughts told curious things, half-realized things that formed images in his brain unbidden, drawn from some far source beyond his understanding. He knew, for instance, that the thing at their heels was inescapable. He knew that it would never cease its relentless pursuit, silent, invisible, remorseless, until the thick waves of it had swallowed up its quarry, and what followed that—what unimaginable horror—he somehow knew, but could not form even into thought-pictures. It was something too far outside any experience for the mind to grasp it.

The horror he felt instinctively was entirely within himself. He could see nothing pursuing him, feel nothing, hear nothing. No tremor of menace reached toward him from the following nothingness. But within him horror swelled and swelled balloonlike, a curious horror akin to something that was part of him, so it was as if he fled in terror of himself, and with no more hope of ever escaping than if indeed he fled his own shadow.

The panic had passed. He no longer ran blindly, but he knew now that he must run and run forever, hopelessly . . . but his mind refused to picture the end. He thought the woman's panic had abated, too. Her breathing was evener, not the frantic gasping of that first frenzy, and he no longer felt the shaking waves of pure terror beating out from her against the ephemeral substance that was himself.

And now, as the gray landscape slid past changelessly and the thin shapes still wavered from their path and the piping went by overhead, he became conscious as he ran of a changing in the revulsion that spurred him on. There were little moments when the horror behind drew him curiously, tightening its hold on that part of his being so strangely akin to it. As a man might stare over a precipice edge and feel the mounting urge to fling himself over, even in the face of his horror of falling, so Smith felt the strong pull of the thing that followed, if thing it might be called. Without abatement in his horror the curious desire grew to turn and face it, let it come lapping over him, steep himself in the thick invisibility—even though his whole being shuddered violently from the very thought.

Without realizing it, his pace slackened. But the woman knew, and gripped his hand fiercely, a frantic appeal rippling through him from the contact. At her touch, the pull abated for a while and he ran on in an access of revulsion, very conscious of the invisibility lapping at their heels.

While the access was at its height he felt the grip of her hand loosen a little and knew that the strange tugging at something within was reaching out for her. His hand tightened over hers and he felt the little shake she gave to free herself of that blind pull.

So they fled, the strength in each bearing the other up. Behind them relentlessly the Something followed. Twice a forward lapping wave of it brushed Smith's heel. And stronger and stronger grew the blind urge within him to turn, to plunge into the heavy flow of what followed, to steep himself in invisibility until—until— He could form no picture of that ultimate, but each time he reached the point of picturing it a shudder went over him and blankness clouded his mind.

And ever within him that thing akin to the Follower strengthened and grew, a blind urge from his innermost being. It grew so strong that only the grip of the werewoman's hand held him from turning, and the plain faded from about him like a gray dream and he ran through a curving void—a void that he somehow knew was bending back upon itself so that he must eventually, if he ran on, come round behind his pursuer and overtake it, wade head-on into the thick deeps of invisibility . . . yet he dared not slacken his running, for then it would catch him from behind. So he spun in the treadmill, terror ahead, terror behind, with no choice but to run and no hope for all his running.

When he saw the plain at all it was in dim flashes, unaccountably blurred and not always at the correct angles. It tilted without reason. Once he saw a dark pool of water slanting before him like a door, and once a whole section of landscape hung miragelike above his head. Sometimes he panted up steeper inclines, sometimes he skimmed fleetly down steeper slopes—yet he knew the plain in reality lay flat and featureless from edge to edge.

And now, though he had long ago left those misty towers and walls far behind, he began to be aware that his flight had somehow twisted and they loomed once more, shadowily, overhead. With a sickening sense of futility he fled again down the dream-vague marble pavements between rows of cloudy palaces.

Through all these dizzy metamorphoses the pursuer flowed relentlessly behind, lapping at his heels when he slowed. He began to realize, very dimly, that it might have overtaken him with ease, but that he was being spurred on thus for some vast, cloudy purpose—perhaps so that he might complete the circle he was so vaguely aware of and plunge of his own effort headlong into the very thing from which he fled. But he was not fleeing now, he was being driven.

The dim shapes of buildings reeled past. The woman running at his side had become something cloudy and vague too, a panting presence flying from the same peril —into the same peril—but unreal as a dream. He felt himself unreal too, a phantom fleeing hand in hand with another phantom through the streets of a phantom city. And all reality was melting away save the unreal, invisible thing that pursued him, and only it had reality while everything else faded to shapes of nothingness. Like driven ghosts they fled.

And as reality melted about them, the shadowy city took firmer shape. In the reversal everything real became cloudy, grass and trees and pools dimming like some forgotten dream, while the unstable outlines of the towers loomed up more and more clearly in the pale dark, colors flushing them as if reviving blood ran through the stones. Now the city stood firm and actual around them, and vague trees thrust themselves mistily through unbroken masonry, shadows of grass waved over firm marble pavements. Superimposed upon the unreal, the real world seemed vague as a mirage.

It was a curious architecture that rose around them now, so old and so forgotten that the very shapes of it were fantastic to Smith's eyes. Men in silk and steel moved down the streets, wading to their greave-clad knees in shadowy grass they did not seem to see. Women, too, brushed by in mail as fine-linked and shining as gowns of silver tissue, belted with swords like the men. Their faces were set in a strained stare, and though they hurried they gave an impression of aimlessness, as if moved by some outer compulsion they did not understand.

And through the hurrying crowd, past the strange-colored towers, over the grass-shadowed streets, werewoman and wolfman fled like the shadows they had become, pale wraiths blowing through the crowds unseen, the invisible follower lapping at their feet when they faltered. That force within which had urged them to turn and meet the pursuer now commanded them irresistibly to flee—to flee toward that same ending, for they knew now that they ran toward what they fled, roundaboutly; yet dared not stop running for deadly fear of what flowed along behind.

Yet in the end they did turn. The werewoman ran now in blind submission, all the strength dissolved that at first had carried her on. She was like a ghost blowing along on a gale, unresisting, unquestioning, hopeless. But in Smith a stouter spirit dwelt. And something strong and insistent was urging him to turn—an insistence that had no relation to the other urge to wait. It may have been a very human revolt against being driven, it may have been a deeply ingrained dislike of running from anything, or of allowing death to overtake him from behind. It had been bred in him to face danger when he could not escape it, and the old urge that every fighting thing knows—even a cornered rat will turn—drove him at last to face what followed him and die resisting—not in flight. For he felt that the end must be very near now. Some instinct stronger than the force that harried them told that.

And so, ignoring the armored crowd that eddied round them, he gripped the werewoman's wrist hard and slackened his speed, fighting against the urge that would have driven him on, choking down the panic that rose involuntarily as he waited for the thick waves to begin their surging round his feet. Presently he saw the shadow of a tree leaning through the smooth stone of a building, and instinctively he chose that misty thing he knew to be real for a bulwark to set his back against, rather than the unreal wall that looked so solid to his eyes. He braced his shoulders, holding a firm grip on the woman's wrist as she struggled and whimpered and moaned in her wolf voice, straining to break the hold and run on. About, the mailclad crowd hurried by heedlessly.

And very soon he felt it—the lapping wavelets touching his toes. He shuddered through all his unreal body at the feel, but he stood steady, gripping the struggling wolfwoman in a resolute hold, feeling the thick waves flowing around his feet, creeping up to his ankles, lapping higher and higher round his legs.

For a while he stood at bay, feeling terror choke up and up in his throat as the waves rose round him, scarcely heeding the woman's struggles to be free. And then a further rebellion began to stir. If die he must, let it be neither in headlong flight nor in dazed and terrified quiescence, but violently, fighting against it, taking some toll, if he could, to pay for the life he was to lose. He gasped a deep breath and plunged forward into the quaking, unseen mass that had risen almost to his waist. Behind him at arm's length the werewoman stumbled unwillingly.

He lurched forward. Very swiftly the unseen rose about him, until arms and shoulders were muffled in thickness, until the heavy invisibility brushed his chin, his closed mouth, sealed his nostrils . . . closed over his head.

Through the clear deeps he forged on, moving like a man in a nightmare of retarded motion. Every step was an immense effort against that flow, dragged through resisting depths of jellylike nothingness. He had all but forgotten the woman he dragged along behind. He had wholly forgotten the colored city and the shining, armored people hurrying past. Blinded to everything but the deep-rooted instinct to keep moving, he forced his slow way onward against the flow. And indescribably he felt it begin to permeate him, seeping in slowly through the atoms of his ephemeral being. He felt it, and felt a curious change coming over him by degrees, yet could not define it or understand what was happening. Something urged him fiercely to go on, to struggle ahead, not to surrender—and so he fought, his mind whirling and the strange stuff of the thing that engulfed him soaking slowly through his being.

Presently the invisibility took on a faint body, a sort of clear opaqueness, so that the things outside were streaked and blurred a little and the splendid dream city with its steel-robed throngs wavered through the walls of what had swallowed him up. Everything was shaking and blurring and somehow changing. Even his body no longer obeyed him completely, as if it trembled on the verge of transition into something different and unknown. Only the driving instinct to fight on held clear in his dazed mind. He struggled forward.

And now the towered city was fading again, its mailed people losing their outlines and melting into the grayness. But the fading was not a reversal—the shadow grass and trees grew more shadowy still. It was as if by successive steps he was leaving all matter behind. Reality had faded almost to nothing, even the cloudy unreality of the city was going now, and nothing but a gray blankness remained, a blankness through which he forged stubbornly against the all-engulfing flow that steeped him in nothingness.

Sometimes in flashes he ceased to exist—joined the gray nothing as part of it. The sensation was not that of unconsciousness. Somehow utter nirvana swallowed him up and freed him again, and between the moments of blank he fought on, feeling the transition of his body taking place very slowly, very surely, into something that even now he could not understand.

For gray eternities he struggled ahead through the clogging resistance, through darknesses of nonexistence, through flashes of near-normality, feeling somehow that the path led in wild loops and whorls through spaces without name. His time sense had stopped. He could hear and see nothing, he could feel nothing but the immense effort of dragging his limbs through the stuff that enfolded him, and the effort was so great that he welcomed those spaces of blankness when he did not exist even as an unconsciousness. Yet stubbornly, unceasingly, the blind intinct drove him on.

There was a while when the flashes of nonexistence crowded closer and closer, and the metamorphosis of his body was all but complete, and only during brief winks of consciousness did he realize himself as an independent being. Then in some unaccountable way the tension slackened. For a long moment without interludes he knew himself a real being struggling upstream through invisibility and dragging a half-fainting woman by the wrist. The clarity of it startled him. For a while he could not understand—then it dawned upon him that his head and shoulders were free—free! What had happened he could not imagine, but he was free of it.

The hideous gray nothingness had gone—he looked
out over a plain dotted with low trees and low, white,
columned villas like no architecture he had ever seen before. A little way ahead a stone slab no higher than
himself leaned against a great boulder in a hollow fringed
with trees. Upon the slab an indescribable symbol was
incised. It was like no symbol of any writing he had ever
seen before. It was so different from all the written
characters men make that it scarcely seemed akin to writing at all, nor traced by any human hand. Yet there was
a curious familiarity about it, that did not even puzzle
him. He accepted it without question. He was somehow
akin to it.

And between him and the engraved slab the air writhed
and undulated. Streamers of invisibility flowed toward
him, mounting as they flowed. He struggled forward, exultation surging within him. For—he knew, now. And as
he advanced the thick resistance fell away from him, sliding down his shoulders, ebbing lower and lower about his
struggling body. He knew that whatever the invisibility
was, its origin lay in that symbol on the stone. From that
it flowed. Half visibly, he could see it. And toward that
stone he made his way, a dim purpose forming in his
brain.

He heard a little gasp and quickened breathing behind
him, and turned his head to see the werewoman, moon
white in the undulating, almost-visible flow, staring about
with wakened eyes and incomprehension clouding her
face. He saw that she did not remember anything of what
had happened. Her green-glowing eyes were empty as if
they had just opened from deep slumber.

He forged on swiftly now through the waves that lapped
futilely around his waist. He had won. Against what he
did not yet know, nor from what cloudy terror he had
saved himself and her, but he was not afraid now. He
knew what he must do, and he struggled on eagerly toward the slab.

He was still waist-deep in the resisting flow when he reached it, and for a dizzy instant he thought he could not stop; that he must wade on into the very substance of that unnameable carving out of which came the engulfing nothingness. But with an effort he wrenched himself round and waded cross-stream, and after a while of desperate struggle he broke free into the open air.

It was like a cessation of gravity. In the release from that dragging weight he felt he must scarcely be touching the ground, but there was no time now to exult in his freedom. He turned purposefully toward the slab.

The werewoman was just floundering clear of the stream when she saw what he intended, and she flung up her hands with a shriek of protest that startled Smith into a sidewise leap, as if some new terror were coming upon him. Then he saw what it was and gave her an amazed stare as he turned again to the stone, lifting his arms to grapple with it. She reeled forward and seized him in a cold, desperate embrace, dragging backward with all her might. Smith glared at her and shook his shoulders impatiently. He had felt the rock give a little. But when she saw that, she screamed again piercingly, and her arms twined like snakes as she struggled to drag him away.

She was very strong. He paused to unwind the fierce clasp and she fought savagely to prevent it. He needed all his strength to break her grip, and he pushed her from him then with a heavy shove that sent her reeling. The pale eyes followed her, puzzling why, though she had fled in such a frenzy of terror from what flowed out of the stone, she still strove to prevent him from destroying it. For he was quite sure that if the slab were broken and the symbol destroyed that stream would cease to flow. He could not understand her. He shook his shoulders impatiently and turned again to the stone.

This time she was on him with an animal spring, snarling low in her throat and clawing with frantic hands. Her fangs snapped just clear of his throat. Smith wrenched free with a great effort, for she was steel strong and very desperate, and gripped her by the shoulder, swinging her away. Then he set his teeth and drove a heavy fist into her face, smashing against the fangs. She yelped, short and sharply, and collapsed under his hand, sinking to the grass in a huddle of whiteness and wild black hair.

He turned to the stone again. This time he got a firm grip on it, braced his legs wide, heaved. And he felt it give. He heaved again. And very slowly, very painfully, he uprooted its base from the bed where for ages it must have lain. Rock ground protestingly against rock. One edge rose a little, then settled. And the slab tilted. He heaved again, and very deliberately he felt it slipping from his hands. He stood back, breathing slowly, and watched.

Majestically, the great slab tottered. The stream flowing invisibly from its incised symbol twisted in a streaked path through the air, long whorls of opacity blurring the landscape beyond. Smith thought he felt a stirring in the air, a shiver as of warning. All the white villas dimly seen through the dark wavered a little before his eyes, and something hummed through the air like a thin, high wailing too sharp to be heard save as a pain to the ears. The chattering overhead quickened suddenly. All this in the slow instant while the slab tottered.

Then it fell. Deliberately slow, it leaned outward and down. It struck the ground with a rush and a splintering crash. He saw the long cracks appear miraculously upon its surface as the great fantastic symbol broke into fragments. The opacity that had flowed outward from it writhed like a dragon in pain, flung itself high-arching into the shivering air—and ceased. In that moment of cessation the world collapsed around him. A mighty wind swooped down in a deafening roar, blurring the landscape. He thought he saw the white villas melting like dreams, and he knew the werewoman on the grass must have recovered consciousness, for he heard a wolf yell of utter agony from behind him. Then the great wind blotted out all other things, and he was whirling through space in a dizzy flight.

In that flight understanding overtook him. In a burst of illumination he knew quite suddenly what had happened and what would happen now—realized without surprise, as if he had always known it, that the denizens of this wasteland had dwelt here under the protection of that mighty curse laid upon the land in the long-past century when the city fell. And he realized that it must have been a very powerful curse, laid down by skill and knowledge that has long vanished even from the legends of man, for in all the ages since, this accursed moor had been safe haven for all the half-real beings that haunt mankind, akin to the evil that lay like a blanket over the moor.

And he knew that the curse had its origin in the nameless symbol which some sorcerer of forgotten times had inscribed upon the stone, a writing from some language which can have no faintest kinship with man. He knew that the force flowing out from it was a force of utter evil, spreading like a river over the whole salt waste. The stream of it lapped to and fro in changing courses over the land, and when it neared some dweller of the place the evil that burnt for a life force in that dweller acted as a magnet to the pure evil which was the stream. So, evil answering to evil, the two fused into one, the unfortunate dweller swallowed up into a nirvana of nonexistence in the heart of that slow-flowing stream.

It must have worked strange changes in them. That city whose shapes of shadow still haunted the place assumed reality, taking on substance and becoming more and more actual as the reality of the captive waned and melted into the power of the stream.

He thought, remembering those hurrying throngs with their strained, pale faces, that the spirits of the people who had died in the lost city must be bound tenuously to the spot of their death. He remembered that young, richly garmented warrior he had been one with in fleeting moments, running golden-sandaled through the streets of the forgotten city in a panic of terror from something too long past to be remembered—the jeweled woman in her colored sandals and rippling robes running at his side—and wondered in the space of a second what their story had been so many ages ago. He thought that curse must somehow have included the dwellers in the city, chaining them in earthbound misery for centuries. But of this he was not sure.

Much of all this was not clear to him, and more he realized without understanding, but he knew that the instinct which guided him to turn upstream had not been a false one—that something human and alien in him had been a talisman to lead his staggering feet back toward the source of his destroyer. And he knew that with the breaking up of the symbol that was a curse, the curse ceased to be, and the warm, sweet, life-giving air that humanity breathes swept in a flood across the barrens, blowing away all the shadowy, unclean creatures to whom it had been haven for so long. He knew—he knew . . .

Grayness swooped round him, and all knowledge faded from his mind and the wind roared mightily in his ears. Somewhere in that roaring flight oblivion overtook him.

When he opened his eyes again he could not for an instant imagine where he lay or what had happened. Weight pressed upon his entire body suffocatingly, pain shot through it in jagged flashes. His shoulder ached deeply. And the night was dark, dark about him. Something muffling and heavy had closed over his senses, for no longer could he hear the tiny, sharp sounds of the plain or scent those tingling odors that once blew along the wind. Even the chattering overhead had fallen still. The place did not even smell the same. He thought he could catch from afar the odor of smoke, and somehow the air, as nearly as he could tell with his deadened senses, no longer breathed of desolation and loneliness. The smell of life was in the wind, very faintly. Little pleasant odors of flower scent and kitchen smoke seemed to tinge it.

"—wolves must have gone," someone was saying above him. "They stopped howling a few minutes ago—notice? —first time since we came into this damned place. Listen."

With a painful effort Smith rolled his head sideways and stared. A little group of men was gathered around him, their eyes lifted just now to the dark horizon. In the new density of the night he could not see them clearly, and he blinked in irritation, striving to regain that old, keen, clarity he had lost. But they looked familiar. One wore a white fur cap on his head. Someone said, indicating something beyond Smith's limited range of vision, "Fellow here must have had quite a tussle. See the dead she-wolf with her throat torn out? And look—all the wolf tracks everywhere in the dust. Hundreds of them. I wonder . . ."

"Bad luck to talk about them," broke in the fur-capped leader. "Werewolves, I tell you—I've been in this place before, and I know. But I never saw or heard of a thing like what we saw tonight—that big white-eyed one running with the she-wolves. God! I'll never forget those eyes."

Smith moved his head and groaned. The men turned quickly.

"Look, he's coming to," said someone, and Smith was vaguely conscious of an arm under his head and some liquid, hot and strong, forced between his lips. He opened his eyes and looked up. The fur-capped man was bending over him. Their eyes met. In the starlight, Smith's were colorless as pale steel.

The man choked something inarticulate and leaped back so suddenly that the flask spilled its contents half over

Smith's chest. He crossed himself frankly with a hand that shook.

"Who—who are you?" he demanded unsteadily.

Smith grinned wearily and closed his eyes.

THEODORE STURGEON, (b. 1918), was one of the earliest discoveries of John W. Campbell, and Sturgeon's first stories for him appeared in the pages of *Astounding Science Fiction*. But as with many of his contemporaries, Sturgeon was equally at home in the sister genre of fantasy, and some of his most delightful stories appeared in *Unknown* (later *Unknown Worlds)* and after World War II, in *Weird Tales* and the other fantasy magazines of the day. Unlike *Weird Tales, Unknown* was concerned less with atmosphere than with story line; Campbell rarely published the grisly tale that relied on the reeking odor of grave mold to frighten the reader. Instead, he and his writers set out to prove that horror existed in the everyday world and could be discovered even in the bright sunlight. The following story of a shop that sold bottles with things in them is a perfect example of the *Unknown* brand of horror.

Shottle Bop

Theodore Sturgeon

I'd never seen the place before, and I lived just down the block and around the corner. I'll even give you the address, if you like. "The Shottle Bop," between Twentieth and Twenty-first Streets, on Tenth Avenue in New York City. You can find it if you go there looking for it. Might even be worth your while, too.

But you'd better not.

"The Shottle Bop." It got me. It was a small shop with a weather-beaten sign swung from a wrought crane, creaking dismally in the late fall wind. I walked past it, thinking of the engagement ring in my pocket and how it had just been handed back to me by Audrey, and my mind was far removed from such things as shottle bops. I was thinking that Audrey might have used a gentler term than "useless" in describing me; and her neatly turned remark about my being a "constitutional psychopathic incompetent" was as uncalled-for as it was spectacular. She must have read it somewhere, balanced as it was by "And I wouldn't marry you if you were the last man on earth!" which is a notably worn cliché.

"Shottle Bop!" I muttered, and then paused, wondering where I had picked up such oddly rhythmic syllables with which to express myself. I'd seen it on that sign, of course, and it had caught my eye. "And what," I asked myself, "might be a Shottle Bop?" Myself replied promptly, "Dunno. Toddle back and have a look." So toddle I did, back along the east side of Tenth, wondering what manner of man might be running such an establishment in pursuance of what kind of business. I was enlightened on the second point by a sign in the window, all but obscured by the dust and ashes of apparent centuries, which read:

WE SELL BOTTLES

There was another line of smaller print there. I rubbed at the crusted glass with my sleeve and finally was able to make out:

With things in them.

Just like that:

WE SELL BOTTLES
With things in them.

Well of course I went in. Sometimes very delightful things come in bottles, and the way I was feeling, I could stand a little delighting.

"Close it!" shrilled a voice, as I pushed through the door. The voice came from a shimmering egg adrift in the air behind the counter, low-down. Peering over, I saw that it was not an egg at all, but the bald pate of an old man who was clutching the edge of the counter, his scrawny body streaming away in the slight draft from the open door, as if he were made of bubbles. A mite startled, I kicked the door with my heel. He immediately fell on his face, and then scrambled to his feet.

"Ah, it's good to see you again," he rasped.

I think his vocal cords were dusty, too. Everything else here was. As the door swung to, I felt as if I were inside a great dusty brain that had just opened its eyes. Oh yes, there was light enough. But it wasn't the lamp light and it wasn't daylight. It was like—like reflected from the cheeks of pale people. Can't say I enjoyed it much.

"What do you mean, 'again'?" I asked irritably. "You never saw me before."

"I saw you when you came in and I fell down and got up and saw you again," he quibbled, and beamed. "What can I do for you?"

"Oh," I said. "Well, I saw your sign. What have you got in a bottle that I might like?"

"What do you want?"

"What've you got?"

He broke into a piping chant—I remember it yet, word for word.

For half a buck, a vial of luck
    Or a bottle of nifty breaks
Or a flask of joy, or Myrna Loy
    For luncheon with sirloin steaks.

Pour out a mug from this old jug,
    And you'll never get wet in rains.
I've bottles of grins and racetrack wins
And lotions to ease your pains.

Here's bottles of imps and wet-pack shrimps
    From a sea unknown to men,
And an elixir to banish fear,
    And the sap from the pipes of Pan.

With the powdered horn of a unicorn
    You can win yourself a mate;
With the rich hobnob; or get a job—
    It's yours at a lowered rate.

"Now wait right there!" I snapped. "You mean you actually sell dragon's blood and ink from the pen of Friar Bacon and all such mumbo-jum?"

H nodded rapidly and smiled all over his improbable face.

I went on, "The genuine article?"

He kept on nodding.

I regarded him for a moment. "You mean to stand there with your teeth in your mouth and your bare face hanging out and tell me that in this day and age, in this city and in broad daylight, you sell such trash and then expect me —me, an enlightened intellectual—"

"You are very stupid and twice as bombastic," he said quietly.

I glowered at him and reached for the doorknob—and there I froze. And I mean froze. The old man whipped out an ancient bulb-type atomizer and squeezed a couple of whiffs at me as I turned away; and so help me, *I couldn't move!* I could cuss, though, and boy, did I.

The proprietor hopped over the counter and ran over to

me. He must have been standing on a box back there, for now I could see he was barely three feet tall. He grabbed my coattails, ran up my back and slid down my arm, which was extended doorward. He sat down on my wrist and swung his feet and laughed up at me. As far as I could feel, he weighed absolutely nothing.

When I had run out of profanity—I pride myself on never repeating a phrase of invective—he said, "Does that prove anything to you, my cocky and unintelligent friend? That was the essential oil from the hair of the Gorgon's head. And until I give you an antidote, you'll stand there from now till a week text Neusday!"

"Get me out of this," I roared, "or I'll smack you so hard you'll lose your brains through the pores in your feet!"

He giggled.

I tried to tear loose again and couldn't. It was as if all my epidermis had turned to high-carbon steel. I began cussing again, but quit in despair.

"You think altogether too much of yourself," said the proprietor of the Shottle Bop. "Look at you! Why, I wouldn't hire you to wash my windows. You expect to marry a girl who is accustomed to the least of animal comfort, and then you get miffed because she turns you down. Why does she turn you down? Because you won't get a job. You're a no-good. You're a bum. Hee hee! And you have the nerve to walk around telling people where to get off. Now if I were in your position I would ask politely to be released, and then I would see if anyone in this shop would be good enough to sell you a bottle full of something that might help out."

Now I never apologize to anybody, and I never back down, and I never take any guff from mere tradesmen. But this was different. I'd never been petrified before, nor had my nose rubbed in so many galling truths. I relented. "Okay, okay; let me break away then. I'll buy something."

"Your tone is sullen," he said complacently, dropping

lightly to the floor and holding his atomizer at the ready. "You'll have to say 'Please. Pretty please.'"

"Pretty please," I said, almost choking with humiliation.

He went back to the counter and returned with a paper of powder which he had me sniff. In a couple of seconds I began to sweat, and my limbs lost their rigidity so quickly that it almost threw me. I'd have been flat on my back if the man hadn't caught me and solicitously led me to a chair. As strength dribbled back into my shocked senses, it occurred to me that I might like to flatten this hobgoblin for pulling a trick like that. But a strange something stopped me—strange because I'd never had the experience before. It was simply the idea that once I got outside I'd agree with him for having such a low opinion of me.

He wasn't worrying. Rubbing his hands briskly, he turned to his shelves. "Now let's see . . . what would be best for you, I wonder? Hm-m-m. Success is something you couldn't justify. Money? You don't know how to spend it. A good job? You're not fitted for one." He turned gentle eyes on me and shook his head. "A sad case. *Tsk, tsk.*" I crawled. "A perfect mate? Nup. You're too stupid to recognize perfection, too conceited to appreciate it. I don't think that I can— Wait!"

He whipped four or five bottles and jars off the dozens of shelves behind him and disappeared somewhere in the dark recesses of the store. Immediately there came sounds of violent activity—clinkings and little crashes; stirrings and then the rapid susurrant grating of a mortar and pestle; then the slushy sound of liquid being added to a dry ingredient during stirring; and at length, after quite a silence, the glugging of a bottle being filled through a filtering funnel. The proprietor reappeared triumphantly bearing a four-ounce bottle without a label.

"This will do it!" he beamed.

"That will do what?"

"Why, cure you!"

"Cure—" My pompous attitude, as Audrey called it,

had returned while he was mixing. "What do you mean, cure? I haven't got anything!"

"My dear little boy," he said offensively, "you most certainly have. Are you happy? Have you ever been happy? No. Well, I'm going to fix all that up. That is, I'll give you the start you need. Like any other cure, it requires your cooperation.

"You're in a bad way, young fellow. You have what is known in the profession as retrogressive metempsychosis of the ego in its most malignant form. You are a constitutional unemployable; a downright sociophagus. I don't like you. Nobody likes you."

Feeling a little bit on the receiving end of a blitz, I stammered, "W-what do you aim to do?"

He extended the bottle. "Go home. Get into a room by yourself—the smaller the better. Drink this down, right out of the bottle. Stand by for developments. That's all."

"But—what will it do to me?"

"It will do nothing *to* you. It will do a great deal *for* you. It can do as much for you as you want it to. But mind me, now. As long as you use what it gives you for your self-improvement, you will thrive. Use it for self-gratification, as a basis for boasting, or for revenge, and you will suffer in the extreme. Remember that, now."

"But what is it? How—"

"I am selling you a talent. You have none now. When you discover what kind of a talent it is, it will be up to you to use it to your advantage. Now go away. I still don't like you."

"What do I owe you?" I muttered, completely snowed under by this time.

"The bottle carries its own price. You won't pay anything unless you fail to follow my directions. Now will you go, or must I uncork a bottle of jinn—and I don't mean London Dry?"

"I'll go," I said. I'd seen something swirling in the

depths of a ten-gallon carboy at one end of the counter, and I didn't like it a bit. "Good-bye."

"Bood-gye," he returned.

I went out and I headed down Tenth Avenue and I turned east up Twentieth Street and I never looked back. And for many reasons I wish now that I had, for there was, without doubt, something very strange about that Shottle Bop.

I didn't simmer down until I got home; but once I had a cup of black Italian coffee under my belt I felt better. I was skeptical about it at last. I was actually inclined to scoff. But somehow I didn't want to scoff too loudly. I looked at the bottle a little scornfully, and there was a certain something about the glass of it that seemed to be staring back at me. I sniffed and threw it up behind some old hats on top of the closet, and then sat down to unlax. I used to love to unlax. I'd put my feet on the doorknob and slide down in the upholstery until I was sitting on my shoulder blades, and as the old saying has it, "Sometimes I sets and thinks, and sometimes I just sets." The former is easy enough, and is what even an accomplished loafer has to go through before he reaches the latter and more blissful state. It takes years of practice to relax sufficiently to be able to "just set." I'd learned it years ago.

But just as I was about to slip into the vegetable status, I was annoyed by something. I tried to ignore it. I manifested a superhuman display of lack of curiosity, but the annoyance persisted. A light pressure on my elbow, where it draped over the arm of the chair. I was put in the unpleasant predicament of having to concentrate on what it was; and realizing that concentration on anything was the least desirable thing there could be. I gave up finally, and with a deep sigh, opened my eyes and had a look.

It was the bottle.

I screwed up my eyes and then looked again, but it was still there. The closet door was open as I had left it, and its shelf almost directly above me. Must have fallen out.

Feeling that if the damn thing were on the floor it couldn't fall any farther, I shoved it off the arm of my chair with my elbow.

It bounced. It bounced with such astonishing accuracy that it wound up in exactly the same spot it had started from—on the arm of the easy chair, by my elbow. Startled, I shoved it violently. This time I pushed it hard enough to send it against the wall, from which it rebounded to the shelf under my small table, and thence back to the chair arm—and this time it perched cozily against my shoulder. Jarred by the bouncing, the stopper hopped out of the bottle mouth and rolled into my lap; and there I sat, breathing the bittersweet fumes of its contents, feeling frightened and silly as hell.

I grabbed the bottle and sniffed. I'd smelled that somewhere before—where was it? Uh—oh, yes; that mascara the Chinese honkytonk girls use in Frisco. The liquid was dark—smoky black. I tasted it cautiously. It wasn't bad. If it wasn't alcoholic, then the old man in the shop had found a darn good substitute for alcohol. At the second sip I liked it and at the third I really enjoyed it and there wasn't any fourth because by then the little bottle was a dead marine. That was about the time I remembered the name of the black ingredient with the funny smell. Kohl. It is an herb the Orientals use to make it possible to see supernatural beings. Silly superstition!

And then the liquid I'd just put away, lying warm and comfortable in my stomach, began to fizz. Then I think it began to swell. I tried to get up and couldn't. The room seemed to come apart and throw itself at me piecemeal, and I passed out.

Don't you ever wake up the way I did. For your own sake, be careful about things like that. Don't swim up out of a sodden sleep and look around you and see all those things fluttering and drifting and flying and creeping and crawling around you—puffy things dripping blood, and filmy, legless creatures, and little bits and snatches of pasty human anatomy. It was awful. There was a human hand afloat in the air an inch away from my nose; and at my startled gasp it drifted away from me, fingers fluttering in the disturbed air from my breath. Something veined and bulbous popped out from under my chair and rolled across the floor. I heard a faint clicking, and looked up into a gnashing set of jaws without any face attached. I think I broke down and cried a little. I know I passed out again.

The next time I awoke—must have been hours later, because it was broad daylight and my clock and watch had both stopped—things were a little better. Oh, yes, there were a few horrors around. But somehow they didn't bother me much now. I was practically convinced that I was nuts; now that I had the conviction, why worry about it? I dunno; it must have been one of the ingredients in the bottle that had calmed me down so. I was curious and excited, and that's about all. I looked around me and I was almost pleased.

The walls were green! The drab wallpaper had turned to something breathtakingly beautiful. They were covered with what seemed to be moss; but never moss like that grew for human eyes to see before. It was long and thick, and it had a slight perpetual movement—not that of a breeze, but of growth. Fascinated, I moved over and looked closely. Growing indeed, with all the quick magic of spore and cyst and root and growth again to spore; and the swift magic of it was only a part of the magical whole, for never was there such a green. I put out my hand to touch and stroke it, but I felt only the wallpaper. But when I closed my fingers on it, I could feel that light touch of it in the palm of my hand, the weight of twenty sunbeams, the soft resilience of jet darkness in a closed place. The sensation was a delicate ecstasy, and never have I been happier than I was at that moment.

Around the baseboards were little snowy toadstools, and the floor was grassy. Up the hinged side of the closet door climbed a mass of flowering vines, and their petals were hued in tones indescribable. I felt as if I had been blind until now, and deaf, too; for now I could hear the whispering of scarlet, gauzy insects among the leaves and the constant murmur of growth. All around me was a new and lovely world, so delicate that the wind of my movements tore petals from the flowers, so real and natural that it defied its own impossibility. Awestruck, I turned and turned, running from wall to wall, looking under my old furniture, into my old books; and everywhere I looked I found newer and more beautiful things to wonder at. It was while I was flat on my stomach looking up at the bed springs, where a colony of jewellike lizards had nested, that I first heard the sobbing.

It was young and plaintive, and had no right to be in my room where everything was so happy. I stood up and looked around, and there in the corner crouched the translucent figure of a little girl. She was leaning back against the wall. Her thin legs were crossed in front of her, and she held the leg of a tattered toy elephant dejectedly in one hand and cried into the other. Her hair was long and dark, and it poured and tumbled over her face and shoulders.

I said, "What's the matter, kiddo?" I hate to hear a child cry like that.

She cut herself off in the middle of a sob and shook the hair out of her eyes, looking up and past me, all fright and olive skin and big, filled violet eyes. "Oh!" she squeaked.

I repeated, "What's the matter? Why are you crying?"

She hugged the elephant to her breast defensively, and whimpered, "W-where are you?"

Surprised, I said, "Right here in front of you, child. Can't you see me?"

She shook her head. "I'm scared. Who are you?"

"I'm not going to hurt you. I heard you crying, and I wanted to see if I could help you. Can't you see me at all?"

"No," she whispered. "Are you an angel?"

I guffawed. "By no means!" I stepped closer and put my hand on her shoulder. The hand went right through her and she winced and shrank away, uttering a little wordless cry. "I'm sorry," I said quickly. "I didn't mean . . . you can't *see* me at all? I can see you."

She shook her head again. "I think you're a ghost," she said.

"Do tell," I said. "And what are you?"

"I'm Ginny," she said. "I have to stay here, and I have no one to play with." She blinked, and there was a suspicion of further tears.

"Where did you come from?" I asked.

"I came here with my mother," she said. "We lived in lots of other rooming houses. Mother cleaned floors in office buildings. But this is where I got so sick. I was sick a long time. Then one day I got off the bed and come over here but then when I looked back I was still on the bed. It was awful funny. Some men came and put the 'me' that was on the bed onto a stretcher and took it— me—out. After a while mummy left, too. She cried for a long time before she left, and when I called to her she couldn't hear me. She never came back, and I just got to stay here."

"Why?"

"Oh, I got to. I—don't know why. I just—got to."

"What do you do here?"

"I just stay here and think about things. Once a lady lived here, had a little girl just like me. We used to play together until the lady watched us one day. She carried on somethin' awful. She said her little girl was possessed. The girl kept callin' me, 'Ginny! Ginny! Tell mamma you're here!'; an' I tried, but the lady couldn't see me. Then the lady got scared an' picked up her little girl an' cried, an' so I was sorry. I ran over here an' hid, an' after a while the other little girl forgot about me, I guess. They moved," she finished with pathetic finality.

I was touched. "What will become of you, Ginny?"

"I dunno," she said, and her voice was troubled. "I guess I'll just stay here and wait for mummy to come back. I been here a long time. I guess I deserve it, too."

"Why, child?"

She looked guiltily at her shoes. "I couldn' stand feelin' so awful bad when I was sick. I got up out of bed before it was time. I shoulda stayed where I was. This is what I get for quittin'. But mummy'll be back; just you see."

"Sure she will," I muttered. My throat felt tight. "You take it easy, kid. Any time you want someone to talk to, you just pipe up. I'll talk to you any time I'm around."

She smiled, and it was a pretty thing to see. What a raw deal for a kid! I grabbed my hat and went out.

Outside things were the same as in the room to me. The hallways, the dusty stair carpets wore new garments of brilliant, nearly intangible foliage. They were no longer dark, for each leaf had its own pale and different light. Once in a while I saw things not quite so pretty. There was a giggling thing that scuttled back and forth on the third floor landing. It was a little indistinct, but it looked a great deal like Barrel-head Brogan, a shanty Irish bum who'd returned from a warehouse robbery a year or so ago, only to shoot himself accidentally with his own gun. I wasn't sorry.

Down on the first floor, on the bottom step, I saw two youngsters sitting. The girl had her head on the boy's shoulders, and he had his arms around her, and I could see the banister through them. I stopped to listen. Their voices were faint, and seemed to come from a long way away.

He said, "There's one way out."

She said, "Don't talk that way, Tommy!"

"What else can we do? I've loved you for three years, and we still can't get married. No money, no hope—no nothing. Sue, if we did do it, I just *know* we'd always be together. Always and always—"

After a long time she said, "All right, Tommy. You get

a gun, like you said." She suddenly pulled him even closer. "Oh, Tommy, are you sure we'll always be together just like this?"

"Always," he whispered, and kissed her. "Just like this."

Then there was a long silence, while neither moved. Suddenly they were as I had first seen them, and he said:

"There is only one way out."

And she said, "Don't talk that way, Tommy!"

And he said, "What else can we do? I've loved you for three years—" It went on like that, over and over and over.

I felt lousy. I went on out into the street.

It began to filter through to me what had happened. The man in the shop had called it a "talent." I couldn't be crazy, could I? I didn't *feel* crazy. The draught from the bottle had opened my eyes on a new world. What was this world?

It was a thing peopled by ghosts. There they were— storybook ghosts, and regular haunts, and poor damned souls—all the fixings of a storied supernatural, all the things we have heard about and loudly disbelieved and secretly wonder about. So what? What had it all to do with me?

As the days slid by, I wondered less about my new, strange surroundings, and gave more and more thought to that question. I had bought—or been given—a talent. I could see ghosts. I could see all parts of a ghostly world, even the vegetation that grew in it. That was perfectly reasonable—the trees and birds and fungi and flowers. A ghost world is a world as we know it, and a world as we know it must have vegetation. Yes, I could see them. But they couldn't see me!

Okay; what could I get out of it? I couldn't talk about it or write about it because I wouldn't be believed; and besides, I had this thing exclusive, as far as I knew; why cut a lot of other people in on it?

On what, though?

No, unless I could get a steer from somewhere, there was no percentage in it for me that I could see. And then, about six days after I took that eye-opener, I remembered the one place where I might get that steer.

The Shottle Bop!

I was on Sixth Avenue at the time, trying to find something in a five-and-dime that Ginny might like. She couldn't touch anything I brought her but she enjoyed things she could look at—picture books and such. By getting her a little book on photographs of trains since the "De Witt Clinton," and asking her which of them was like ones she had seen, I found out approximately how long it was she'd been there. Nearly eighteen years. Anyway, I got my bright idea and headed for Tenth Avenue and the Shottle Bop. I'd ask the old man—he'd tell me. And when I got to Twenty-first Street, I stopped and stared. Facing me was a blank wall. The whole side of the block was void of people. There was no sign of a shop.

I stood there for a full two minutes not even daring to think. Then I walked downtown toward Twentieth, and then uptown to Twenty-first. Then I did it again. No shop. I wound up without my question answered—what was I going to do with this "talent"?

I was talking to Ginny one afternoon about this and that when a human leg, from the knee down, complete and puffy, drifted between us. I recoiled in horror, but Ginny pushed it gently with one hand. It bent under the touch, and started toward the window, which was open a little at the bottom. The leg floated toward the crack and was sucked through like a cloud of cigarette smoke, reforming again on the other side. It bumbled against the pane for a moment and then ballooned away.

"My gosh!" I breathed. "What *was* that?"

Ginny laughed. "Oh, just one of the Things that's all 'e time flying around. Did it scare you? I used to be scared, but I saw so many of them that I don't care any more, so's they don't light on me."

"But what in the name of all that's disgusting are they?"

"Parts." Ginny was all childish *savoir faire*.

"Parts of what?"

"People, silly. It's some kind of a game, I think. You see, if someone gets hurt and loses something—a finger or an ear or something, why, the ear—the *inside* part of it, I mean, like me being the inside of the 'me' they carried out of here—it goes back to where the person who owned it lived last. Then it goes back to the place before that, and so on. It doesn't go very fast. Then when something happens to a whole person, the 'inside' part comes looking for the rest of itself. It picks up bit after bit— Look!" she put out a filmy forefinger and thumb and nipped a flake of gossamer out of the air.

I leaned over and looked closely; it was a small section of semitransparent human skin, ridged and whorled.

"Somebody must have cut his finger," said Ginny matter-of-factly, "while he was living in this room. When something happens to um—you see! He'll be back for it!"

"Good heavens!" I said. "Does this happen to everyone?"

"I dunno. Some people have to stay where they are— like me. But I guess if you haven't done nothing to deserve bein' kept in one place, you have to come all around pickin' up what you lost."

I'd thought of more pleasant things in my time.

For several days I'd noticed a gray ghost hovering up and down the block. He was always on the street, never inside. He whimpered constantly. He was—or had been— a little inoffensive man of the bowler hat and starched collar type. He paid no attention to me—none of them did, for I was apparently invisible to them. But I saw him so often that pretty soon I realized that I'd miss him if he went away. I decided I'd chat with him the next time I saw him.

I left the house one morning and stood around for a few minutes in front of the brownstone steps. Sure enough, pressing through the flotsam of my new, weird coexistent world, came the slim figure of the wraith I had noticed, his rabbit face screwed up, his eyes deep and sad, and his swallowtail coat and striped waistcoat immaculate. I stepped up behind him and said, "Hi!"

He started violently and would have run away, I'm sure, if he'd known where my voice was coming from.

"Take it easy, pal," I said. "I won't hurt you."

"Who are you?"

"You wouldn't know if I told you," I said. "Now stop shivering and tell me about yourself."

He mopped his ghostly face with a ghostly handkerchief, and then began fumbling nervously with a gold toothpick. "My word," he said. "No one's talked to me for years. I'm not quite myself, you see."

"I see," I said. "Well, take it easy. I just happen to've noticed you wandering around here lately. I got curious. You looking for somebody?"

"Oh, no," he said. Now that he had a chance to talk about his troubles, he forgot to be afraid of this mysterious voice from nowhere that had accosted him. "I'm looking for my home."

"Hm-m-m," I said. "Been looking for a long time?"

"Oh, yes." His nose twitched. "I left for work one morning a long time ago, and when I got off the ferry at Battery Place I stopped for a moment to watch the work on that newfangled elevated railroad they were building down there. All of a sudden there was a loud noise—my goodness! It was terrible—and the next thing I knew I was standing back from the curb and looking at a man who looked just like me! A girder had fallen, and—my word!" He mopped his face again. "Since then I have been looking and looking. I can't seem to find anyone who knows where I might have lived, and I don't understand all the things I see floating around me, and I never thought I'd see the day when grass would grow on lower Broadway—oh, it's terrible." He began to cry.

I felt sorry for him. I could easily see what had happened. The shock was so great that even his ghost had amnesia! Poor little egg—until he was whole, he could find no rest. The thing interested me. Would a ghost react to the usual cures for amnesia? If so, then what would happen to him?

"You say you got off a ferryboat?"

"Yes."

"Then you must have lived on the Island . . . Staten Island, over there across the bay!"

"You really think so?" He stared through me, puzzled and hopeful.

"Why sure! Say, how'd you like me to take you over there? Maybe we can find your house."

"Oh, that would be splendid! But—oh, my, what will my wife say?"

I grinned. "She might want to know where you've been. Anway, she'll be glad to see you back, I imagine. Come on; let's get going!"

I gave h... a shove in the direction of the subways and strolled along behind him. Once in a while I got a stare from a passerby for walking with one hand out in front of me and talking into thin air. It didn't bother me very much. My companion, though, was very self-conscious about it, for the inhabitants of his world screeched and giggled when they saw him doing practically the same thing. Of all the humans, only I was invisible to them, and the little ghost in the bowler hat blushed from embarrassment until I thought he'd burst.

We hopped a subway—it was a new experience for him, I gathered—and went down to South Ferry. The subway system in New York is a very unpleasant place to one gifted as I was. Everything that enjoys lurking in the dark hangs out there, and there is quite a crop of dismembered human remains. After this day I took the bus.

We got a ferry without waiting. The little gray ghost got a real kick out of the trip. He asked me about the ships in the harbor and their flags, and marveled at the dearth of sailing vessels. He *tsk tsked* at the Statue of Liberty; the last time he had seen it, he said, was while it still had its original brassy gold color, before it got its patina. By this I placed him in the late 70s; he must have been looking for his home for over sixty years!

We landed at the Island, and from there I gave him his head. At the top of Fort Hill he suddenly said "My name is John Quigg. I live at 45 Fourth Avenue!" I've never seen anyone quite so delighted as he was by the discovery. And from then on it was easy. He turned left again, straight down for two blocks and again right. I noticed— he didn't—that the street was marked "Winter Avenue." I remembered vaguely that the streets in this section had been numbered years ago.

He trotted briskly up the hill and then suddenly stopped and turned vaguely. "I say, are you still with me?"

"Still here," I said.

"I'm all right now. I can't tell you how much I appreciate this. Is there anything I could do for you?"

I considered. "Hardly. We're of different times, you know. Things change."

He looked, a little pathetically, at the new apartment house on the corner and nodded. "I think I know what happened to me," he said softly. "But I guess it's all right . . . I made a will, and the kids were grown." He sighed. "But if it hadn't been for you I'd still be wandering around Manhattan. Let's see—ah; come with me!"

He suddenly broke into a run. I followed as quickly as I could. Almost at the top of the hill was a huge old shingled house, with a silly cupola and a complete lack of paint. It was dirty and it was tumbledown, and at the sight of it the little fellow's face twisted sadly. He gulped and turned through a gap in the hedge and down beside the house. Casting about in the long grass, he spotted a boulder sunk deep into the turf.

"This is it," he said. "Just you dig under that. There is no mention of it in my will, except a small fund to keep paying the box rent. Yes, a safety deposit box, and the key and an authority are under that stone. I hid it"—he giggled—"from my wife one night, and never did get a chance to tell her. You can have whatever's any good to you." He turned to the house, squared his shoulders, and marched in the side door, which banged open for him in a convenient gust of wind. I listened for a moment and then smiled at the tirade that burst forth. Old Quigg was catching real hell from his wife, who'd sat waiting for over sixty years for him! It was a bitter stream of invective, but—well, she must have loved him. She couldn't leave the place until she was complete, if Ginny's theory was correct, and she wasn't really complete until her husband came home! It tickled me. They'd be all right now!

I found an old pinch bar in the drive and attacked the ground around the stone. It took quite a while and made my hands bleed, but after a while I pried the stone up and was able to scrabble around under it. Sure enough, there was an oiled silk pouch under there. I caught it up and carefully unwrapped the strings around it. Inside was a key and a letter addressed to a New York bank, designating only "Bearer" and authorizing me to use the key. I laughed aloud. Little old meek and mild John Quigg, I'd bet, had set aside some "mad money." With a layout like that, a man could take a powder without leaving a single sign. The son of a gun! I would never know just what it was he had up his sleeve, but I'll bet there was a woman in the case. Even fixed up with his will! Ah, well—I should kick!

It didn't take me long to get over to the bank. I had a little trouble getting into the vaults, because it took quite a while to look up the box in the old records. But I finally cleared the red tape, and found myself the proud possessor of just under eight thousand bucks in small bills—and not a yellowback among 'em!

Well, from then on I was pretty well set. What did I do? Well, first I bought clothes, and then, I started out to cut ice for myself. I clubbed around a bit and got to know a lot of people, and the more I knew the more I realized what a lot of superstitious dopes they were. I couldn't blame anyone for skirting a ladder under which crouched a genuine basilisk, of course, but what the heck—not one in a thousand have beasts under them! Anyway, my question was answered. I dropped two grand on an elegant office with drapes and dim indirect lighting, and I got me a phone installed and a little quiet sign on the door—Psychic Consultant. And, boy, I did all right.

My customers were mostly upper crust, because I came high. It was generally no trouble to get contact with people's dead relatives, which was usually what they wanted. Most ghosts are crazy to get in contact with this world anyway. That's one of the reasons that almost anyone can become a medium of sorts if he tries hard enough; Lord knows that it doesn't take much to contact the average ghost. Some of course, were not available. If a man leads a pretty square life, and kicks off leaving no loose ends, he gets clear. I never did find out where these clear spirits went to. All I knew was that they weren't to be contacted. But the vast majority of people have to go back and tie up those loose ends after they die—righting a little wrong here, helping someone they've hindered, cleaning up a little bit of dirty work. That's where luck itself comes from, I do believe. You don't get something for nothing.

If you get a nice break, it's been arranged that way by someone who did you dirt in the past, or someone who did wrong to your father or your grandfather or your great-uncle Julius. Everything evens up in the long run, and until it does, some poor damned soul is wandering around the earth trying to do something about it. Half of humanity is walking around crabbing about its tough breaks. If you and you and you only knew what dozens of powers were begging for the chance to help you if you'll let them! And if you let them, you'll help clear up the mess they've made of their lives here, and free them to go wherever it is they go when they've cleaned up. Next time you're in a jam, go away somewhere by yourself and open your mind to these folks. They'll cut in and guide you all right, if you can drop your smugness and your mistaken confidence in your own judgment.

I had a couple of ghostly stooges to run errands for me. One of them, an ex-murderer by the name of One-eye Rachuba, was the fastest spook I ever saw, when it came to locating a wanted ancestor; and then there was Professor Grafe, a frog-faced teacher of social science who'd embezzled from a charity fund and fallen into the Hudson trying to make a getaway. He could trace the most devious genealogies in mere seconds, and deduce the most likely whereabouts of the ghost of a missing relative. The pair of them were all the office force I could use, and although every time they helped out one of my clients they came closer to freedom for themselves, they were both so entangled with their own sloppy lives that I was sure of their services for years.

But do you think I'd be satisfied to stay where I was, making money hand over fist without really working for it? Oh, no. Not me. No, I had to big-time. I had to brood over the events of the last few months, and I had to get dramatic about that screwball Audrey, who really wasn't worth my trouble. It wasn't enough that I'd prove Audrey wrong when she said I'd never amount to anything. And I wasn't happy when I thought about the gang. I had to show them up.

I even remembered what the little man in the Shottle Bop had said to me about my using my "talent" for bragging or for revenge. I figured I had the edge on everyone, everything. Cocky, I was. Why, I could send one of my ghostly stooges out any time and find out exactly what anyone had been doing three hours ago come Michaelmas. With the shade of the professor at my shoulder, I could backtrack on any far-fetched statement and give immediate and logical reasons for backtracking. No one had anything on me, and I could outtalk, outmaneuver, and outsmart anyone on earth. I was really quite a fellow. I began to think, "What's the use of my doing as well as this when the gang on the West Side don't know anything about it?" and "Man, would that half-wit Happy Sam burn up if he saw me drifting down Broadway in my new six-thousand-dollar roadster!" and "To think I used to waste my time and tears on a dope like Audrey!" In other words, I was tripping up on an inferiority complex. I acted like a veridam fool, which I was. I went over to the West Side.

It was a chilly, late winter night. I'd taken a lot of trouble to dress myself and my car so we'd be bright and shining and would knock some eyes out. Pity I couldn't brighten my brains up a little.

I drove up in front of Casey's pool room, being careful to do it too fast, and concentrating on shrieks from the tires and a shuddering twenty-four-cylinder roar from the engine before I cut the switch. I didn't hurry to get out of the car, either. Just leaned back and lit a fifty-cent cigar, and then tipped my hat over one ear and touched the horn button, causing it to play "Tuxedo Junction" for forty-eight seconds. Then I looked over toward the pool hall.

Well, for a minute I thought that I shouldn't have come, if that was the effect my return to the fold was going to have. And from then on I forgot about everything except how to get out of here.

There were two figures slouched in the glowing doorway of the pool room. It was up a small side street, so short that the city had depended on the place, an old institution, to supply the street lighting. Looking carefully,

I made out one of the silhouetted figures as Happy Sam, and the other was Fred Bellew. They just looked out at me; they didn't move; they didn't say anything, and when I said, "Hiya, small fry—remember me?" I noticed that along the darkened walls flanking the bright doorway were ranked the whole crowd of them—the whole gang. It was a shock; it was a little too casually perfect. I didn't like it.

"Hi," said Fred quietly. I knew he wouldn't like the big-timing. I didn't expect any of them to like it, of course, but Fred's dislike sprang from distaste, and the others from resentment, and for the first time I felt a little cheap. I climbed out over the door of the roadster and let them have a gander at my fine feathers.

Sam snorted and said, "Jelly bean!" very clearly. Someone else giggled, and from the darkness beside the building came a high-pitched, "Woo-woo!"

I walked up to Sam and grinned at him. I didn't feel like grinning. "I ain't seen you in so long I almost forgot what a heel you were," I said. "How you making?"

"I'm doing all right," he said, and added offensively, "I'm still *working* for a living."

The murmur that ran through the crowd told me that the really smart thing to do was to get back into that shiny new automobile and hoot along out of there. I stayed.

"Wise, huh?" I said weakly.

They'd been drinking, I realized—all of them. I was suddenly in a spot. Sam put his hands in his pockets and looked at me down his nose. He was the only short man that ever could do that to me. After a thick silence he said:

"Better get back to yer crystal balls, phony. We like guys that sweat. We even like guys that have rackets, if they run them because they're smarter or tougher than the next one. But luck and gab ain't enough. Scram."

I looked around helplessly. I was getting what I'd begged for. What had I expected, anyway? Had I thought that these boys would crowd around and shake my hand off for acting this way?

They hardly moved, but they were all around me suddenly. If I couldn't think of something quickly, I was going to be mobbed. And when those mugs started mobbing a man, they did it up just fine. I drew a deep breath.

"I'm not asking for anything from you, Sam. Nothing; that means advice; see?"

"You're gettin' it!" he flared. "You and your seeanses. We heard about you. Hanging up widdow-women for fifty bucks a throw to talk to their 'dear departed'! P-sykik investigator! What a line! Go on; beat it!"

I had a leg to stand on now. "A phony, huh? Why I'll bet I could put a haunt on you that would make that hair of yours stand up on end, if you have guts enough to go where I tell you to."

"You'll bet? That's a laugh. Listen to that, gang." He laughed, then turned to me and talked through one side of his mouth. "All right, you wanted it. Come on, rich guy; you're called. Fred'll hold stakes. How about ten of your lousy bucks for every one of mine? Here, Fred— hold this sawbuck."

"I'll give you twenty to one," I said half-hysterically. "And I'll take you to a place where you'll run up against the homeliest, plumb-meanest old haunt you ever heard of."

The crowd roared. Sam laughed with them, but didn't try to back out. With any of that gang, a bet was a bet. He'd taken me up, and he'd set the odds, and he was bound. I just nodded and put two century notes into Fred Bellew's hand. Fred and Sam climbed into the car, and just as we started, Sam leaned out and waved.

"See you in hell, fellas," he said. "I'm goin' to raise me a ghost, and one of us is going to scare the other one to death!"

I honked my horn to drown out the whooping and

hollering from the sidewalk and got out of there. I turned up the parkway and headed out of town.

"Where to?" Fred asked after a while.

"Stick around," I said, not knowing.

There must be some place not far from here where I could find an honest-to-God haunt, I thought, one that would make Sam backtrack and set me up with the boys again. I opened the compartments in the dashboard and let Ikey out. Ikey was a little twisted imp who'd got his tail caught in between two sheets of steel when they were assembling the car, and had to stay there until it was junked.

"Hey, Ike," I whispered. He looked up, the gleam of the compartment light shining redly in his bright little eyes. "Whistle for the professor, will you? I don't want to yell for him because those mugs in the back seat will hear me. They can't hear you."

"Okay, boss," he said; and putting his fingers to his lips, he gave vent to a bloodcurdling, howling scream.

That was the prof's call letters, as it were. The old man flew ahead of the car, circled around and slid in beside me through the window, which I'd opened a crack for him.

"My goodness," he panted, "I wish you wouldn't summon me to a location which is traveling with this high degree of celerity. It was all I could do to catch up with you."

"Don't give me that, professor," I whispered. "You can catch a stratoliner if you want to. Say, I have a guy in the back who wants to get a real scare from a ghost. Know of any around here?"

The professor put on his ghostly pince-nez. "Why, yes. Remember my telling you about the Wolfmeyer place?"

"Golly—he's bad."

"He'll serve your purpose admirably. But don't ask me to go there with you. None of us ever associates with Wolfmeyer. And for Heaven's sake, be careful."

"I guess I can handle him. Where is it?"

He gave me explicit directions, bade me good night and left. I was a little surprised; the professor traveled around with me a great deal, and I'd never seen him refuse a chance to see some new scenery. I shrugged it off and went my way. I guess I just didn't know any better.

I headed out of town and into the country to a certain old farmhouse. Wolfmeyer, a Pennsylvania Dutchman, had hung himself there. He had been, and was, a bad egg. Instead of being a nice guy about it all, he was the rebel type. He knew perfectly well that unless he did plenty of good to make up for the evil, he'd be stuck where he was for the rest of eternity. That didn't seem to bother him at all. He got surly and became a really bad spook. Eight people had died in that house since the old man rotted off his own rope. Three of them were tenants who had rented the place, and three were hobos, and two were psychic investigators. They'd all hung themselves. That's the way Wolfmeyer worked. I think he really enjoyed haunting. He certainly was thorough about it anyway.

I didn't want to do any real harm to Happy Sam. I just wanted to teach him a lesson. And look what happened!

We reached the place just before midnight. No one had said much, except that I told Fred and Sam about Wolfmeyer, and pretty well what was to be expected from him. They did a good deal of laughing about it, so I just shut up and drove. The next item of conversation was Fred's, when he made the terms of the bet. To win, Sam was to stay in the house until dawn. He wasn't to call for help and he wasn't to leave. He had to bring in a coil of rope, tie a noose in one end and string the other up on "Wolfmeyer's Beam"—the great oaken beam on which the old man had hung himself, and eight others after him. This was an added temptation to Wolfmeyer to work on Happy Sam, and was my idea. I was to go in with Sam, to watch him in case the thing became too dangerous. Fred was to stay in the car a hundred yards down the road and wait.

I parked the car at the agreed distance and Sam and I got out. Sam had my tow rope over his shoulder, already noosed. Fred had quieted down considerably, and his face was dead serious.

"I don't think I like this," he said, looking up the road at the house. It hunched back from the highway, and looked like a malign being deep in thought.

I said, "Well, Sam? Want to pay up now and call it quits?"

He followed Fred's gaze. It sure was a dreary-looking place, and his liquor had fizzed away. He thought a minute, then shrugged and grinned. I had to admire the rat. "Hell, I'll go through with it. Can't bluff me with scenery, phony."

Surprisingly, Fred piped up, "I don't think he's a phony, Sam."

The resistance made Sam stubborn, though I could see by his face that he knew better. "Come on, phony," he said and swung up the road.

We climbed into the house by way of a cellar door that slanted up to a window on the first floor. I hauled out a flashlight and lit the way to the beam. It was only one of many that delighted in turning the sound of one's footsteps into laughing whispers that ran round and round the rooms and halls and would not die. Under the famous beam the dusty floor was dark-stained.

I gave Sam a hand in fixing the rope, and then clicked off the light. It must have been tough on him then. I didn't mind because I knew I could see anything before it got to me, and even then, no ghost could see me. Not only that, for me the walls and floors and ceilings were lit with the phosphorescent many-hued glow of the ever-present ghost plants. For its eerie effect I wished Sam could see the ghost molds feeding greedily on the stain under the beam.

Sam was already breathing heavily, but I knew it would take more than just darkness and silence to get his goat.

He'd have to be alone, and then he'd have to have a visitor or so.

"So long, kid," I said, slapping him on the shoulder, and I turned and walked out of the room.

I let him hear me go out of the house and then I crept silently back. It was without doubt the most deserted place I have ever seen. Even ghosts kept away from it, excepting, of course, Wolfmeyer's. There was just the luxurious vegetation, invisible to all but me, and the deep silence rippled by Sam's breath. After ten minutes or so I knew for certain that Happy Sam had more guts than I'd ever have credited him with. He had to be scared. He couldn't —or wouldn't—scare himself.

I crouched down against the walls of an adjoining room and made myself comfortable. I figured Wolfmeyer would be along pretty soon. I hoped earnestly that I could stop the thing before it got too far. No use in making this any more than a good lesson for a wiseacre. I was feeling pretty smug about it all, and I was totally unprepared for what happened.

I was looking toward the doorway opposite when I realized that for some minutes there had been the palest of pale glows there. It brightened as I watched; brightened and flickered gently. It was green, the green of things moldy and rotting away; and with it came a subtly harrowing stench. It was the smell of flesh so very dead that it had ceased to be really odorous. It was utterly horrible, and I was honestly scared out of my wits. It was some moments before the comforting thought of my invulnerability came back to me, and I shrank lower and closer to the walls and watched.

And Wolfmeyer came in.

His was the ghost of an old, old man. He wore a flowing, filthy robe, and his bare forearms thrust out in front of him were stringy and strong. His head, with its tangled hair and beard, quivered on a broken, ruined neck like the blade of a knife thrown into soft wood. Each slow step as he crossed the room set his head to quivering again. His eyes were alight; red they were, with deep green flames buried in them. His canine teeth had lengthened into yellow, blunt tusks, and they were like pillars supporting his crooked grin. The putrescent green glow was a horrid halo about him.

He passed me completely unconscious of my presence and paused at the door of the room where Sam waited by the rope. He stood just outside it, his claws extended, the quivering of his head slowly dying. He stared in at Sam, and suddenly opened his mouth and howled. It was a quiet, deadly sound, one that might have come from the throat of a distant dog, but, though I couldn't see into the other room, I knew that Sam had jerked his head around and was staring at the ghost. Wolfmeyer raised his arms a trifle, seemed to totter a bit, and then moved into the room.

I snapped myself out of the crawling terror that gripped me and scrambled to my feet. If I didn't move fast—

Tiptoeing swiftly to the door, I stopped just long enough to see Wolfmeyer beating his arms about erratically over his head, a movement that made his robe flutter and his whole figure pulsate in the green light; just long enough to see Sam on his feet, wide-eyed, staggering back and back toward the rope. He clutched his throat and opened his mouth and made no sound, and his head tilted, his neck bent, his twisted face gaped at the ceiling as he clumped backward away from the ghost and into the ready noose. And then I leaned over Wolfmeyer's shoulder, put my lips to his ear, and said:

"*Boo!*"

I almost laughed. Wolfmeyer gave a little squeak, jumped about ten feet, and, without stopping to look around, hightailed out of the room so fast that he was just a blur. That was one scared old spook!

At the same time Happy Sam straightened, his face relaxed and relieved, and sat down with a bump under the noose. That was as close a thing as ever I want to see. He sat there, his face soaking wet with cold sweat, his hands between his knees, staring limply at his feet.

"That'll show you!" I exulted, and walked over to him. "Pay up, scum, and you may starve for that week's pay!" He didn't move. I guess he was plenty shocked.

"Come on!" I said. "Pull yourself together, man! Haven't you seen enough? That old fellow will be back any second now. On your feet!"

He didn't move.

"Sam!"

He didn't move.

"Sam!" I clutched at his shoulder. He pitched over sideways and lay still. He was quite dead.

I didn't do anything and for a while I didn't say anything. Then I said hopelessly, as I knelt there, "Aw, Sam. Sam—cut it out, fella."

After a minute I rose slowly and started for the door. I'd taken three steps when I stopped. Something was happening! I rubbed my hand over my eyes. Yes, it is— it was getting dark! The vague luminescence of the vines and flowers of the ghost world was getting dimmer, fading, fading—

But that had never happened before!

No difference. I told myself desperately, it's happening now, all right. *I got to get out of here!*

See? You see. It was the stuff—the damn stuff from the Shottle Bop. It was wearing off! When Sam died it . . . it stopped working on me! Was this what I had to pay for the bottle? Was this what was to happen if I used it for revenge?

The light was almost gone—and now it was gone. I couldn't see a thing in the room but one of the doors. Why could I see the doorway? What was that pale green light that set off its dusty frame?

Wolfmeyer! *I got to get out of here!*

I couldn't see ghosts any more. Ghosts could see me

now. I ran. I darted across the dark room and smashed into the wall on the other side. I reeled back from it, blood spouting from between the fingers I slapped to my face. I ran again. Another wall clubbed me. Where was that other door? I ran again, and again struck a wall. I screamed and ran again. I tripped over Sam's body. My head went through the noose. It whipped down on my windpipe, and my neck broke with an agonizing crunch. I floundered there for half a minute, and then dangled.

Dead as hell, I was. Wolfmeyer, he laughed and laughed.

Fred found me and Sam in the morning. He took our bodies away in the car. Now I've got to stay here and haunt this damn old house. Me and Wolfmeyer.

FREDRIC BROWN, (1906–1972), spent his early years knocking around the country, working at times for a carnival and then again as a printer. Each of the occupations appears repeatedly in his writing, in such short stories as *Etaoin Shrdlu* and *The Angelic Angleworm* and in the series of novels featuring Ed and Am Hunter that started with *The Fabulous Clipjoint*. Brown began writing for the detective and science-fiction pulps in the late 1930s and published more than three hundred short stories and about thirty novels. His most famous science-fiction novels are *What Mad Universe?* and *Martian, Go Home!* In his shorter stories he was particularly noted for his mastery of the vignette and short-short story and for his humor, an ingredient seldom encountered in the pulps except on a very broad slapstick level. Most of his novels appeared during the ten years following publication of *The Fabulous Clipjoint* in 1947. Many can still be found on the shelves of large libraries and will pleasantly reward the reader who hunts them out.

Armageddon

Fredric Brown

It happened—of all places—in Cincinnati. Not that there is anything wrong with Cincinnati, save that it is not the center of the Universe, nor even of the State of Ohio. It's a nice old town and, in its way, second to none. But even its Chamber of Commerce would admit that it lacks cosmic significance. It must have been mere coincidence that Gerber the Great—what a name!—was playing Cincinnati when things slipped elsewhere.

Of course, if the episode had become known, Cincinnati would be the most famous city of the world, and little Herbie would be hailed as a modern St. George and get more acclaim, even, than a quiz kid. But no member of that audience in the Bijou Theater remembers a thing about it. Not even little Herbie Westerman, although he had the water pistol to show for it.

He wasn't thinking about the water pistol in his pocket as he sat looking up at the prestidigitator on the other side of the footlights. It was a new water pistol, bought en route to the theater when he'd inveigled his parents into a side trip into the five-and-dime on Vine Street, but at the moment, Herbie was much more interested in what went on upon the stage.

His expression registered qualified approval. The front-and-back palm was no mystery to Herbie. He could do it himself. True, he had to use pony-sized cards that came with his magic set and were just the right size for his nine-year-old hands. And true, anyone watching could see the card flutter from the front-palm position to the back as he turned his hands. But that was a detail.

He knew, though, that front-and-back palming seven cards at a time required great finger strength as well as dexterity, and that was what Gerber the Great was doing. There wasn't a telltale click in the shift, either, and Herbie nodded approbation. Then he remembered what was coming next.

He nudged his mother and said, "Ma, ask Pop if he's gotta extra handkerchief."

Out of the corner of his eye, Herbie saw his mother turn her head and in less time than it would take to say "Presto" Herbie was out of his seat and skinning down the aisle. It had been, he felt, a beautiful piece of misdirection and his timing had been perfect.

It was at this stage of the performance—which Herbie had seen before, alone—that Gerber the Great asked if some little boy from the audience would step to the stage. He was asking it now.

Herbie Westerman had jumped the gun. He was well in motion before the magician had asked the question. At the previous performance, he'd been a bad tenth in reaching the steps from aisle to stage. This time he'd been ready, and he hadn't taken any chances with parental restraint. Perhaps his mother would have let him go and perhaps not; it had seemed wiser to see that she was looking the other way. You couldn't trust parents on things like that. They had funny ideas sometimes.

"—will please step up on the stage?" And Herbie's foot touched the first of the steps upward right smack on the interrogation point of that sentence. He heard the disappointed scuffle of other feet behind him, and grinned smugly as he went on up across the footlights.

It was the three-pigeon trick, Herbie knew from the previous performance, that required an assistant from the audience. It was almost the only trick he hadn't been able to figure out. There *must,* he knew, have been a concealed compartment somewhere in that box, but where it could be he couldn't even guess. But this time he'd be holding the box himself. If from that range, he couldn't spot the gimmick, he'd better go back to stamp collecting.

He grinned confidently up at the magician. Not that he, Herbie, would give him away. He was a magician, too, and he understood that there was a freemasonry among magicians and that one never gave away the tricks of another.

He felt a little chilled, though, and the grin faded as he caught the magician's eyes. Gerber the Great, at close range, seemed much older than he had seemed from the other side of the footlights. And somehow different. Much taller, for one thing.

Anyway, here came the box for the pigeon trick. Gerber's regular assistant was bringing it in on a tray. He remembered, even, his reason for being on the stage. The servant limped. Herbie ducked his head to catch a glimpse of the under side of the tray, just in case. Nothing there.

Gerber took the box. The servant limped away and Herbie's eyes followed him suspiciously. Was the limp genuine or was it a piece of misdirection?

The box folded out flat as the proverbial pancake. All four sides hinged to the bottom, the top hinged to one of the sides. There were little brass catches.

Herbie took a quick step back so he could see behind it while the front was displayed to the audience. Yes, he saw it now. A triangular compartment built against one side of the lid, mirror-covered, angles calculated to achieve invisibility. Old stuff. Herbie felt a little disappointed.

The prestidigitator folded the box, mirror-concealed compartment inside. He turned slightly. "Now, my fine young man—"

What happened in Tibet wasn't the only factor; it was merely the final link of a chain.

The Tibetan weather had been unusual that week, highly unusual. It had been warm. More snow succumbed to the gentle warmth than had melted in more years than man could count. The streams ran high, they ran wide and fast.

Along the streams some prayer wheels whirled faster than they had ever whirled. Others, submerged, stopped altogether. The priests, knee-deep in the cold water, worked frantically, moving the wheels nearer to shore where again the rushing torrent would turn them.

There was one small wheel, a very old one that had revolved without cease for longer than any man knew. So long had it been there that no living lama recalled what had been inscribed upon its prayer plate, nor what had been the purpose of that prayer.

The rushing water had neared its axle when the lama Klarath reached for it to move it to safety. Just too late. His foot slid in the slippery mud and the back of his hand touched the wheel as he fell. Knocked loose from its moorings, it swirled down with the flood, rolling along the bottom of the stream, into deeper and deeper waters.

While it rolled, all was well.

The lama rose, shivering from his momentary immersion, and went after other of the spinning wheels. What, he thought, could one small wheel matter? He didn't know that—now that other links had broken—only that tiny thing stood between Earth and Armageddon.

The prayer wheel of Wangur Ul rolled on, and on, until—a mile farther down—it struck a ledge and stopped. That was the moment.

"And now, my fine young man—"

Herbie Westerman—we're back in Cincinnati now— looked up, wondering why the prestidigitator had stopped in mid-sentence. He saw the face of Gerber the Great contorted as though by a great shock. Without moving, without changing, his face began to change. Without appearing different, it became different.

Quietly, then, the magician began to chuckle. In the overtones of that soft laughter was all of evil. No one who heard it could have doubted who he was. No one did doubt. The audience, every member of it, knew in that awful moment who stood before them, knew it—even the most skeptical among them—beyond a shadow of doubt.

No one moved, no one spoke, none drew a shuddering breath. There are things beyond fear. Only uncertainty causes fear and the Bijou Theater was filled, then, with a dreadful certainty.

The laughter grew. Crescendo, it reverberated into the

far dusty corners of the gallery. Nothing—not a fly on the ceiling—moved.

Satan spoke.

"I thank you for your kind attention to a poor magician." He bowed, ironically low. "The performance is ended."

He smiled. "All performances are ended."

Somehow the theater seemed to darken, although the electric lights still burned. In dead silence, there seemed to be the sound of wings, leathery wings, as though invisible Things were gathering.

On the stage was a dim red radiance. From the head and from each shoulder of the tall figure of the magician there sprang a tiny flame. A naked flame.

There were other flames. They flickered along the proscenium of the stage, along the footlights. One sprang from the lid of the folded box little Herbie Westerman still held in his hands.

Herbie dropped the box.

Did I mention that Herbie Westerman was a Safety Cadet? It was purely a reflex action. A boy of nine doesn't know much about things like Armageddon, but Herbie Westerman should have known that water would never have put out that fire.

But, as I said, it was purely a reflex action. He yanked out his new water pistol and squirted it at the box of the pigeon trick. And the fire *did* vanish, even as a spray from the stream of water ricocheted and dampened the trouser leg of Gerber the Great, who had been facing the other way.

There was a sudden, brief, hissing sound. The lights were growing bright again, and all the other flames were dying, and the sound of wings faded, blended into another sound—the rustling of the audience.

The eyes of the prestidigitator were closed. His voice sounded strangely strained as he said: "This much power I retain. None of you will remember this."

Then, slowly, he turned and picked up the fallen box. He held it out to Herbie Westerman. "You must be more careful, boy," he said. "Now hold it so."

He tapped the top lightly with his wand. The door fell open. Three white pigeons flew out of the box. The rustle of their wings was not leathery.

Herbie Westerman's father came down the stairs and, with a purposeful air, took his razor strop off the hook on the kitchen wall.

Mrs. Westerman looked up from stirring the soup on the stove. "Why, Henry," she asked, "are you really going to punish him with that—just for squirting a little water out of the window of the car on the way home?"

Her husband shook his head grimly. "Not for that, Marge. But don't you remember we bought him that water gun on the way downtown, and that he wasn't near a water faucet after that? Where do you think he filled it?"

He didn't wait for an answer. "When we stopped in at the cathedral to talk to Father Ryan about his confirmation, that's when the little brat filled it. Out of the baptismal font! Holy water he uses in his water pistol!"

He clumped heavily up the stairs, strop in hand.

Rhythmic thwacks and wails of pain floated down the staircase. Herbie—who had saved the world—was having his reward.

ROBERT BLOCH, (b. 1917), is best known as author of the psychological horror novel, *Psycho,* which was translated to the screen by Alfred Hitchcock; it remains today as one of the best of the famed director's works. Bloch's own career started in the *Weird Tales* of the early 1930s when he became a member of the Lovecraft circle of correspondents. Like Fredric Brown, Bloch became noted for his humor, and particularly for his fondness for puns. Humor, however, rarely appeared in the pages of *Weird Tales,* although *The Cheaters* represents the growing trend, under the editorship of Dorothy McIlwraith, away from the excesses of the Lovecraftian style.

The Cheaters

Robert Bloch

1. Joe Henshaw

The way I got those spectacles, I bought a blind lot off the City for twenty bucks.

Maggie hollered fit to raise the dead when I told her.

"What you wanna load up on some more junk for? The store's full of it now. Get yourself a lot of raggedy old clothes and some busted furniture, that's what you'll get. Why, that dump's over two hunnert years old! Ain't nobody been inside it since Prohibition, it's padlocked tight shut. And you have to throw away twenty bucks for whatever you find for salvage."

And so on and so on, about what a bum I was and why had she ever married me and who wanted to be stuck away for life in the junk and second-hand business.

Well, I just walked out on her and let her keep right on jawing to Jake. He'd listen to her—listen for hours, sitting in back of the shop, drinking coffee when he should have been working.

But I knew what I was doing. Delehanty at City Hall tipped me off about this old house and told me to get in my bid, he'd take care of it.

The dump was near the wharf and it must have been class once, even though they made a speak out of it back in Prohibition days and slapped a padlock on it ever since. Delehanty told me that upstairs, where nobody ever went while it was a rummy hangout, there was all kinds of old furniture from way back. So maybe Maggie was right about it being junk and maybe she was wrong. You never can tell. What I figured, there might be some real antique pieces up there. You got to take a chance once in a while, so I slapped in my bid and got the lot. City gave me three days to move the stuff out before they started razing and Delehanty slipped me a key.

I walked out on Maggie and took the truck down there. Usual thing, I have Jake drive and help me load, but this time I wanted to case the joint myself. If there really was something valuable in there—well, Jake would want a cut. So I let him stay back there and listen to Maggie. Maybe I am a dried-up old jerk like she tells it. And maybe I'm also a pretty smart guy. Just because Jake liked to dress up Saturdays and go down to the Bright Spot—

Anyway, I'm not talking about that, I'm talking about these glasses, these cheaters* I found.

That's all I found, too. All I could use. Downstairs was just rubbish and slats; they must have ripped out the bar when the Feds raided it. I kind of counted on finding bar stools and maybe some scrap metal, but no dice.

Upstairs was even worse. Eight big rooms, all dust and broken sticks of furniture. Busted beds, chairs with the springs sprung, nothing I could use. Old rags in some of the closets, and rotted shoes; it looked as if the people who lived here cleared out in a hurry a long time ago. Delehanty tipped me off this was supposed to be a haunted house, but in my line that's strictly a gag. I salvaged maybe two hundred haunted houses in my time—every old dump is supposed to be haunted. But I never run into anything in these places except maybe some cockroaches.

Then I came to this end room with the locked door. This looked a little better; all the other doors was open, but this one was locked tight. I had to use a crowbar on it. Got kind of excited, because you never can tell what a locked door means. Worked and sweated and finally pried it open.

Dust hits me in the face, and an awful stink. I switched on the flashlight and saw a big room with mounds of dirt all over the floor and bookshelves lining the walls. There must of been a thousand books in that room, no kidding, a regular library like.

I waded through the dust and pulled out a couple of the nearest books. The bindings were some kind of leather— that is, they used to be. Now the things just sort of crumbled in my hands, and so did the pages. All yellow and musty, which was why the stink was so bad in here.

I began to swear. I'm no *schmoe,* I know there's dough

*A 1930s expression for spectacles.

in old books. But not unless they're in good condition. And this stuff was rotten.

Then I saw this here desk in the corner and so help me, right on top of it was a human skull. A human skull, all yellow and grinning up at me under the light, and for a minute I almost went for that haunted house routine.

Then I noticed how the top was bored out for one of them oldfashion goose-quill pens. The guy who collected all these books used the skull for an inkwell. Screwy, hey?

But the desk was what really interested me because it was antique all right. Solid mahogany and all kinds of fancy scrollwork on it; little goofy faces carved in the wood. There was a drawer, too, and it wasn't locked. I got excited, figuring you never can tell what you find in such places, so I didn't waste much time pulling it open.

Only it was empty. I was so mad I let out a couple of words and kicked the side of the desk.

That's how I found them. The cheaters, that is. Because I hit one of the little goofy faces and a sort of panel swung open on the left side and there was this other drawer.

I reached in and pulled out the spectacles.

Just a pair of glasses, is all, but real funny ones. Little square-shaped lenses with big ear pieces—books, I guess they call them. And a silver bridge over the middle.

I didn't get it. Sure, there was silver in the frames but not more than a couple of bucks worth. So why hide the cheaters away in a secret drawer?

I held the glasses up and wiped the dust off the lenses, which was yellow glass instead of the regular clear kind, but not very thick. I noticed little designs in the temples, like engraving. And right across the bridge for the nose was a word carved into the silver. I remember that word because I never saw it before.

"Veritas" was the word, in funny square letters. Could that be Greek? Maybe the old guy was Greek—the guy who had the locked library and the skull for an inkwell and the glasses in the secret drawer, I mean.

I had to squint at the lettering to see it in the gloom there because my eyes weren't so hot—and that gave me an idea.

Get to be my age, sometimes you're kind of shortsighted. I always figured on going to the eye doctor but kept putting it off. So looking at the cheaters I said to myself, why not?

I put them on.

At first my eyes hurt a little. Not hurt, exactly, but something else like hurting inside of me. Like I was being all pulled and twisted. The whole room went far away for a minute and then it came up close and I blinked fast.

After that it was all right and I could see pretty good. Everything was sharp and clear.

So I left the cheaters on and went downstairs, figuring to come back tomorrow with Jake and the truck. At least we could haul the desk and maybe sell the bed-frames for scrap. No sense in me lifting, when I had Jake for the heavy stuff.

I went on home, then.

I come in the shop and sure enough there was Jake and Maggie sitting in back having coffee.

Maggie kind of grinned at me. Then she said, "How did you make out, Joe, you lousy old baboon? I'm glad we're going to kill you."

No, she didn't *say* all that. She just said, "How did you make out, Joe?"

But she was *thinking* the rest.

I know because I *saw* it.

Don't ask me to explain. I *saw* it. Not words, or anything. And I didn't *hear*. I saw. I knew by looking at her what she was thinking and planning.

"Find a lot of stuff?" Jake asked, and I *saw*, "I hope you did because it's all mine as soon as we bump you and we're gonna bump you for sure tonight."

"What you look so funny for, Joe, you sick or something?" Maggie asked. And she said, to herself, "Who cares, he's gonna be a lot sicker soon, all right, does he suspect anything, no of course not, the old goat never got wise to us for a whole year now, just wait until Jake and I own this place together and his insurance too, it's all set."

"What you need, you need a little drink," Jake said to me, and to himself he was saying, "That's the way, get him drunk, and when he gets upstairs I'll push him down and if that don't finish him I'll clobber him with a board, it leaves the same kind of marks. Everybody knows he drinks, it'll look like an accident."

I made myself smile.

"Where'd you get the cheaters?" Maggie asked, saying also, "God, what a homely mug on him, I get sick just looking at that face but it won't be long now."

"Picked them up over at the house," I said.

Jake got out a fifth and some water glasses. "Drink up," he said.

I sat there trying to figure it out. Why could I read their minds? I didn't know, but I could see what they were up to. I could *see* it. Could it be—the cheaters?

Yes, the cheaters. *They* were the cheaters, carrying on behind my back. Waiting now until I got drunk enough so they could kill me. Pretending to drink a lot while they got me loaded.

But I couldn't get drunk, not as long as I was *seeing* them. The thoughts going through their heads made everything turn to ice, and I was cold sober. I knew just what to do. I made them drink with me.

That helped, only their thoughts got worse. I listened to them talk but all the time I saw their thoughts.

"We'll kill him, just a little while now, why doesn't he hurry up and pass out, got to keep him from suspecting. God how I hate that puss of his. I want to see it smashed open, wait until he's out of the way and I have Maggie all to myself, he's going to die, die, die—"

I listened and I knew just what to do. After dark I said I'd put the truck in the garage for the night, and they stayed behind, thinking about how to get me upstairs now, how to keep people from suspecting them.

Me, I didn't worry about people suspecting. I put the truck away and I came back into the kitchen carrying the crowbar. I locked the door and they saw me with the crowbar, standing there.

"Hey, Joe—" said Jake.

"Joe, what's wrong?" said Maggie.

I didn't say a word.

There wasn't any time to talk, because I was smashing Jake's face with the crowbar, smashing his nose and eyes and jaw, and then I was hammering Maggie over the head and the thoughts came out but not in words, just in screams now, and then there weren't even any screams left to see.

So I sat down and took off the cheaters to polish them. I was still scrubbing at the red stains when the squad car came and the fuzz took me in.

They wouldn't let me keep the glasses and I never did see them again. It didn't matter much, anyway. I could have worn them at the trial, but who cares what the jury thought? And at the end I would have had to take them off anyway.

When they put the black hood over my head . . .

2. Miriam Spencer Olcott

I distinctly remember it was on Thursday afternoon, because that's when Olive has her bridge club over, and of course she simply *must* have Miss Tooker help with the serving.

Olive is much too diplomatic to lock me in my room even when Miss Tooker isn't there, and I always wondered why I seemed to get so sleepy on Thursdays, just when I might have a chance to slip out without anyone noticing. Finally I realized she must be putting something into my tea at luncheon—more of Dr. Cramer's work, no doubt.

Well, I'm not a complete fool by any means, no matter what they think, and this Thursday I simply poured the tea down the you-know-what. So Olive was none the wiser, and when I lay down on the bed and closed my eyes she went away satisfied. I waited until her guests arrived, then tiptoed down the stairs.

Olive and her friends were in the parlor with the door closed. I had to rest a moment at the foot of the stairs because of my heart, you know, and for an instant I had the most peculiar temptation to open the parlor door and stick my tongue out at the guests.

But that wouldn't have been very ladylike. After all Olive and her husband Percy had come to live with me when Herbert died and they got Miss Tooker to help care for me after I had my first heart attack. I mustn't be rude to them.

Besides, I knew Olive would never permit me to go out alone anymore. So it would be wiser if I didn't disturb her.

I managed to leave without being seen, and took a bus at the corner. There were several people on the bus and they kept staring at me—people are so rude nowadays! I know my clothing is not in the latest style, but there is no

call for vulgar curiosity. I wear highbutton shoes for the
support they afford my ankles, and if I choose to be
sensible regarding draughts, that is my affair. My coat is
fur and very expensive; it needs relining and possibly
some mending, that is true, but for all strangers know I
might be quite impoverished. They need not be so rude.
Even my bag attracts their attention; my fine reticule
which Herbert brought back for me from abroad, in '37!

I didn't like the way they stared at my bag. It was almost as if they knew. But how could they know, or even
suspect?

I sniffed and sat back, trying to decide whether to walk
north or south when I got off the bus.

If I walked north, I'd need my bag.

If I walked south, like the last time—

No, I couldn't do that. The last time was frightful, I
remember being in that awful place, and then the men
laughing, and I had been singing, I believe, was still singing when Percy and Olive came for me in the taxicab.
How they found me I'll never know; perhaps the tavern-
keeper telephoned them. They got me home and I had one
of my attacks and Dr. Cramer told them never to even
mention it to me again. So there were no discussions. I
hate discussions.

But I knew this time I must walk north. When I left
the bus I began to get that tingly feeling all over. It frightened me but it felt—nice.

It felt even nicer when I went into Warram's and began
to look at the cameos. The clerk was a man. I told him
what I wanted and he went to look. He brought back a
wide selection. I told him about my trip to Baden-Baden
with Herbert and what we had seen in the jewelry stores
there. He was very patient and understanding. I thanked
him politely for his trouble and walked out, tingling.
There was a brooch, a really lovely thing, in my reticule.

At Slade's I got a scarf. The clerk was an impertinent

young snip and so I felt I really must buy a corsage to distract her attention. They were vulgar things, and cost sixty-nine cents. Not nearly worth it. But the scarf in my bag was of imported silk.

It was very exciting. I walked in and out of the shops and the bag began to fill. Then I started going into those second-hand stores near the City Hall. One never knows. My reticule was almost full, but I could still make purchases, too.

In Henshaw's I saw this lively escritoire, obviously solid mahogany and beautifully carved. I smiled at the proprietor.

"I noticed that escritoire in your window, Mr. Henshaw," I began, but he shook his head.

"It's sold, lady. Beside, my name's Burgin. Henshaw's dead—didn't you read about it in the papers? Hanged him. I bought the place out—"

I held up my hand and sniffed. "Please spare me. But I'll glance around a bit, if I may."

"Sure, lady."

I had seen the table with the ceramics and now I approached it, but he never let his eyes stray from me. I was tingling again and very nervous. There was one piece I simply adored. I had the bag open and it only needed an instant—

He was right behind me, watching my hand move.

"How much is this?" I asked, very quickly, picking up an object at random from one of the trays on the table.

"Two bits!" he snapped.

I fumbled in my pocket and gave him a quarter, then marched out of the store and slammed the door. It was only when I reached the street that I stopped to examine the object in my hand.

It was a pair of spectacles. How in the world had I ever managed to snatch eyeglasses from that tray? Still, they were rather unusual—quite heavy, with tarnished silver frames. I held them up to the light and in the sunset I noticed a word etched across the bridge.

"Veritas." Latin. *Truth*. Strange.

At the same moment I noticed the clock on the City Hall. It was past five. This would never do. I should be found out and there might be a distressing scene—

I hailed a taxicab, and as I rode I remembered that Olive and Percy were dining out tonight, and Dr. Cramer was to come over and examine me. Surely by this time they would have ascertained my absence. How could I ever explain?

Fumbling in my pocket for the fare, my hands encountered the spectacles again. And that, of course, was the solution. I placed them firmly on the bridge of my nose and adjusted the bows just as we turned into the driveway. For a moment the tingling increased and I felt I might have another attack, but then I could see clearly again and the tingling drained away.

I paid the driver and walked into the house quickly, before he had time to comment on the absence of a "tip."

Olive and Percy were waiting for me at the door. I could see them so clearly, so very clearly; Olive so tall and thin, and Percy so short and fat. Both of them had pale skins, like leeches.

Why not? They *were* leeches. Moving into my house when Herbert died, using my property, living on my income. Getting Miss Tooker to come and keep her eye on me, encouraging Dr. Cramer to make an invalid out of me. Ever since Herbert died they had been waiting for *me* to die.

"Here's the old —— now."

I won't *repeat* the word.

For a moment I was shocked beyond all belief, to think that Percy would stand there smiling and *say* such a thing to my face! Then I realized he wasn't saying it. He was *thinking* it. Somehow, I was reading his mind.

He said, "Mother, darling, where on earth have you been?"

"Yes," said Olive. "We worried so. Why you might have been run over." Her tone was the familiar one of daughterly affection. And behind it, the thought came. "Why *wasn't* she run over, the old ———"

That word again!

I began to tremble.

"Where were you?" Olive murmured. Thinking, "Did you go off on another bat, you doddering old fool? Or were you making trouble for us, stealing from the shops again? The times Percy has had to go down and make good on merchandise—"

I caught the thought and blinked behind the spectacles. I hadn't suspected *that*. Did they *know,* in the stores, what I did? And did they permit it as long as Percy paid for what I had taken? But then I wasn't profiting at all! They were all against me. I saw it for the first time—could it be the spectacles?

"If you must know," I said, very rapidly, "I went downtown to be fitted for a pair of glasses."

And before they had time to reply, I brushed past them and went up to my room.

I was really quite upset. Not only by their thoughts but because I could tell what they were thinking. It couldn't be the spectacles. It couldn't be. Such things aren't really possible. It was only that I was so very tired and so very old—

I took off the glasses and lay down on the bed and suddenly I was crying. Perhaps I fell asleep, for when I awoke it was quite dark and Miss Tooker was coming into the room, carrying a tray. On the tray was a teapot and some biscuits. Dr. Cramer had put me on a strict diet; he knew I loved to eat and wouldn't permit it.

"Go away," I said.

Miss Tooker smiled weakly. "Mr. and Mrs. Dean have

left for their dinner engagement. But I thought you might be hungry—"

"Go away," I repeated. "When Dr. Cramer comes, send him up. But you keep out of here."

Her smile faded and she started for the door. For a moment I had the queerest urge to put on the spectacles and *really* see her. But that was all an illusion, wasn't it? I watched her depart, then sat up and reached for my bag. I began to go through my souvenirs of the afternoon and was quite engrossed by the time Dr. Cramer appeared.

He knocked first, giving me time to hide the reticule and its contents, and then entered quietly. "What's all this I hear about you, young lady?" he chuckled. He always called me "young lady." It was our private joke.

"I hear you took a little trip this afternoon," he continued, sitting down next to the bed. "Mrs. Dean mentioned something about spectacles—"

I shrugged. He leaned closer. "And you haven't eaten your dinner. You were crying." He sounded so sympathetic. A wonderful personality, Dr. Cramer. One couldn't help but respond.

"I just wasn't hungry. You see, Olive and Percy just don't understand. I do so enjoy getting out into the fresh air and I hate to trouble them. I can explain about the glasses."

He smiled and winked. "First, some tea. I'd better heat it up again, eh?"

Dr. Cramer set the teapot on the little electric hotplate over on the endtable. He worked quickly, efficiently, humming under his breath. It was a pleasure to watch him, a pleasure to have him visit me. We would sit down now and have a cup of tea together and I would tell him everything. He would understand. It would be all right.

I sat up. The glasses clicked on the bed beside me. I slipped them on.

Dr. Cramer turned and winked at me again. When he winked I felt the glasses pulling on my eyes and closed them for a moment. Then I opened them again and I knew.

I knew Dr. Cramer was here to kill me.

He smiled at me and poured two cups of tea. I watched him stoop over the cup on the left side of the tray and slip the powder into the hot tea.

He brought the tray over to the bed and I said, "A napkin, please." He went back, got the napkin, sat down beside me and handed me the cup from the left side of the tray.

We drank.

My hand didn't tremble, even though he watched me. I emptied my cup. He emptied his.

He winked once more. "Well, young lady—feeling better?"

I winked right back at him. "Much better. And you?"

"First rate. Now we can talk, eh? You were going to tell me something?"

"Yes," I said. "I was going to tell you something. I was going to tell you that I know all about it. Percy and Olive had the plan and they put you up to this. They will inherit and give you one-third. The time for action was indefinite, but when I came home distraught tonight they thought it a good idea if you acted at once. Miss Tooker knew I might have an attack, anyway, and she would be convenient as a witness. Not that witnesses would be needed. You could certify as to the cause of death. My heart, you know."

Dr. Cramer was perspiring. The tea had been quite hot. He raised his hand. "Mrs. Olcott, please—"

"Don't bother to speak. You see, I can read your mind. You don't believe that, do you? You're wondering why, knowing these things, I permitted you to poison me."

His eyes bulged and he turned red as a beet.

"Yes," I whispered. "You wonder why I allowed it. And the answer is—I didn't."

He tugged at his collar and half-rose from his chair. "You—didn't?" he croaked.

"No." I smiled sweetly. "When you brought me the napkin I switched our teacups."

I do not know what poison he employed, but it was quite efficacious. Of course his excitement helped speed the process along. He managed to stand erect, but only for an instant, and then sank back into his chair.

His voice failed almost immediately. His head began to wobble. He frothed and retched and made little sounds. Then he began to bite his lips.

I wanted to read his thoughts, but there were no coherent thoughts any more, only images. Words of prayer and blasphemy commingled, and then the overpowering mastery of pain blotted out everything. It made me tingle all over.

At the end he had convulsions and tried to claw out his own throat. I stood over him and laughed. Not a very ladylike thing to do, I admit, but there was justification. Besides, it made me tingle.

Afterwards I went downstairs. Miss Tooker was sleeping and there was no one to stop me. I deserved a little celebration. So I raided the refrigerator and took up a tray loaded with turkey and dressing and truffles and kumquats—oh, they feasted well downstairs, my loving daughter and son-in-law!

I brought the brandy decanter, too.

It was enough to make me quite giddy, climbing the stairs with that load, but once I was back in my room I felt better.

I filled my teacup with brandy and toasted the figure sprawled in the chair before me. I inquired politely did he want a snack, would he care for some brandy, it was delicious and how was his heart behaving these days?

The brandy was strong. I finished all the food, every last bit of it, and drank again. The tingling was mixed with warmth. I felt like singing, shouting. I did both.

The teacup broke. I drank out of the decanter. No one to see me. I reached out and closed his eyes. Bulging eyes. My own eyes ached. I took off the spectacles. Shouldn't have worn them. But if I hadn't, I'd be dead. Now he was dead. I was alive, and tingling.

More brandy. Heartburn. Too much food. Brandy burned too. I lay back on the bed. Everything went round and round, burning. I could see him sprawled there with his mouth open, laughing at me.

Why did he laugh? He was dead. I was the one who should laugh. He had poison. I had brandy. "Liquor is poison to you, Mrs. Olcott."

Who said that? Dr. Cramer said that, the last time. But I wasn't poisoned. So why did it hurt when I laughed?

Why did it hurt my chest so and why did the room go around when I tried to sit up and fell face downwards on the floor why did I tear at the rug until my fingers bent backwards and snapped one by one like pretzel sticks but I couldn't feel them because the pain in my chest was so much stronger than anything, stronger than life itself—

Because it was death.

I died at 10:18 p.m.

3. Percy Dean

After the whole affair was hushed up, Olive and I went away for a while. We could afford to travel now and I made arrangements to have the whole place remodeled while we were gone.

When we returned Olive and I could really hold our heads up in the community. No more snubs, no more covert insults, no more gossip about, "Mrs. Olcott's son-in-law . . . *parvenu* . . . not altogether the sort of person who belongs."

We had the means now to take our rightful place in

society at last. To entertain. That was the first step. The costume party was really Olive's idea, although I was the one who tied it in with our "housewarming."

It was important to invite the right people. Thorgeson, Harker, Pfluger, Hattie Rooker, the Misses Christie. I checked the list with Olive most carefully before we sent invitations.

"If we have Hattie Rooker we must invite Sebastian Grimm," she reminded me. "The writer, you know. He's visiting at her home for the summer."

We planned it all carefully, so carefully in fact that we almost forgot to select our own costumes. At the last moment Olive mentioned the fact. I asked her what she intended to wear.

"Something Spanish, with a mantilla. Then I can wear the earrings." She peered at me quizzically. "But you're going to be a problem. Frankly, Percy, you're too tubby for the usual things. Unless you choose to dress as a clown."

I almost spoke harshly to her, but it was true. I regarded my portliness in the mirror; my receding hairline, my double chin. She peered over my shoulder.

"Just the thing!" she exclaimed. "You shall be Benjamin Franklin."

Benjamin Franklin. I had to admit it wasn't a bad idea. After all, Franklin was a symbol of dignity, stability and wisdom—I am inclined to discount those absurd rumors about his mistresses—and that was the very effect I was seeking. I depended upon this evening to impress my guests. It might be an important first step.

The upshot of the matter was that I went to the costumer, told him my needs, and returned that evening with a Colonial costume, including a partial wig.

Olive was ecstatic over the results. I dressed hastily after dinner and she inspected me at the last moment. "Quite a striking likeness," she said. "But didn't Franklin always wear spectacles?"

"So he did. Unfortunately, it's too late now to procure a pair. I trust the guests will forgive the oversight."

They did.

I spent a most enjoyable evening. Everyone arrived, the liquor was good and plentiful, our catering service excellent, and the costumes added the proper note of frivolity. Although a total abstainer myself, I saw to it that old man Harker, Judge Pfluger, Thorgeson and the others imbibed freely, and their cordiality increased as the evening progressed.

It was particularly important to gain Thorgeson's friendship. Through him I could gain membership in the Gentry Club, and sooner or later I'd worm my way into Room 1200—the fabulous "poker room" where the really big deals were made; millions of dollars in contracts assigned casually as the powers-that-be dealt their cards.

The writer, Sebastian Grimm, put the next idea into my head. "Party's going nicely," he drawled. "Almost think it would be safe to leave the ladies to their own devices for an hour or so, now that the dancing has started. You haven't a poker table available, have you, Dean?"

"There's a room upstairs," I ventured. "Away from the crowd and the noise. If you gentlemen are interested—"

They were. We ascended the stairs.

I hate poker. I dislike all games of chance. But this was too perfect an opportunity to miss. Wouldn't it be natural for my guests to suggest another meeting in the future? Perhaps Thorgeson would mention the Gentry Club games, and I could remind him I was not a member. "That's easily remedied, Dean," he would boom. "Tell you what I'll do—"

Oh, it was an inspiration, and no mistake! I secured cards and chips and we gathered around the big table in the upstairs study—Thorgeson, Dr. Cassit, Judge Pfluger, Harker, Grimm and myself. I would have excluded Grimm if possible; the tall, thin sardonic writer was a disturbing element, and his presence was of no value to me. But it had been his suggestion and I couldn't very well shake him off.

Olive tapped on the door before we started to play.

"Oh here you are," she said. "I see you're in good company. Would anyone care to have buffet luncheon sent up?"

There was an awkward silence. I felt annoyance.

"Very well, then, I shan't disturb you. Oh, Percy—I found something for you just now. In—in Mother's room." She came up behind me and slipped something over my nose and ears. "Spectacles," she giggled. "You remember, we couldn't find a pair for you? But these were in Mother's bureau drawer."

She stood back and surveyed me. "Now, that does it. He really looks like Benjamin Franklin, don't you think?"

I didn't want the spectacles. They hurt my eyes. But I was too embarrassed to reprove her; merely grateful when she slipped out of the room again. The men were already intent on the distribution of chips. Thorgeson was banking. I pulled out my wallet and placed a hundred dollar bill on the table. I received ten white chips.

Obviously, they played for "blood." Very well. I smiled and placed five hundred dollars more before me. "Now for some reds." Thorgeson gave me twenty red chips.

"That's better," I commented. And it was, for I meant to lose tonight. A thousand dollars or so invested properly here would almost guarantee my acceptance by this group, if I lost graciously, like a gentleman. That was my strategy for the evening.

But it didn't work.

I have heard of clairvoyance, of telepathy, of ESP, and these phenomena I have always discounted. Yet *something* was at work tonight. For as I squinted through my spectacles at the cards, I could read the hands of the other players. Not their hands, but their *minds*.

"Pair of eights under . . . raise, I'll get another . . . two queens . . . wonder if he's going for a straight? . . . better stay in . . . never make an inside . . . raise again, bluff them out."

It came to me in a steady stream. I knew when to drop, when to stay, when to raise, when to call.

Of course I meant to lose. But when a man *knows* what to do he's a fool to abandon his advantage. That's logic, isn't it? Sound business. These men respected shrewdness, good judgment. How could I help myself?

I do not wish to dwell upon the actual incidents of the game. Sufficient to say that I won almost every hand. This psychic sense never deserted me, and I must have been over nine thousand dollars ahead when Harker cheated.

I had paid no heed to any extraneous thought or circumstance; merely concentrated on the game and the bets. And then, "I'll keep the ace until the next hand," Harker thought. I could feel it, feel the strength and the desperate avariciousness behind it. Old Harker, worth close to a million dollars, cheating over the poker table.

It stunned me. Before I could make up my mind how to react, the next hand was in play—had been played—and I was sitting there calling with a full house, queens over fours, getting ready to rake in a three-thousand-dollar pot.

Harker's monkey face creased into a grin. "Not so fast, my friend. I have"—he licked his thin lips eagerly—"four aces."

I coughed. "Sorry, Mr. Harker. But has it come to your attention that this is a seven-card stud game and you also have—eight cards?"

Everybody gasped. Gasped, then fell silent.

"An oversight, no doubt. But if you will be good enough to raise your left arm from the table—there, underneath your sleeve—"

The silence deepened. Yet suddenly it was filled with a clamor; not a clamor of words but of *thoughts*.

"The cur . . . accusing Harker, of all people . . . probably planted the card there himself . . . cheating . . . no gentleman . . . nasty little fat-faced fool . . . never should have come . . . barred from decent society . . . vulgar . . . probably drove the old lady to her grave . . .

My head hurt.

I thought if I could talk, the hurting would go away. So I told them what I knew and what I felt about them, and they only stared. So I thought if I shouted it might relieve the pressure in my head, and I shouted and ordered them out of my house and named them for what they were, but they gaped at me as if I were mad. And they kept on *thinking*.

Harker was the worst. He thought things about me which no man could endure. No man could endure such thoughts, even if his head weren't splitting and he didn't know it was all lost, they all hated him, they were mocking and sneering inside.

So I knocked over the table and I took him by the collar, and then they were all on me at once, but I had his wizened throat between my fingers and I wouldn't let go until I squeezed out all the hurting, all of it, and my glasses fell off and everything seemed to go dim. I looked up just in time to see Thorgeson aiming the water carafe at my head.

I tried to move to one side, but it was too late. The carafe came down and everything went away.

Forever.

4. Sebastian Grimm

This will be very brief.

When I picked up those peculiar yellow-lensed spectacles from the floor—slipping them into my pocket unobserved, in the confusion attendant upon calling the doctor and the police—I was motivated by mere curiosity.

That curiosity grew when, at the inquest, Olive Dean

spoke of her mother and how she had brought a pair of glasses home with her on the night of her tragic death.

Certain aspects of that poker game had piqued my fancy, and the statements at the inquest further intrigued me.

The legend, *"Veritas,"* inscribed upon the bridge of the spectacles, was also interesting.

I shall not bore you with my researches. Amateur detection is a monotonous, albeit sometimes a rewarding procedure. It is sufficient to say that my private inquiry led me to a second-hand store and eventually to a partially-razed house near the docks. Research with the local historical society enabled me to ascertain that the spectacles had once been the property of Dirk Van Prinn; legends of his reputed interest in sorcery are common knowledge amongst antiquarians who delve into the early history of the community. I need not bother to underscore the obvious.

At any rate, my rather careful investigations bore fruit. I was able, taking certain liberties based upon circumstantial evidence, to "reconstruct" the thoughts and actions of the various persons who had inadvertently worn the spectacles since the time of their discovery in the secret drawer of old Van Prinn's escritoire. These thoughts and actions have formed the basis of this narrative, in which I have assumed the characters of Mr. Joseph Henshaw, Mrs. Miriam Spencer Olcott, and Mr. Percy Dean—all deceased.

Unfortunately, a final chapter remains to be written. I had no idea of this necessity when I started; had I suspected, I would have desisted immediately. But now I know, as Dirk Van Prinn must have known when he hid the spectacles away in that drawer, that there is danger in wisdom; that knowledge of the thoughts of others leads only to disillusion and destruction.

I mused upon the triteness of this moral, and not for anything in the world would I have emulated poor Joe

Henshaw, or Mrs. Olcott, or Percy Dean, and put on the spectacles to gaze at other men and other minds.

But pride goeth before a fall, and as I wrote of the tragic fate of those poor fools whose search for wisdom ended in disaster, I could not help but reflect upon the actual purpose for which these singular spectacles had somehow been created by a long-dead savant and seer.

"Veritas." The truth.

The truth about others brought evil consequences. But suppose the spectacles were meant to be employed to discover the truth about one's self?

"Know thyself." Could it be that this was the secret purpose of the spectacles—to enable the wearer to look *inward?*

Surely there could be no harm in that. Not in the hands of an intelligent man.

I have always fancied that I "knew" myself in the ordinary sense of the word; was perhaps more aware, through constant introspection, of my inner nature. Thus I *fancied,* but I had to *know.*

And that is why I put them on, just now. Put them on and stared at myself in the hall mirror. Stared, and saw, and knew.

There are things about subliminal intelligence, about the so-called "subconscious," which psychiatry and psychology cannot encompass. I know these things now, and a great deal more. I know that the actual agony undergone by the victims who read the minds of others is as nothing compared to that which is born of reading one's own mind.

I stood before the mirror and looked *into* myself— seeing there the atavistic memories, the desires, the fears, the self-defeat, the seeds of madness, the lurking filth and cruelty; the slimy, crawling, secret shapes which dare not rise even in dreams. I saw the unutterable foulness beneath all the veneer of consciousness and intellect, and knew it for my true nature. Every man's nature. Perhaps it can be suppressed and controlled, if one remains unaware. But merely to realize that *it is there* is a horror which must not be permitted.

When I conclude this account I shall take the "cheaters," as Joe Henshaw so appropriately called them, and destroy them forever. I shall use a revolver for that purpose; aiming it quite steadily and deliberately at these accursed instruments, and shattering them with a single shot.

And I shall be wearing them at the time . . .

ISAAC ASIMOV and FREDERICK POHL, (b. 1920 and 1919 respectively), are two of the leading writers of today. Although their fictional works have been primarily within the science-fiction genre, their names are recognized by a much broader audience. Friends for more than thirty years, their professional careers began at almost the same time, in the late 1930s. Asimov has almost never worked with a collaborator, Pohl being the sole exception; Pohl has done so a number of times, most successfully in the case of his long collaboration with C. M. Kornbluth. Neither has worked often in fantasy, the following story being a rare occurrence—and one of the few instances in which *Weird Tales* presented a story that examined the lighter side of the supernatural.

Legal Rites

Isaac Asimov and Frederik Pohl

I

Already the stars were out, though the sun had just dipped under the horizon, and the sky of the west was a blood-stuck gold behind the Sierra Nevadas.

"Hey!" squawked Russell Harley. "Come back!"

But the one-lunged motor of the old Ford was making too much noise; the driver didn't hear him. Harley cursed as he watched the old car careen along the sandy ruts on its half-flat tires. Its taillight was saying a red *no* to him. *No, you can't get away tonight; no, you'll have to stay here and fight it out.*

Harley grunted and climbed back up the porch stairs of the old wooden house. It was well made, anyhow. The stairs, though half a century old, neither creaked beneath him nor showed cracks.

Harley picked up the bags he'd dropped when he experienced his abrupt change of mind—fake leather and worn out, they were—and carted them into the house. He dumped them on a dust-jacketed sofa and looked around.

It was stifling hot, and the smell of the desert outside had permeated the room. Harley sneezed.

"Water," he said out loud. "That's what I need."

He'd prowled through every room on the ground floor before he stopped still and smote his head. Plumbing—naturally there'd be no plumbing in this hole eight miles out on the desert! A well was the best he could hope for—

If that.

It was getting dark. No electric lights either, of course. He blundered irritatedly through the dusky rooms to the back of the house. The screen door shrieked metallically as he opened it. A bucket hung by the door. He picked it up, tipped it, shook the loose sand out of it. He looked over the "back yard"—about thirty thousand visible acres of hilly sand, rock and patches of sage and flame-tipped ocotillo.

No well.

The old fool got water from somewhere, he thought savagely. Obstinately he climbed down the back steps and wandered out into the desert. Overhead the stars were blinding, a million billion of them, but the sunset was over already and he could see only hazily. The silence was murderous. Only a faint whisper of breeze over the sand, and the slither of his shoes.

He caught a glimmer of starlight from the nearest clump of sage and walked to it. There was a pool of water, caught in the angle of two enormous boulders. He stared at it doubtfully, then shrugged. It was water. It was better than nothing. He dipped the bucket in the little pool. Knowing nothing of the procedure, he filled it with a quart of loose sand as he scooped it along the bottom. When he lifted it, brimful, to his lips, he spat out the first mouthful and swore violently.

Then he used his head. He set the bucket down, waited a second for the sand grains to settle, cupped water in his hands, lifted it to his lips. . . .

Pat. HISS. Pat. HISS. Pat. HISS—

"What the hell!" Harley stood up, looking around in abrupt puzzlement. It sounded like water dripping from somewhere, onto a red-hot stove, flashing into sizzling steam. He saw nothing, only the sand and the sage and the pool of tepid, sickly water.

Pat. HISS—

Then he saw it, and his eyes bulged. Out of nowhere it was dripping, a drop a second, a sticky, dark drop that was thicker than water, that fell to the ground lazily, in slow defiance of gravity. And when it struck each drop sizzled and skittered about, and vanished. It was perhaps eight feet from him, just visible in the starlight.

And then, "Get off my land!" said the voice from nowhere.

Harley got. By the time he got to Rebel Butte three hours later, he was barely managing to walk, wishing desperately that he'd delayed long enough for one more good drink of water, despite all the fiends of hell. But he'd run the first three miles. He'd had plenty of encouragement. He remembered with a shudder how the clear desert air had taken milky shape around the incredible trickle of dampness and had advanced on him threateningly.

And when he got to the first kerosene-lighted saloon of Rebel Butte, and staggered inside, the saloonkeeper's fascinated stare at the front of his shoddy coat showed him strong evidence that he hadn't been suddenly taken with insanity, or drunk on the unaccustomed sensation of fresh desert air. All down the front of him it was, and the harder he rubbed the harder it stayed, the stickier it got. Blood!

"Whiskey!" he said in a strangled voice, tottering to the bar. He pulled a threadbare dollar bill from his pocket, flapped it onto the mahogany.

The blackjack game at the back of the room had stopped. Harley was acutely conscious of the eyes of the players, the bartender and the tall, lean man leaning on the bar. All were watching him.

The bartender broke the spell. He reached for a bottle behind him without looking at it, placed it on the counter before Harley. He poured a glass of water from a jug, set it down with a shot glass beside the bottle.

"I could of told you that would happen," he said casually. "Only you wouldn't of believed me. You had to meet Hank for yourself before you'd believe he was there."

Harley remembered his thirst and drained the glass of water, then poured himself a shot of the whiskey and swallowed it without waiting for the chaser to be refilled. The whiskey felt good going down, almost good enough to stop his internal shakes.

"What are you talking about?" he said finally. He twisted his body and leaned forward across the bar to partly hide the stains on his coat. The saloonkeeper laughed.

"Old Hank," he said. "I knowed who you was right away, even before Tom came back and told me where he'd took you. I knowed you was Zeb Harley's no-good nephew, come to take Harley Hall an' sell it before he was cold in the grave."

The blackjack players were still watching him, Russell Harley saw. Only the lean man farther along the bar seemed to have dismissed him. He was pouring himself another drink, quite occupied with his task.

Harley flushed. "Listen," he said, "I didn't come in here for advice. I wanted a drink. I'm paying for it. Keep your mouth out of this."

The saloonkeeper shrugged. He turned his back and walked away to the blackjack table. After a couple of seconds one of the players turned, too, and threw a card down. The others followed suit.

Harley was just getting set to swallow his pride and talk to the saloonkeeper again—he seemed to know something about what Harley'd been through, and might be helpful—when the lean man tapped his shoulder. Harley whirled and almost dropped his glass. Absorbed and jumpy, he hadn't seen him come up.

"Young man," said the lean one, "my name's Nicholls. Come along with me, sir, and we'll talk this thing over. I think we may be of service to each other."

Even the twelve-cylinder car Nicholls drove jounced like a hay wagon over the sandy ruts leading to the place old Zeb had—laughingly—named "Harley Hall."

Russell Harley twisted his neck and stared at the heap of paraphernalia in the open rumble seat. "I don't like it," he complained. "I never had anything to do with ghosts. How do I know this stuff'll work?"

Nicholls smiled. "You'll have to take my word for it. I've had dealings with ghosts before. You could say that I might qualify as a ghost exterminator, if I chose."

Harley growled. "I still don't like it."

Nicholls turned a sharp look on him. "You like the prospect of owning Harley Hall, don't you? And looking for all the money your late uncle is supposed to have hidden around somewhere?" Harley shrugged. "Certainly you do," said Nicholls, returning his eyes to the road. "And with good reason. The local reports put the figure pretty high, young man."

"That's where you come in, I guess," Harley said sullenly. "I find the money—that I own anyhow—and give some of it to you. How much?"

"We'll discuss that later," Nicholls said. He smiled absently as he looked ahead.

"We'll discuss it right now!"

The smile faded from Nicholls' face. "No," he said. "We won't. I'm doing you a favor, young Harley. Remember that. In return—you'll do as I say, all the way!"

Harley digested that carefully, and it was not a pleasant meal. He waited a couple of seconds before he changed the subject.

"I was out here once when the old man was alive," he said. "He didn't say nothing about any ghost."

"Perhaps he felt you might think him—well, peculiar," Nicholls said. "And perhaps you would have. When were you here?"

"Oh, a long time ago," Harley said evasively. "But I was here a whole day, and part of the night. The old man was crazy as a coot, but he didn't keep any ghosts in the attic."

"This ghost was a friend of his," Nicholls said. "The gentleman in charge of the bar told you that, surely. Your late uncle was something of a recluse. He lived in this house a dozen miles from nowhere, came into town hardly ever, wouldn't let anyone get friendly with him. But he wasn't exactly a hermit. He had Hank for company."

"Fine company."

Nicholls inclined his head seriously. "Oh, I don't know," he said. "From all accounts, they got on well together. They played pinochle and chess—Hank's supposed to have been a great pinochle player. He was killed that way, according to the local reports. Caught somebody dealing from the bottom and shot it out with him. He lost. A bullet pierced his throat and he died quite bloodily." He turned the car out of the ruts of the "road," sent it jouncing across unmarked sand to the old frame house to which they were going.

"That," he finished as he pulled up before the porch, "accounts for the blood that accompanies his apparition."

Harley opened the door slowly and got out, looking uneasily at the battered old house. Nicholls cut the motor, got out and walked at once to the back of the car.

"Come on," he said, dragging things out of the compartment. "Give me a hand with this. I'm not going to carry this stuff all by myself."

Harley came around reluctantly, regarded the curious assortment of bundles of dried faggots, lengths of colored cord, chalk, pencils, ugly little bunches of wilted weeds, bleached bones of small animals and a couple of less pleasant things without pleasure.

Pat. HISS. Pat. HISS—

"He's here!" Harley yelped. "Listen! He's someplace around here watching us."

"Ha!"

The laugh was deep, unpleasant and—bodiless. Harley looked around desperately for the tell-tale trickle of blood. And he found it; from the air it issued, just beside the car, sinking gracefully to the ground and sizzling, vanishing, there.

"I'm watching you, all right," the voice said grimly. "Russell, you worthless piece of corruption, I've got no more use for you than you used to have for me. Dead or alive, this is my land! I shared it with your uncle, you young scalawag, but I won't share it with you. Get out!"

Harley's knees weakened and he tottered dizzily to the rear bumper, sat on it. "Nicholls—" he said confusedly.

"Oh, brace up," Nicholls said with irritation. He tossed a ball of gaudy twine, red and green, with curious knots tied along it, to Harley. Then he confronted the trickle of blood and made a few brisk passes in the air before it. His lips were moving silently, Harley saw, but no words came out.

There was a gasp and a chopped-off squawk from the source of the blood drops. Nicholls clapped his hands sharply, then turned to young Harley. .

"Take that cord you have in your hands and stretch it around the house," he said. "All the way around, and make sure it goes right across the middle of the doors and windows. It isn't much, but it'll hold him till we can get the good stuff set up."

Harley nodded, then pointed a rigid finger at the drops of blood, now sizzling and fuming more angrily than before. "What about *that?*" he managed to get out.

Nicholls grinned complacently. "I'll hold him here till the cows come home," he said. "Get moving!"

Harley inadvertently inhaled a lungful of noxious white smoke and coughed till the tears rolled down his cheeks. When he recovered he looked at Nicholls, who was reading silently from a green leather book with dog-eared pages. He said, "Can I stop stirring this now?"

Nicholls grimaced angrily and shook his head without looking at him. He went on reading, his lips contorting over syllables that were not in any language Harley had ever heard, then snapped the book shut and wiped his brow.

"Fine," he said. "So far, so good." He stepped over to windward of the boiling pot Harley was stirring on the hob over the fireplace, peered down into it cautiously.

"That's about done," he said. "Take it off the fire and let it cool a bit."

Harley lifted it down, then squeezed his aching biceps

with his left hand. The stuff was the consistency of sickly green fudge.

"Now what?" he asked.

Nicholls didn't answer. He looked up in mild surprise at the sudden squawk of triumph from outside, followed by the howling of a chill wind.

"Hank must be loose," he said casually. "He can't do us any harm, I think, but we'd better get a move on." He rummaged in the dwindled pile of junk he'd brought from the car, extracted a paint brush. "Smear this stuff around all the windows and doors. All but the front door. For that I have something else." He pointed to what seemed to be the front axle of an old Model T. "Leave that on the doorsill. Cold iron. You can just step over it, but Hank won't be able to pass it. It's been properly treated already with the very best thaumaturgy."

"Step over it," Harley repeated. "What would I want to step over it for? *He's* out there."

"He won't hurt you," said Nicholls. "You will carry an amulet with you—that one, there—that will keep him away. Probably he couldn't really hurt you anyhow, being a low-order ghost who can't materialize to any great density. But just to take no chances, carry the amulet and don't stay out too long. It won't hold him off forever, not for more than half an hour. If you ever have to go out and stay for any length of time, tie that bundle of herbs around your neck." Nicholls smiled. "That's only for emergencies, though. It works on the asafoetida principle. Ghosts can't come anywhere near it—but you won't like it much yourself. It has—ah—a rather definite odor."

He leaned gingerly over the pot again, sniffing. He sneezed.

"Well, that's cool enough," he said. "Before it hardens, get moving. Start spreading the stuff upstairs—and make sure you don't miss any windows."

"What are you going to do?"

"I," said Nicholls sharply, "will be here. Start."

But he wasn't. When Harley finished his disagreeable task and came down, he called Nicholls' name, but the man was gone. Harley stepped to the door and looked out; the car was gone, too.

He shrugged. "Oh, well," he said, and began taking the dust-cloths off the furniture.

II

Somewhere within the cold, legal mind of Lawyer Turnbull, he weighed the comparative likeness of nightmare and insanity.

He stared at the plush chair facing him, noted with distinct uneasiness how the strangely weightless, strangely sourceless trickle of redness disappeared as it hit the floor, but left long, mud-ochre streaks matted on the upholstery. The sound was unpleasant, too; *Pat. HISS. Pat. Hiss*—

The voice continued impatiently, "Damn your human stupidity! I may be a ghost, but heaven knows I'm not trying to haunt you. Friend, you're not that important to me. Get this—I'm here on business."

Turnbull learned that you cannot wet dry lips with a dehydrated tongue. "Legal business?"

"Sure. The fact that I was once killed by violence, and have to continue my existence on the astral plane, doesn't mean I've lost my legal rights. Does it?"

The lawyer shook his head in bafflement. He said, "This would be easier on me if you weren't invisible. Can't you do something about it?"

There was a short pause. "Well, I could materialize for

a minute," the voice said. "It's hard work—damn hard, for me. There are a lot of us astral entities that can do it easy as falling out of bed, but—Well, if I have to I shall try to do it once."

There was a shimmering in the air above the armchair, and a milky, thin smoke condensed into an intangible seated figure. Turnbull took no delight in noting that, through the figure, the outlines of the chair were still hazily visible. The figure thickened. Just as the features took form—just as Turnbull's bulging eyes made out a prominent hooked nose and a crisp beard—it thinned and exploded with a soft pop.

The voice said weakly, "I didn't think I was that bad. I'm way out of practice. I guess that's the first daylight materialization I've made in seventy-five years."

The lawyer adjusted his rimless glasses and coughed. *Hell's binges,* he thought, *the worst thing about this is that I'm believing it!*

"Oh, well," he said aloud. Then he hurried on before the visitor could take offense: "Just what did you want? I'm just a small-town lawyer, you know. My business is fairly routine—"

"I know all about your business," the voice said. "You can handle my case—it's a land affair. I want to sue Russell Harley."

"Harley?" Turnbull fingered his cheek. "Any relation to Zeb Harley?"

"His nephew—and his heir, too."

Turnbull nodded. "Yes, I remember now. My wife's folks live in Rebel Butte, and I've been there. Quite a coincidence you should come to me—"

The voice laughed. "It was no coincidence," it said softly.

"Oh." Turnbull was silent for a second. Then, "I see," he said. He cast a shrewd glance at the chair. "Lawsuits cost money, Mr.—I don't think you mentioned your name?"

"Hank Jenkins," the voice prompted. "I know that. Would—let's see. Would six hundred and fifty dollars be sufficient?"

Turnbull swallowed. "I think so," he said in a relatively unemotional tone—relative to what he was thinking.

"Then suppose we call that your retainer. I happen to have cached a considerable sum in gold when I was—that is to say, before I became an astral entity. I'm quite certain it hasn't been disturbed. You will have to call it treasure trove, I guess, and give half of it to the state, but there's thirteen hundred dollars altogether."

Turnbull nodded judiciously. "Assuming we can locate your trove," he said, "I think that would be quite satisfactory." He leaned back in his chair and looked legal. His aplomb had returned.

And half an hour later he said slowly, "I'll take your case."

Judge Lawrence Gimbel had always liked his job before. But his thirteen honorable years on the bench lost their flavor for him as he grimaced wearily and reached for his gavel. This case was far too confusing for his taste.

The clerk made his speech, and the packed courtroom sat down en masse. Gimbel held a hand briefly to his eyes before he spoke.

"Is the counsel for the plaintiff ready?"

"I am, your honor." Turnbull, alone at his table, rose and bowed.

"The counsel for the defendant?"

"Ready, your honor!" Fred Wilson snapped. He looked with a hard flicker of interest at Turnbull and his solitary table, then leaned over and whispered in Russell Harley's ear. The youth nodded glumly, then shrugged.

Gimbel said, "I understand the attorneys for both sides have waived jury trial in this case of Henry Jenkins versus Russell Joseph Harley."

Both lawyers nodded. Gimbel continued, "In view of

the unusual nature of this case, I imagine it will prove necessary to conduct it with a certain amount of informality. The sole purpose of this court is to arrive at the true facts at issue, and to deliver a verdict in accord with the laws pertaining to these facts. I will not stand on ceremony. Nevertheless, I will not tolerate any disturbances or unnecessary irregularities. The spectators will kindly remember that they are here on privilege. Any demonstration will result in the clearing of the court."

He looked severely at the white faces that gleamed unintelligently up at him. He suppressed a sigh as he said, "The counsel for the plaintiff will begin."

Turnbull rose quickly to his feet, faced the judge.

"Your honor," he said, "we propose to show that my client, Henry Jenkins, has been deprived of his just rights by the defendant. Mr. Jenkins, by virtue of a sustained residence of more than twenty years in the house located on Route 22, eight miles north of the town of Rebel Butte, with the full knowledge of its legal owner, has acquired certain rights. In legal terminology we define these as the rights of adverse possession. The layman would call them common-law rights—squatters' rights."

Gimbel folded his hands and tried to relax. Squatters' rights—for a ghost! He sighed, but listened attentively as Turnbull went on.

"Upon the death of Zebulon Harley, the owner of the house involved—it is better known, perhaps, as Harley Hall—the defendant inherited title to the property. We do not question his right to it. But my client has an equity in Harley Hall; the right to free and full existence. The defendant has forcefully evicted my client, by means which have caused my client great mental distress, and have even endangered his very existence."

Gimbel nodded. If the case only had a precedent somewhere. . . . But it hadn't; he remembered grimly the hours he'd spent thumbing through all sorts of unlikely law books, looking for anything that might bear on the case. It had been his better judgment that he throw the case out of court outright—a judge couldn't afford to have himself laughed at, not if he were ambitious. And public laughter was about the only certainty there was to this case. But Wilson had put up such a fight that the judge's temper had taken over. He never did like Wilson, anyhow.

"You may proceed with your witnesses," he said.

Turnbull nodded. To the clerk he said, "Call Henry Jenkins to the stand."

Wilson was on his feet before the clerk opened his mouth.

"Objection!" he bellowed. "The so-called Henry Jenkins cannot qualify as a witness!"

"Why not?" demanded Turnbull.

"Because he's dead!"

The judge clutched his gavel with one hand, forehead with the other. He banged on the desk to quiet the court-room.

Turnbull stood there, smiling. "Naturally," he said, "you'll have proof of that statement."

Wilson snarled. "Certainly." He referred to his brief. "The so-called Henry Jenkins is the ghost, spirit or specter of one Hank Jenkins, who prospected for gold in this ter-ritory a century ago. He was killed by a bullet through the throat from the gun of one Long Tom Cooper, and was declared legally dead on September 14, 1850. Cooper was hanged for his murder. No matter what hocus-pocus you produce for evidence to the contrary now, that status of legal death remains completely valid."

"What evidence have you of the identity of my client with this Hank Jenkins?" Turnbull asked grimly.

"Do you deny it?"

Turnbull shrugged. "I deny nothing. I'm not being cross-examined. Furthermore, the sole prerequisite of a witness is that he understand the value of an oath. Henry Jenkins was tested by John Quincy Fitzjames, professor of psy-chology at the University of Southern California. The results—I have Dr. Fitzjames' sworn statement of them here, which I will introduce as an exhibit—show clearly that my client's intelligence quotient is well above normal, and that a psychiatric examination discloses no important aberrations which would injure his validity as a witness. I insist that my client be allowed to testify in his own behalf."

"But he's dead!" squawked Wilson. "He's invisible right now!"

"My client," said Turnbull stiffly, "is not present just now. Undoubtedly that accounts for what you term his invisibility." He paused for the appreciative murmur that swept through the court. Things were breaking perfectly, he thought, smiling. "I have here another affidavit," he said. "It is signed by Elihu James and Terence MacRae, who respectively head the departments of physics and biology at the same university. It states that my client exhibits all the vital phenomena of life. I am prepared to call all three of my expert witnesses to the stand, if necessary."

Wilson scowled but said nothing. Judge Gimbel leaned forward.

"I don't see how it is possible for me to refuse the plaintiff the right to testify," he said. "If the three experts who prepared these reports will testify on the stand to the facts contained in them, Henry Jenkins may then take the stand."

Wilson sat down heavily. The three experts spoke briefly —and dryly. Wilson put them through only the most formal cross-examination.

The judge declared a brief recess. In the corridor outside, Wilson and his client lit cigarettes and looked unsympathetically at each other.

"I feel like a fool," said Russell Harley. "Bringing suit against a ghost."

"The ghost brought the suit," Wilson reminded him. "If only we'd been able to hold fire for a couple more weeks, till another judge came on the bench, I could've got this thing thrown right out of court."

"Well, why couldn't we wait?"

"Because you were in such a damn hurry!" Wilson said. "You and that idiot Nicholls—so confident that it would never come to trial."

Harley shrugged, and thought unhappily of their failure in completely exorcising the ghost of Hank Jenkins. That had been a mess. Jenkins had somehow escaped from the charmed circle they'd drawn around him, in which they'd hoped to keep him till the trial was forfeited by non-appearance.

"That's another thing," said Wilson. "Where is Nicholls?"

Harley shrugged again. "I dunno. The last I saw of him was in your office. He came around to see me right after the deputy slapped the show-cause order on me at the house. He brought me down to you—said you'd been recommended to him. Then you and him and I talked about the case for a while. He went out, after he lent me a little money to help meet your retainer. Haven't seen him since."

"I'd like to know who recommended me to him," Wilson said grimly. "I don't think he'd ever recommend anybody else. I don't like this case—and I don't much like you."

Harley growled but said nothing. He flung his cigarette away. It tasted of the garbage that hung around his neck—everything did. Nicholls had told no lies when he said Harley wouldn't much like the bundle of herbs that would ward off the ghost of old Jenkins. They smelled.

The court clerk was in the corridor, bawling something and people were beginning to trickle back in. Harley and his attorney went with them.

When the trial had been resumed, the clerk said, "Henry Jenkins!"

Wilson was on his feet at once. He opened the door of the judge's chamber, said something in a low tone. Then he stepped back, as if to let someone through.

Pat. HISS. Pat. HISS—

There was a concerted gasp from the spectators as the weirdly appearing trickle of blood moved slowly across the open space to the witness chair. This was the ghost— the plaintiff in the most eminently absurd case in the history of jurisprudence.

"All right, Hank," Turnbull whispered. "You'll have to materialize long enough to let the clerk swear you in."

The clerk drew back nervously at the pillar of milky fog that appeared before him, vaguely humanoid in shape. A phantom hand, half-transparent, reached out to touch the Bible. The clerk's voice shook as he administered the oath, and heard the response come from the heart of the cloudpillar.

The haze drifted into the witness chair, bent curiously at about hip-height, and popped into nothingness.

The judge banged his gavel wildly. The buzz of alarm that had arisen from the spectators died out.

"I'll warn you again," he declared, "that unruliness will not be tolerated. The counsel for the plaintiff may proceed."

Turnbull walked to the witness chair and addressed its emptiness.

"Your name?"

"My name is Henry Jenkins."

"Your occupation?"

There was a slight pause. "I have none. I guess you'd say I'm retired."

"Mr. Jenkins, just what connection have you with the building referred to as Harley Hall?"

"I have occupied it for ninety years."

"During this time, did you come to know the late Zebulon Harley, owner of the Hall?"

"I knew Zeb quite well."

Turnbull nodded. "When did you make his acquaintance?" he asked.

"In the spring of 1907. Zeb had just lost his wife. After that, you see, he made Harley Hall his year-round home. He became—well, more or less of a hermit. Before that we had never met, since he was only seldom at the Hall. But we became friendly then."

"How long did this friendship last?"

"Until he died last fall. I was with him when he died. I still have a few keepsakes he left me then." There was a distinct nostalgic sigh from the witness chair, which by now was liberally spattered with muddy red liquid. The falling drops seemed to hesitate for a second, and their sizzling noise was muted as with a strong emotion.

Turnbull went on, "Your relations with him were good, then?"

"I'd call them excellent," the emptiness replied firmly. "Every night we sat up together. When we didn't play pinochle or chess or cribbage, we just sat and talked over the news of the day. I still have the book we used to keep records of the chess and pinochle games. Zeb made the entries himself, in his own handwriting."

Turnbull abandoned the witness for a moment. He faced the judge with a smile. "I offer in evidence," he said, "the book mentioned. Also a ring given to the plaintiff by the late Mr. Harley, and a copy of the plays of Gilbert and Sullivan. On the flyleaf of this book is inscribed, 'To Old Hank,' in Harley's own hand."

He turned again to the empty, blood-leaking witness chair.

He said, "In all your years of association, did Zebulon Harley ever ask you to leave, or to pay rent?"

"Of course not. Not Zeb!"

Turnbull nodded. "Very good," he said. "Now, just one or two more questions. Will you tell in your own words what occurred, after the death of Zebulon Harley, that caused you to bring this suit?"

"Well, in January young Harley—"

"You mean Russell Joseph Harley, the defendant?"

"Yes. He arrived at Harley Hall on January fifth. I asked him to leave, which he did. On the next day he returned with another man. They placed a talisman upon the threshold of the main entrance, and soon after sealed every threshold and windowsill in the Hall with a substance which is noxious to me. These activities were accompanied by several of the most deadly spells in the Ars Magicorum. He further added an Exclusion Circle with a radius of a little over a mile, entirely surrounding the Hall."

"I see," the lawyer said. "Will you explain to the court the effects of these activities?"

"Well," the voice said thoughtfully, "it's a little hard to put in words. I can't pass the Circle without a great expenditure of energy. Even if I did I couldn't enter the building because of the talisman and the seals."

"Could you enter by air? Through a chimney, perhaps?"

"No. The Exclusion Circle is really a sphere. I'm pretty sure the effort would destroy me."

"In effect, then, you are entirely barred from the house you have occupied for ninety years, due to the wilful acts of Russell Joseph Harley, the defendant, and an unnamed accomplice of his."

"That is correct."

Turnbull beamed. "Thank you. That's all."

He turned to Wilson, whose face had been a study in dourness throughout the entire examination. "Your witness," he said.

Wilson snapped to his feet and strode to the witness chair.

He said belligerently, "You say your name is Henry Jenkins?"

"Yes."

"That is your name now, you mean to say. What was your name before?"

"Before?" There was surprise in the voice that emanated from above the trickling blood drops. "Before when?"

Wilson scowled. "Don't pretend ignorance," he said sharply. "Before you *died,* of course."

"Objection!" Turnbull was on his feet, glaring at Wilson. "The counsel for the defense has no right to speak of some hypothetical death of my client!"

Gimbel raised a hand wearily to cut off the words that were forming on Wilson's lips. "Objection sustained," he said. "No evidence has been presented to identify the plaintiff as the prospector who was killed in 1850—or anyone else."

Wilson's mouth twisted into a sour grimace. He continued on a lower key.

"You say, Mr. Jenkins, that you occupied Harley Hall for ninety years."

"Ninety-two years next month. The Hall wasn't built—in its present form, anyhow—until 1876, but I occupied the house that stood on the site previously."

"What did you do before then?"

"Before then?" The voice paused, then said doubtfully, "I don't remember."

"You're under oath!" Wilson flared.

The voice got firmer. "Ninety years is a long time," it said. "I don't remember."

"Let's see if I can't refresh your memory. Is it true that ninety-one years ago, in the year in which you claim to have begun your occupancy of Harley Hall, Hank Jenkins was killed in a gun duel?"

"That may be true, if you say so. I don't remember."

"Do you remember that the shooting occurred not fifty feet from the present site of Harley Hall?"

"It may be."

"Well, then," Wilson thundered, "is it not a fact that when Hank Jenkins died by violence his ghost assumed existence? That it was then doomed to haunt the site of its slaying throughout eternity?"

The voice said evenly, "I have no knowledge of that."

"Do you deny that it is well known throughout that section that the ghost of Hank Jenkins haunts Harley Hall?"

"Objection!" shouted Turnbull. "Popular opinion is not evidence."

"Objection sustained. Strike the question from the record."

Wilson, badgered, lost his control. In a dangerously uneven voice, he said, "Perjury is a criminal offense. Mr. Jenkins, do you deny that you are the ghost of Hank Jenkins?"

The tone was surprised. "Why, certainly."

"You *are* a ghost, aren't you?"

Stiffly, "I'm an entity on the astral plane."

"That, I believe, is what is called a ghost?"

"I can't help what it's called. I've heard you called a lot of things. Is that proof?"

There was a surge of laughter from the audience. Gimbel slammed his gavel down on the bench.

"The witness," he said, "will confine himself to answering questions."

Wilson bellowed, "In spite of what you say, it's true, isn't it, that you are merely the spirit of a human being who had died through violence?"

The voice from above the blood drops retorted, "I repeat that I am an entity of the astral plane. I am not aware that I was ever a human being."

The lawyer turned an exasperated face to the bench.

"Your honor," he said, "I ask that you instruct the witness to cease playing verbal hide-and-seek. It is quite evident that the witness is a ghost, and that he is therefore the relict of some human being, ipso facto. Circumstantial evidence is strong that he is the ghost of the Hank Jenkins who was killed in 1850. But this is a nonessential point. What is definite is that he is the ghost of someone who is dead, and hence is unqualified to act as witness! I demand his testimony be stricken from the record!"

Turnbull spoke up at once. "Will the counsel for the defense quote his authority for branding my client a ghost —in the face of my client's repeated declaration that he is an entity of the astral plane? What is the legal definition of a ghost?"

Judge Gimbel smiled. "Counsel for the defense will proceed with the cross-examination," he said.

Wilson's face flushed dark purple. He mopped his brow with a large bandanna, then glared at the dropping, sizzling trickle of blood.

"Whatever you are," he said, "answer me this question. Can you pass through a wall?"

"Why, yes. Certainly." There was a definite note of surprise in the voice from nowhere. "But it isn't as easy as some people think. It definitely requires a lot of effort."

"Never mind that. Can you do it?"

"Yes."

"Could you be bound by any physical means? Would handcuffs hold you? Or ropes, chains, prison walls, a hermetically sealed steel chest?"

Jenkins had no chance to answer. Turnbull, scenting danger, cut in hastily. "I object to this line of questioning. It is entirely irrelevant."

"On the contrary," Wilson cried loudly, "it bears strongly on the qualifications of the so-called Henry Jenkins as a witness! I demand that he answer the question."

Judge Gimbel said, "Objection overruled. Witness will answer the question."

The voice from the chair said superciliously, "I don't mind answering. Physical barriers mean nothing to me, by and large."

The counsel for the defense drew himself up triumphantly.

"Very good," he said with satisfaction. *"Very* good." Then to the judge, the words coming sharp and fast, "I claim, your honor, that the so-called Henry Jenkins has no legal status as a witness in court. There is clearly no value in understanding the nature of an oath if a violation of the oath can bring no punishment in its wake. The statements of a man who can perjure himself freely have no worth. I demand they be stricken from the record!"

Turnbull was at the judge's bench in two strides.

"I had anticipated that, your honor," he said quickly. "From the very nature of the case, however, it is clear that my client can be very definitely restricted in his movements—spells, pentagrams, talismans, amulets, Exclusion Circles and what-not. I have here—which I am prepared to deliver to the baliff of the court—a list of the various methods of confining an astral entity to a restricted area for periods ranging from a few moments to all eternity. Moreover, I have also signed a bond for five thousand dollars, prior to the beginning of the trial, which I stand ready to forfeit should my client be confined and make his escape, if found guilty of any misfeasance as a witness."

Gimbel's face, which had looked startled for a second, slowly cleared. He nodded. "The court is satisfied with the statement of the counsel for the plaintiff," he declared. "There seems no doubt that the plaintiff can be penalized for any misstatements, and the motion of the defense is denied."

Wilson looked choleric, but shrugged. "All right," he said. "That will be all."

"You may step down, Mr. Jenkins," Gimbel directed, and watched in fascination as the blood-dripping column rose and floated over the floor, along the corridor, out the door.

Turnbull approached the judge's bench again. He said, "I would like to place in evidence these notes, the diary of the late Zebulon Harley. It was presented to my client by Harley himself last fall. I call particular attention to the entry for April 6, 1917, in which he mentions the entrance of the United States into the First World War, and records the results of a series of eleven pinochle games played with a personage identified as 'Old Hank.' With the court's permission, I will read the entry for that day, and also various other entries for the next four years. Please note the references to someone known variously as 'Jenkins', 'Hank Jenkins' and—in one extremely significant passage —'Old Invisible.' "

Wilson stewed silently during the slow reading of Harley's diary. There was anger on his face, but he paid close attention, and when the reading was over he leaped to his feet.

"I would like to know," he asked, "if the counsel for the plaintiff is in possession of any diaries *after* nineteen twenty?"

Turnbull shook his head. "Harley apparently never kept a diary, except during the four years represented in this."

"Then I demand that the court refuse to admit this diary as evidence on two counts," Wilson said. He raised two fingers to tick off the points. "In the first place, the evidence presented is frivolous. The few vague and unsatisfactory references to Jenkins nowhere specifically describe him as what he is—ghost, astral entity or what you will. Second, the evidence, even were the first point overlooked, concerns only the years up to 1921. The case concerns itself only with the supposed occupation of Harley Hall by the so-called Jenkins in the last twenty years— *since* '21. Clearly, the evidence is therefore irrelevant."

Gimbel looked at Turnbull, who smiled calmly.

"The reference to 'Old Invisible' is far from vague," he said. "It is a definite indication of the astral character of my client. Furthermore, evidence as to the friendship of my client with the late Mr. Zebulon Harley before 1921 is entirely relevant, as such a friendship, once established,

would naturally be presumed to have continued indefi-
nitely. Unless, of course, the defense is able to present
evidence to the contrary."

Judge Gimbel said, "The diary is admitted as evidence."

Turnbull said, "I rest my case."

There was a buzz of conversation in the courtroom
while the judge looked over the diary, and then handed
it to the clerk to be marked and entered.

Gimbel said, "The defense may open its case."

Wilson rose. To the clerk he said, "Russell Joseph Harley."

But young Harley was recalcitrant. "Nix," he said, on
his feet, pointing at the witness chair. "That thing's got
blood all over it! You don't expect me to sit down in that
large puddle of blood, do you?"

Judge Gimbel leaned over to look at the chair. The
drip-drop trickle of blood from the apparition who'd been
testifying had left its mark. Muddy brown all down the
front of the chair. Gimbel found himself wondering how
the ghost managed to replenish its supply of the fluid, but
gave it up.

"I see your point," he said. "Well, it's getting a bit late
anyhow. The clerk will take away the present witness
chair and replace it. In the interim, I declare the court
recessed till tomorrow morning at ten o'clock."

III

Russell Harley noticed how the elevator boy's back registered repulsion and disapproval, and scowled. He was not
a popular guest in the hotel, he knew well. Where he
made his mistake, though, was in thinking that the noxious
bundle of herbs about his neck was the cause of it. His
odious personality had a lot to do with the chilly attitude
of the management and his fellow guests.

He made his way to the bar, ignoring the heads that turned in surprise to follow the reeking comet tail of his passage. He entered the red-leather-and-chromium drinking room, and stared about for Lawyer Wilson.

And blinked in surprise when he saw him. Wilson wasn't alone. In the booth with him was a tall, dark figure, with his back to Harley. The back alone was plenty for recognition. Nicholls!

Wilson had seen him. "Hello, Harley," he said, all smiles and affability in the presence of the man with the money. "Come on and sit down. Mr. Nicholls dropped in on me a little while ago, so I brought him over."

"Hello," Harley said glumly, and Nicholls nodded. The muscles of his cheeks pulsed, and he seemed under a strain, strangely uncomfortable in Harley's presence. Still there was a twinkle in the look he gave young Harley, and his voice was friendly enough—though supercilious— as he said:

"Hello, Harley. How is the trial going?"

"Ask him," said Harley, pointing a thumb at Wilson as he slid his knees under the booth's table and sat down. "He's the lawyer. He's supposed to know these things."

"Doesn't he?"

Harley shrugged and craned his neck for the waitress. "Oh, I guess so. . . . Rye and water!" He watched the girl appreciatively as she nodded and went off to the bar, then turned his attention back to Nicholls. "The trouble is," he said, "Wilson may think he knows, but I think he's all wet."

Wilson frowned. "Do you imply—" he began, but Nicholls put up a hand.

"Let's not bicker," said Nicholls. "Suppose you answer my question. I have a stake in this, and I want to know. How's the trial going?"

Wilson put on his most open-faced expression. "Frankly," he said, "not too well. I'm afraid the judge is on the other side. If you'd listened to me and stalled till another judge came along—"

"I had no time to stall," said Nicholls. "I have to be elsewhere within a few days. Even now, I should be on my way. Do you think we might lose the case?"

Harley laughed sharply. As Wilson glared at him he took his drink from the waitress' tray and swallowed it. The smile remained on his face as he listened to Wilson say smoothly:

"There is a good deal of danger, yes."

"Hum." Nicholls looked interestedly at his fingernails. "Perhaps I chose the wrong lawyer."

"Sure you did." Harley waved at the waitress, ordered another drink. "You want to know what else I think? I think you picked the wrong client, spelled s-t-o-o-g-e. I'm getting sick of this. This damn thing around my neck smells bad. How do I know it's any good, anyhow? Far as I can see, it just smells bad, and that's all."

"It works," Nicholls said succinctly. "I wouldn't advise you to go without it. The late Hank Jenkins is not a very strong ghost—a strong one would tear you apart and chew up your herbs for dessert—but without the protection of what you wear about your neck, you would become a very uncomfortable human as soon as Jenkins heard you'd stopped wearing it."

He put down the glass of red wine he'd been inhaling without drinking, looked intently at Wilson. "I've put up the money in this," he said. "I had hoped you'd be able to handle the legal end. I see I'll have to do more. Now listen intently, because I have no intention of repeating this. There's an angle to this case that's got right by your blunted legal acumen. Jenkins claims to be an astral entity, which he undoubtedly is. Now, instead of trying to prove him a ghost, and legally dead, and therefore unfit to testify, which you have been doing, suppose you do this. . . ."

He went on to speak rapidly and to the point.

And when he left them a bit later, and Wilson took Harley up to his room and poured him into bed, the lawyer felt happy for the first time in days.

Russell Joseph Harley, a little hung over and a lot nervous, was called to the stand as first witness in his own behalf.

Wilson said, "Your name?"

"Russell Joseph Harley."

"You are the nephew of the late Zebulon Harley, who bequeathed the residence known as Harley Hall to you?"

"Yes."

Wilson turned to the bench. "I offer this copy of the late Mr. Zebulon Harley's will in evidence. All his possessions are left to his nephew and only living kin, the defendant."

Turnbull spoke from his desk. "The plaintiff in no way disputes the defendant's equity in Harley Hall."

Wilson continued, "You passed part of your childhood in Harley Hall, did you not, and visited it as a grown man on occasion?"

"Yes."

"At any time, has anything in the shape of a ghost, specter or astral entity manifested itself to you in Harley Hall?"

"No. I'd remember it."

"Did your late uncle ever mention any such manifestation to you?"

"Him? No."

"That's all."

Turnbull came up for the cross-examination.

"When, Mr. Harley, did you last see your uncle before his death?"

"It was in 1938. In September, some time—around the tenth or eleventh of the month."

"How long a time did you spend with him?"

Harley flushed unaccountably. "Ah—just one day," he said.

"When before that did you see him?"

"Well, not since I was quite young. My parents moved to Pennsylvania in 1920."

"And since then—except for that one-day visit in 1938 —has any communication passed between your uncle and yourself?"

"No, I guess not. He was a rather queer duck—solitary. A little bit balmy, I think."

"Well, you're a loving nephew. But in view of what you've just said, does it sound surprising that your uncle never told you of Mr. Jenkins? He never had much chance to, did he?"

"He had a chance in 1938, but he didn't," Harley said defiantly.

Turnbull shrugged. "I'm finished," he said.

Gimbel began to look bored. He had anticipated something more in the way of fireworks. He said, "Has the defense any further witnesses?"

Wilson smiled grimly. "Yes, your honor," he said. This was his big moment, and he smiled again as he said gently, "I would like to call Mr. Henry Jenkins to the stand."

In the amazed silence that followed, Judge Gimbel leaned forward. "You mean you wish to call the plaintiff as a witness for the defense?"

Serenely, "Yes, your honor."

Gimbel grimaced. "Call Henry Jenkins," he said wearily to the clerk, and sank back in his chair.

Turnbull was looking alarmed. He bit his lip, trying to decide whether to object to this astonishing procedure, but finally shrugged as the clerk bawled out the ghost's name.

Turnbull sped down the corridor, out the door. His voice was heard in the anteroom, then he returned more slowly. Behind him came the trickle of blood drops: *Pat. HISS. Pat. HISS—*

"One moment," said Gimbel, coming to life again. "I have no objection to your testifying, Mr. Jenkins, but the State should not be subjected to the needless expense of reupholstering its witness chair every time you do. Bailiff, find some sort of a rug or something to throw over the chair before Mr. Jenkins is sworn in."

A tarpaulin was hurriedly procured and adjusted to the chair; Jenkins materialized long enough to be sworn in, then sat.

"Tell me, Mr. Jenkins," he said, "just how many 'astral entities'—I believe that is what you call yourself— are there?"

"I have no way of knowing. Many billions."

"As many, in other words, as there have been human beings to die by violence?"

Turnbull rose to his feet in sudden agitation, but the ghost neatly evaded the trap. "I don't know. I only know there are billions." The lawyer's cat-who-ate-canary smile remained undimmed. "And all these billions are constantly about us, everywhere, only remaining invisible. Is that it?"

"Oh, no. Very few remain on Earth. Of those, still fewer have anything to do with humans. Most humans are quite boring to us."

"Well, how many would you say are on Earth? A hundred thousand?"

"Even more, maybe. But that's a good guess."

Turnbull interrupted suddenly. "I would like to know the significance of these questions. I object to this whole line of questioning as being totally irrelevant."

Wilson was a study in legal dignity. He retorted, "I am trying to elicit some facts of major value, your honor. This may change the entire character of the case. I ask your patience for a moment or two."

"Counsel for the defense may continue," Gimbel said curtly.

Wilson showed his canines in a grin. He continued to the blood-dripping before him. "Now, the contention of your counsel is that the late Mr. Harley allowed an 'astral entity' to occupy his home for twenty years or more, with his full knowledge and consent. That strikes me as being entirely improbable, but shall we for the moment assume it to be the case?"

"Certainly! It's the truth."

"Then tell me, Mr. Jenkins, have you fingers?"

"Have I—what?"

"You heard me!" Wilson snapped. "Have you fingers, flesh-and-blood fingers, capable of making an imprint?"

"Why, no. I—"

Wilson rushed on. "Or have you a photograph of yourself—or specimens of your handwriting—or any sort of material identification? Have you any of these?"

The voice was definitely querulous. "What do you mean?"

Wilson's voice became harsh, menacing. "I mean, can you prove that *you* are the astral entity alleged to have occupied Zebulon Harley's home. Was it you—or was it another of the featureless, faceless, intangible unknowns— one of the hundreds of thousands of them that, by your own admission, are all over the face of the earth, rambling where they choose, not halted by any locks or bars? Can you prove that *you* are anyone in particular?"

"Your honor!" Turnbull's voice was almost a shriek as he found his feet at last. "My client's identity was never in question!"

"It is now!" roared Wilson. "The opposing counsel has presented a personage whom he styles 'Henry Jenkins.' Who is this Jenkins? What is he? Is he even an individual —or a corporate aggregation of these mysterious 'astral entities' which we are to believe are everywhere, but which we never see? If he is an individual, is he *the* individual?

And how can we know that, even if he says he is? Let him produce evidence—photographs, a birth certificate, finger-prints. Let him bring in identifying witnesses who have known both ghosts, and are prepared to swear that these ghosts are the same ghost. Failing this, there is no case! Your honor, I demand the court declare an immediate judgment in favor of the defendant!"

Judge Gimbel stared at Turnbull. "Have you anything to say?" he asked. "The argument of the defense would seem to have every merit with it. Unless you can produce some sort of evidence as to the identity of your client, I have no alternative but to find for the defense."

For a moment there was a silent tableau. Wilson triumphant, Turnbull furiously frustrated.

How could you identify a ghost?

And then came the quietly amused voice from the witness chair.

"This thing has gone far enough," it said above the sizzle and splatter of its own leaking blood. "I believe I can present proof that will satisfy the court."

Wilson's face fell with express-elevator speed. Turnbull held his breath, afraid to hope.

Judge Gimbel said, "You are under oath. Proceed."

There was no other sound in the courtroom as the voice said, "Mr. Harley, here, spoke of a visit to his uncle in 1938. I can vouch for that. They spent a night and a day together. They weren't alone. I was there."

No one was watching Russell Harley, or they might have seen the sudden sick pallor that passed over his face.

The voice, relentless, went on. "Perhaps I shouldn't have eavesdropped as I did, but old Zeb never had any secrets from me anyhow. I listened to what they talked about. Young Harley was working for a bank in Philadelphia at the time. His first big job. He needed money, and needed it bad. There was a shortage in his department. A woman named Sally—"

"Hold on!" Wilson yelled. "This has nothing to do with your identification of yourself. Keep to the point!"

But Turnbull had begun to comprehend. He was shouting, too, almost too excited to be coherent. "Your honor, my client must be allowed to speak. If he shows knowledge of an intimate conversation between the late Mr. Harley and the defendant, it would be certain proof that he enjoyed the late Mr. Harley's confidence, and thus, Q.E.D., that he is no other than the astral entity who occupied Harley Hall for so long!"

Gimbel nodded sharply. "Let me remind counsel for the defense that this is his own witness. Mr. Jenkins, continue."

The voice began again, "As I was saying, the woman's name—"

"Shut up, damn you!" Harley yelled. He sprang upright, turned beseechingly toward the judge. "He's twisting it! Make him stop! Sure, I knew my uncle had a ghost. He's it, all right, curse his black soul! He can have the house if he wants it—I'll clear out. I'll clear out of the whole damned state!"

He broke off into babbling and turned about wildly. Only the intervention of a marshal kept him from hurtling out of the courtroom.

Banging of the gavel and hard work by the court clerk and his staff restored order in the courtroom. When the room had returned almost to normalcy, Judge Gimbel, perspiring and annoyed, said. "As far as I am concerned, identification of the witness is complete. Has the defense any further evidence to present?"

Wilson shrugged morosely. "No, your honor."

"Counsel for the plaintiff?"

"Nothing, your honor. I rest my case."

Gimbel plowed a hand through his sparse hair and blinked. "In that case," he said, "I find for the plaintiff. An order is entered hereby that the defendant, Russell

Joseph Harley, shall remove from the premises of Harley Hall all spells, pentagrams, talismans and other means of exorcism employed; that he shall cease and desist from making any attempts, of whatever nature, to evict the tenant in the future; and that Henry Jenkins, the plaintiff, shall be permitted to full use and occupancy of the premises designated as Harley Hall for the full term of his natural—ah—existence."

The gavel banged. "The case is closed."

"Don't take it so hard," said a mild voice behind Russell Harley. He whirled surlily. Nicholls was coming up the street after him from the courthouse, Wilson in tow.

Nicholls said, "You lost the case, but you've still got your life. Let me buy you a drink. In here, perhaps."

He herded them into a cocktail lounge, sat them down before they had a chance to object. He glanced at his expensive wrist watch. "I have a few minutes," he said. "Then I really must be off. It's urgent."

He hailed a barman, ordered for all. Then he looked at young Harley and smiled broadly as he dropped a bill on the counter to pay for the drinks.

"Harley," he said, "I have a motto that you would do well to remember at times like these. I'll make you a present of it, if you like."

"What is it?"

" 'The worst is yet to come.' "

Harley snarled and swallowed his drink without replying. Wilson said, "What gets me is, why didn't they come to us before the trial with that stuff about this charmingly illicit client you wished on me? We'd have had to settle out of court."

Nicholls shrugged. "They had their reasons," he said. "After all, one case of exorcism, more or less, doesn't matter. But lawsuits set precedents. You're a lawyer, of sorts, Wilson; do you see what I mean?"

"Precedents?" Wilson looked at him slackjawed for a moment; then his eyes widened.

"I see you understand me." Nicholls nodded. "From now on in this state—and by virtue of the full-faith-and-credence of the Constitution, in *every* state of the country —a ghost has a legal right to haunt a house!"

"Good Lord!" said Wilson. He began to laugh, not loud, but from the bottom of his chest.

Harley stared at Nicholls. "Once and for all," he whispered, "tell me—what's your angle on all this?"

Nicholls smiled again.

"Think about it a while," he said lightly. "You'll begin to understand." He sniffed his wine once more, then sat the glass down gently—

And vanished.

MANLY WADE WELLMAN, (b. 1903), in Portuguese
West Africa, was the youngest son of a medical mission-
ary. He was educated in various parts of the United
States, graduated from Columbia University, and for most
of his life has been a freelance writer. Many of his sixty
books and five hundred magazine stories and articles deal
with American folklore and strange beliefs of the past.
O Ugly Bird! became Chapter One of a book about John,
the Wandering Minstrel: *Who Fears the Devil?* (Arkham
House, 1963), and has recently been made into a motion picture under the same title.

O Ugly Bird!

Manly Wade Wellman

I swear I'm licked before I start, trying to tell you all
what Mr. Onselm looked like. Words give out sometimes.
The way you're purely frozen to death for fit words to tell

the favor of the girl you love. And Mr. Onselm and I pure-poison hated each other from the start. That's a way that love and hate are alike.

He's what folks in the country call a low man, meaning he's short and small. But a low man is low other ways than in inches, sometimes. Mr. Onselm's shoulders didn't wide out as far as his big ears, and they sank and sagged. His thin legs bowed in at the knee and out at the shank, like two sickles put point to point. His neck was as thin as a carrot, and on it his head looked like a swollen-up pale gourd. Thin hair, gray as tree moss. Loose mouth, a little bit open to show long, straight teeth. Not much chin. The right eye squinted, mean and dark, while the hike of his brow stretched the left one wide open. His good clothes fitted his mean body as if they were cut to its measure. Those good clothes of his were almost as much out of match to the rest of him as his long, soft, pink hands, the hands of a man who'd never had to work a tap's worth.

You see now what I mean? I can't say just how he looked, only that he looked hateful.

I first met him when I was coming down from that high mountain's comb, along an animal trail—maybe a deer made it. I was making to go on across the valley and through a pass, on to Hark Mountain where I'd heard tell was the Bottomless Pool. No special reason, just I had the notion to go there. The valley had trees in it, and through and among the trees I saw, here and there down the slope, patchy places and cabins and yards.

I hoped to myself I might could get fed at one of the cabins, for I'd run clear out of eating some spell back. I didn't have any money, nary coin of it; just only my hickory shirt and blue jeans pants and torn old army shoes, and my guitar on its sling cord. But I knew the mountain folks. If they've got anything to eat, a decent-spoken stranger can get the half part of it. Town folks ain't always the same way about that.

Down the slope I picked my way, favoring the guitar

just in case I slipped and fell down, and in an hour I'd
made it to the first patch. The cabin was two rooms, dog-
trotted and open through the middle. Beyond it was a shed
and a pigpen. In the yard was the man of the house, talking to who I found out later was Mr. Onselm.

"You don't have any meat at all?" Mr. Onselm inquired
him, and Mr. Onselm's voice was the last you'd expect his
sort of man to have, it was full of broad low music, like an
organ in a big town church. But I decided not to ask him
to sing when I'd taken another closer glimpse of him—
sickle-legged and gourd-headed, and pale and puny in his
fine-fitting clothes. For, small as he was, he looked mad
and dangerous; and the man of the place, though he was a
big, strong-seeming old gentleman with a square jaw,
looked scared.

"I been right short this year, Mr. Onselm," he said, and
it was a half-begging way he said it. "The last bit of meat
I done fished out of the brine on Tuesday. And I'd sure
enough rather not kill the pig till December."

Mr. Onselm tramped over to the pen and looked in. The
pig was a friendly-acting one; it reared up with its front
feet against the boards and grunted up, the way you'd
know he hoped for something nice to eat. Mr. Onselm
spit into the pen.

"All right," he said, granting a favor. "But I want some
meal."

He sickle-legged back toward the cabin. A brown barrel
stood out in the dog trot. Mr. Onselm flung off the cover
and pinched up some meal between the tips of his pink
fingers. "Get me a sack," he told the man.

The man went quick indoors, and quick out he came,
with the sack. Mr. Onselm held it open while the man
scooped out enough meal to fill it up. Then Mr. Onselm
twisted the neck tight shut and the man lashed the neck
with twine. Finally Mr. Onselm looked up and saw me
standing there with my guitar under my arm.

"Who are you?" he asked, sort of crooning.

"My name's John," I said.

"John what?" Then he never waited for me to tell him John what. "Where did you steal that guitar?"

"This was given to me," I replied him. "I strung it with the silver wires myself."

"Silver," said Mr. Onselm, and he opened his squint eye by a trifle bit.

"Yes, sir." With my left hand I clamped a chord. With my right thumb I picked the silver strings to a whisper. I began to make up a song:

> Mister Onselm,
> They do what you tell 'em—

"That will do," said Mr. Onselm, not so singingly, and I stopped with the half-made-up song. He relaxed and let his eye go back to a squint again.

"They do what I tell 'em," he said, halfway to himself. "Not bad."

We studied each other, he and I, for a few ticks of time. Then he turned away and went tramping out of the yard and off among the trees. When he was gone from sight, the man of the house asked me, right friendly enough, what he could do for me.

"I'm just a-walking through," I said. I didn't want to ask him right off for some dinner.

"I heard you name yourself John," he said. "Just so happens my name's John, too. John Bristow."

"Nice place you got here, Mr. Bristow," I said, looking around. "You cropping or you renting?"

"I own the house and the land," he told me, and I was surprised; for Mr. Onselm had treated him the way a mean-minded boss treats a cropper.

"Oh," I said, "then that Mr. Onselm was just a visitor."

"Visitor?" Mr. Bristow snorted out the word. "He visits ary living soul here around. Lets them know what thing he wants, and they pass it to him. I kindly thought you knew him, you sang about him so ready."

"Oh, I just got that up." I touched the silver strings again. "Many a new song comes to me, and I just sing it. That's my nature."

"I love the old songs better," said Mr. Bristow, and smiled; so I sang one:

> I had been in Georgia
> Not a many more weeks than three
> When I fell in love with a pretty fair girl
> And she fell in love with me.
>
> Her lips were red as red could be,
> Her eyes were brown as brown,
> Her hair was like a thundercloud
> Before the rain comes down.

Gentlemen, you'd ought to been there, to see Mr. Bristow's face shine. He said: "By God, John, you sure enough can sing it and play it. It's a pure pleasure to hark at you."

"I do my possible best," I said. "But Mr. Onselm doesn't like it." I thought for a moment, then I inquired him: "What's the way he can get ary thing he wants in this valley?"

"Shoo, can't tell you what way. Just done it for years, he has."

"Doesn't anybody refuse him?"

"Well, it's happened. Once, they say, Old Jim Desbro refused him a chicken. And Mr. Onselm pointed his finger at Old Jim's mules, they was a-plowing at the time. Them mules couldn't move nary hoof, not till Mr. Onselm had the chicken from Old Jim. Another time there was, Miss Tilly Parmer hid a cake she'd just baked when she seen Mr. Onselm a-coming. He pointed a finger and he dumbed her. She never spoke one mumbling word from that day on to the day she laid down and died. Could hear and know what was said to her, but when she tried to talk she could only just gibble."

"Then he's a hoodoo man," I said. "And that means, the law can't do a thing to him."

"No sir, not even if the law worried itself up about anything going on this far from the county seat." He looked at the meal sack, still standing in the dog-trot. "Near about time for the Ugly Bird to come fetch Mr. Onselm's meal."

"What's the Ugly Bird?" I asked, but Mr. Bristow didn't have to tell me that.

It must have been a-hanging up there over us, high and quiet, and now it dropped down into the yard, like a fish hawk into a pond.

First out I could see it was dark, heavy-winged, bigger by right much than a buzzard. Then I made out the shiny gray-black of the body, like wet slate, and how the body looked to be naked, how it seemed there were feathers only on the wide wings. Then I saw the long thin snaky neck and the bulgy head and the long crane beak. And I saw the two eyes set in the front of the head—set man-fashion in the front, not bird-fashion one on each side.

The feet grabbed for the sack and taloned onto it, and they showed pink and smooth, with five grabby toes on each one. Then the wings snapped, like a tablecloth in a high wind, and it went churning up again, and away over the tops of the trees, taking the sack of meal with it.

"That's the Ugly Bird," said Mr. Bristow to me, so low I could just about hear him. "Mr. Onselm's been companioning with it ever since I could recollect."

"Such a sort of bird I never before saw," I said. "Must be a right scared-out one. Do you know what struck me while I was a-watching it?"

"Most likely I do know, John. It's got feet look like Mr. Onselm's hands."

"Could it maybe be," I asked, "that a hoodoo man like Mr. Onselm knows what way to shape himself into a bird thing?"

But Mr. Bristow shook his gray head. "It's known that when he's at one place, the Ugly Bird's been sighted at another." He tried to change the subject. "Silver strings on your guitar; I never heard tell of aught but steel strings."

"In the olden days," I told him, "silver was used a many times for strings. It gives a more singy sound."

In my mind I had it made sure that the subject wasn't going to be changed. I tried a chord on my guitar, and began to sing:

> You all have heard of the Ugly Bird
> So curious and so queer,
> It flies its flight by day and night
> And fills folks' hearts with fear.

"John—" Mr. Bristow began to butt in. But I sang on:

> I never came here to hide from fear,
> And I give you my promised word
> That I soon expect to twist the neck
> Of that God damn Ugly Bird.

Mr. Bristow looked sick at me. His hand trembled as it felt in his pocket.

"I wish I could bid you stop and eat with me," he said, "but—here, maybe you better buy you something."

What he gave me was a quarter and a dime. I near about gave them back, but I saw he wanted me to have them. So I thanked him kindly and walked off down the same trail through the trees Mr. Onselm had gone. Mr. Bristow watched me go, looking shrunk up.

Why had my song scared him? I kept singing it:

> O Ugly Bird! O Ugly Bird!
> You spy and sneak and thieve!
> This place can't be for you and me,
> And one of us got to leave.

Singing, I tried to recollect all I'd heard or read or guessed that might could help toward studying out what the Ugly Bird was.

Didn't witch folks have partner animals? I'd read, and I'd heard tell, about the animals called familiars. Mostly they were cats or black dogs or such matter as that, but sometimes they were birds.

That might could be the secret, or a right much of it. For the Ugly Bird wasn't Mr. Onselm, changed by witching so he could fly. Mr. Bristow had said the two of them were seen different places at one and the same time. So Mr. Onselm could no way turn himself into the Ugly Bird. They were close partners, no more. Brothers. With the Ugly Bird's feet looking like Mr. Onselm's pink hands.

I was ware of something up in the sky, the big black V of something that flew. It quartered over me, half as high as the highest scrap of woolly white cloud. Once or twice it made a turn, seemingly like wanting to stoop for me like a hawk for a rabbit; but it didn't do any such. Looking up at it and letting my feet find the trail on their own, I rounded a bunch of mountain laurel and there, on a rotten log in the middle of a clearing, sat Mr. Onselm.

His gourd head was sunk down on his thin neck. His elbows set on his crooked knees, and the soft, pink, long hands hid his face, as if he felt miserable. The look of him made me feel disgusted. I came walking close to him.

"You don't feel so brash, do you?" I asked him.

"Go away," he sort of gulped, soft and tired and sick.

"What for?" I wanted to know. "I like it here." Sitting on the log next to him, I pulled my guitar across me. "I feel like singing, Mr. Onselm."

I made it up again, word by word as I sang it:

> His father got hung for hog stealing,
> His mother got burnt for a witch,
> And his only friend is the Ugly Bird,
> The dirty son—

Something hit me like a shooting star, a-slamming down from overhead.

It hit my back and shoulder, and it knocked me floundering forward on one hand and one knee. It was only the mercy of God I didn't fall on my guitar and smash it. I crawled forward a few quick scrambles and made to get up again, shaky and dizzy, to see what had happened.

I saw. The Ugly Bird had flown down and dropped the sack of meal on me. Now it skimmed across the clearing, at the height of the low branches. Its eyes glinted at me, and its mouth came open like a pair of scissors. I saw teeth, sharp and mean, like the teeth of a gar fish. Then the Ugly Bird swooped for me, and the wind of its wings was colder than a winter tempest storm.

Without thinking or stopping to think, I flung up my both hands to box it off from me, and it gave back, it flew back from me like the biggest, devilishest humming bird you'd ever see in a nightmare. I was too dizzy and scared to wonder why it pulled off like that; I had barely the wit to be glad it did.

"Get out of here," moaned Mr. Onselm, not stirring from where he sat.

I take shame to say, I got. I kept my hands up and backed across the clearing and to the trail on the far side. Then I halfway thought I knew where my luck had come from. My hands had lifted my guitar up as the Ugly Bird flung itself at me, and some way it hadn't liked the guitar.

Reaching the trail again, I looked back. The Ugly Bird was perching on the log where I'd been sitting. It slaunched along close to Mr. Onselm, sort of nuzzling up to him. Horrible to see, I'll be sworn. They were sure enough close together. I turned and stumbled off away, along the trail down the valley and off toward the pass beyond the valley.

I found a stream, with stones making steps across it. I followed it down to where it made a wide pool. There I got on my knees and washed my face—it looked pales as clabber in the water image—and sat down with my back to a tree and hugged my guitar and had a rest.

I was shaking all over. I must have felt near about as bad for a while as Mr. Onselm had looked to feel, sitting on that rotten log to wait for his Ugly Bird and—what else?

Had he been hungry near to death? Sick? Or maybe had his own evil set back on him? I couldn't rightly say which.

But after a while I felt some better. I got up and walked back to the trail and along it again, till I came to what must have been the only store thereabouts.

It faced one way on a rough gravelly road that could carry wagon traffic, car traffic too if you didn't mind your car getting a good shakeup, and the trail joined on there, right across the doorway. The building wasn't big but it was good, made of sawed planks, and there was paint on it, well painted on. Its bottom rested on big rocks instead of posts, and it had a roofed-open front like a porch, with a bench in there where folks could sit.

Opening the door, I went in. You'll find many such stores in back country places through the land, where folks haven't built their towns up too close. Two-three counters. Shelves of cans and packages. Smoked meat hung up in one corner, a glass-fronted icebox for fresh meat in another. Barrels here and there, for beans or meal or potatoes. At the end of one counter, a sign says U.S. POST OFFICE, and there's a set of maybe half a dozen pigeonholes to put letters in, and a couple of cigar boxes for stamps and money order blanks. That's the kind of place it was.

The proprietor wasn't in just then. Only a girl, scared and shaky back of the counter, and Mr. Onselm, there ahead of me, a-telling her what it was he wanted.

He wanted her.

"I don't care a shuck if Sam Heaver did leave you in charge here," he said with the music in his voice. "He won't stop my taking you with me."

Then he heard me come in, and he swung around and

fixed his squint eye and his wide-open eye on me, like two mismated gun muzzles. "You again," he said.

He looked right hale and hearty again. I strayed my hands over the guitar's silver strings, just enough to hear, and he twisted up his face as if it colicked him.

"Winnie," he told the girl, "wait on this stranger and get him out of here."

Her round eyes were scared in her scared face. I thought inside myself that seldom I'd seen as sweet a face as hers, or as scared a one. Her hair was dark and thick. It was like the thundercloud before the rain comes down. It made her paleness look paler. She was small and slim, and she cowered there, for fear of Mr. Onselm and what he'd been saying to her.

"Yes, sir?" she said to me, hushed and shaky.

"A box of crackers, please, ma'am," I decided, pointing to where they were on the shelf behind her. "And a can of those little sardine fish."

She put them on the counter for me. I dug out the quarter Mr. Bristow had given me up the trail, and slapped it down on the counter top between the scared girl and Mr. Onselm.

"Get away!" he squeaked, shrill and sharp and mean as a bat. When I looked at him, he'd jumped back, almost halfway across the floor from the counter. And for just once, his both eyes were big and wide.

"Why, Mr. Onselm, what's the matter?" I wondered him, and I purely was wondering. "This is a good quarter."

I picked it up and held it out for him to take and study.

But he flung himself around, and he ran out of that store like a rabbit. A rabbit with dogs running it down.

The girl he'd called Winnie just leaned against the wall as if she was bone tired. I asked her: "Why did he light out like that?"

I gave her the quarter, and she took it. "That money isn't a scary thing, is it?" I asked.

"It doesn't much scare me," she said, and rang it up on the old cash register. "All that scares me is—Mr. Onselm."

I picked up the box of crackers and sardines. "Is he courting you?"

She shivered, although it was warm in the store. "I'd sooner be in a hole with a snake than be courted by Mr. Onselm."

"Then why not just tell him to leave you be?"

"He wouldn't hark at that," she said. "He always just does what pleasures him. Nobody dares to stop him."

"So I've heard tell," I nodded. "About the mules he stopped where they stood, and the poor old lady he struck dumb." I returned to the other thing we'd been talking. "But what made him squinch away from that money piece? I'd reckon he loved money."

She shook her head, and the thundercloud hair stirred. "Mr. Onselm never needs any money. He takes what he wants, without paying for it."

"Including you?" I asked.

"Not including me yet." She shuddered again. "He reckons to do that later on."

I put down my dime I had left from what Mr. Bristow had gifted me. "Let's have a coke drink together, you and me."

She rang up the dime too. There was a sort of dried-out chuckle at the door, like a stone flung rattling down a deep dark well. I looked quick, and I saw two long, dark wings flop away outside. The Ugly Bird had come to spy what we were doing.

But the girl Winnie hadn't seen, and she smiled over her coke drink. I asked her permission to open my fish and crackers on the bench outside. She said I could. Out there, I worried open the can with that little key that comes with it, and had my meal. When I'd finished I put the empty can and cracker box in a garbage barrel and tuned my guitar.

Hearing that, Winnie came out. She told me how to make my way to the pass and on beyond to Hark Mountain. Of the Bottomless Pool she'd heard some talk, though she'd never been to it. Then she harked while I picked the music and sang the song about the girl whose hair was like the thundercloud before the rain come down. Harking, Winnie blushed till she was pale no more.

Then we talked about Mr. Onselm and the Ugly Bird, and how they had been seen in two different places at once. "But," said Winnie, "nobody's ever seen the two of them together."

"I have," I told her. "And not an hour back."

And I related about how Mr. Onselm had sat, all sick and miserable, on that rotten log, and how the Ugly Bird had lighted beside him and crowded up to him.

She was quiet to hear about it, with her eyes staring off, the way she might be looking for something far away. When I was done, she said: "John, you tell me it crowded right up to him."

"It did that thing," I said again. "You'd think it was studying how to crawl right inside him."

"Inside him!"

"That's a true fact."

She kept staring off, and thinking.

"Makes me recollect something I heard somebody say once about hoodoo folks," she said after a time. "How there's hoodoo folks can sometimes put a sort of stuff out, mostly in a dark room. And the stuff is part of them, but it can take the shape and mind of some other person— and once in a while, the shape and mind of an animal."

"Shoo," I said, "now you mention it, I've heard some talk of the same thing. And somebody reckoned it might could explain those Louisiana stories about the werewolves."

"The shape and mind of an animal," she repeated herself. "Maybe the shape and mind of a bird. And that stuff, they call it echo—no, ecto—ecto—"

"Ectoplasm." I remembered the word. "That's it. I've even seen a book with pictures in it, they say were taken of such stuff. And it seems to be alive. It'll yell if you grab it or hit it or stab at it or like that."

"Couldn't maybe—" Winnie began, but a musical voice interrupted.

"I say he's been around here long enough," Mr. Onselm was telling somebody.

Back he came. Behind him were three men. Mr. Bristow was one, and there was likewise a tall, gawky man with wide shoulders and a black-stubbly chin, and behind him a soft, smooth-grizzled old man with an old fancy vest over his white shirt.

Mr. Onselm was like the leader of a posse. "Sam Heaver," he crooned at the soft grizzled one, "do you favor having tramps come and loaf around your store?"

The soft old storekeeper looked at me, dead and gloomy. "You better get going, son," he said, as if he'd memorized it.

I laid my guitar on the bench beside me, very careful of it. "You men ail my stomach," I said, looking at them, from one to the next to the next. "You come at the whistle of this half-born, half-bred witch-man. You let him sic you on me like dogs, when I'm hurting nobody and nothing."

"Better go," said the old storekeeper again.

I stood up and faced Mr. Onselm, ready to fight him. He just laughed at me, like a sweetly played horn.

"You," he said, "without a dime in your pocket! What are you a-feathering up about? You can't do anything to anybody."

Without a dime . . .

But I'd had a dime. I'd spent it for the coke drinks for Winnie and me. And the Ugly Bird had spied in to see me spend it, my silver money, the silver money that scared and ailed Mr. Onselm . . .

"Take his guitar, Hobe." Mr. Onselm said an order, and

the gawky man moved, clumsy but quick and grabbed my guitar off the bench and backed away to the inner door.

"There," said Mr. Onselm, sort of purring, "that takes care of him."

He fairly jumped, too, and grabbed Winnie by her wrist. He pulled her along out of the porch toward the trail, and I heard her whimper.

"Stop him!" I yelled out, but the three of them stood and looked, scared to move or say a word. Mr. Onselm, still holding Winnie with one hand, faced me. He lifted his other hand and stuck out the pink forefinger at me, like the barrel of a pistol.

Just the look his two eyes, squint and wide, gave me made me weary and dizzy to my bones. He was going to witch me, as he'd done the mules, as he'd done the woman who'd tried to hide her cake from him. I turned away from his gaze, sick and—sure, I was afraid. And I heard him giggle, thinking he'd won already. I took a step, and I was next to that gawky fellow named Hobe, who held my guitar.

I made a quick long jump and started to wrestle it away from him.

"Hang onto that thing, Hobe!" I heard Mr. Onselm sort of choke out, and, from Mr. Bristow:

"Take care, there's the Ugly Bird!"

Its big dark wings flapped like a storm in the air just behind me. But I'd shoved my elbow into Hobe's belly-pit and I'd torn my guitar from his hands, and I turned on my heel to face what was being brought upon me.

A little way off in the open, Mr. Onselm stood stiff and straight as a stone figure in front of an old court house. He still held Winnie by the wrist. Right betwixt them came a-swooping the Ugly Bird at me, the ugliest ugly of all, its long beak pointing for me like a sticky knife.

I dug my toes and smashed my guitar at it. I swung the way a player swings a ball bat at a pitched ball. Full-slam I struck its bulgy head, right above that sharp beak and across its two eyes, and I heard the loud noise as the polished wood of my music-maker crashed to splinters.

Oh, gentlemen, and down went that Ugly Bird!

Down it went, falling just short of the porch.

Quiet it lay.

Its great big feathered wings stretched out either side, without ary flutter to them. Its beak was driven into the ground like a nail. It didn't kick or flop or stir once.

But Mr. Onselm, where he stood holding Winnie, screamed out the way he might scream if something had clawed out his all insides with one single tearing dig and grab.

He didn't move. I don't even know if his mouth came rightly open to make that scream. Winnie gave a pull with all the strength she had, and tottered back, loose from him. Then, as if only his hold on her had kept him standing, Mr. Onselm slapped right over and dropped down on his face, his arms flung out like the Ugly Bird's wings, his face in the dirt like the Ugly Bird's face.

Still holding onto my broken guitar by the neck, like a club, I walked quick over to him and stooped. "Get up," I bade him, and took hold of what hair he had and lifted up his face to look at it.

One look was a plenty. From the war, I know a dead man when I see one. I let go Mr. Onselm's hair, and his face went back into the dirt the way you'd know it belonged there.

The other men moved at last, slow and tottery like old men. And they didn't act like my enemies now, for Mr. Onselm who'd made them act thataway was down and dead.

Then Hobe gave a sort of shaky scared shout, and we looked where he was looking.

The Ugly Bird looked all of a sudden rotten and mushy, and while we saw that, it was soaking into the ground. To me, anyhow, its body had seemed to turn shadowy and misty, and I could see through it, to pebbles on the ground beneath. I moved close, though I didn't relish moving. The Ugly Bird was melting away, like dirty snow on top of a hot stove; only no wetness left behind.

It was gone, while we watched and wondered and felt bad all over, and at the same time glad to see it go. Nothing left but the hole punched in the dirt by its beak. I stepped closer yet, and with my shoe I stamped the hole shut.

Then Mr. Bristow kneeled on his knee and turned Mr. Onselm over. On the dead face ran lines across, thin and purple, as though he'd been struck down by a blow from a toaster or a gridiron.

"Why," said Mr. Bristow. "Why, John, them's the marks of your guitar strings." He looked at me. "Your silver guitar strings."

"Silver?" said the storekeeper. "Is them strings silver? Why, friends, silver finishes a hoodoo man."

That was it. All of us remembered that at once.

"Sure enough," put in Hobe. "Ain't it a silver bullet that it takes to kill a witch, or hanging or burning? And a silver knife to kill a witch's cat?"

"And a silver key locks out ghosts, doesn't it?" said Mr. Bristow, getting up to stand among us again.

I looked at my broken guitar and the dangling strings of silver.

"What was the word you said?" Winnie whispered to me.

"Ectoplasm," I replied her. "Like his soul coming out of him—and getting itself struck dead outside his body."

Then there was talk, more important, about what to do now. The men did the deciding. They allowed to report to the county seat that Mr. Onselm's heart had stopped on him, which was what it had done, after all. They went over the tale three-four times, to make sure they'd all tell it the same. They cheered up while they talked it. You couldn't ever call for a bunch of gladder folks to get shed of a neighbor.

Then they tried to say their thanks to me.

"John," said Mr. Bristow, "we'd all of us sure enough be proud and happy if you'd stay here. You took his curse off us, and we can't never thank you enough."

"Don't thank me," I said. "I was fighting for my life."

Hobe said he wanted me to come live on his farm and help him work it on half shares. Sam Heaver offered me all the money he had in his old cash register. I thanked them. To each I said, no, sir, thank you kindly, I'd better not. If they wanted their tale to sound true to the sheriff and the coroner, they'd better help it along by forgetting that I'd ever been around when Mr. Onselm's heart stopped. Anyhow, I meant to go look at that Bottomless Pool. All I was truly sorry about was my guitar had got broken.

But while I was saying all that, Mr. Bristow had gone running off. Now he came back, with a guitar he'd had at his place, and he said he'd be honored if I'd take it instead of mine. It was a good guitar, had a fine tone. So I put my silver strings on it and tightened and tuned them, and tried a chord or two.

Winnie swore by all that was pure and holy she'd pray for me by name each night of her life, and I told her that that would sure enough see me safe from any assault of the devil.

"Assault of the devil, John!" she said, almost shrill in the voice, she meant it so truly. "It's been you who drove the devil from out this valley."

And the others all said they agreed her on that.

"It was foretold about you in the Bible," said Winnie, her voice soft again. " 'There was a man sent from God, whose name was John—' "

But that was far too much for her to say, and she dropped her sweet dark head down, and I saw her mouth tremble and two tears sneak down her cheeks. And I was that abashed, I said goodbye all around in a hurry.

Off I walked toward where the pass would be, strumming my new guitar as I walked. Back into my mind I got an old, old song. I've heard tell that the song's written down in an old-timey book called *Percy's Frolics,* or *Relics,* or some such name:

> Lady, I never loved witchcraft,
> Never dealt in privy wile,
> But evermore held the high way
> Of love and honor, free from guile . . .

And though I couldn't bring myself to look back yonder to the place I was leaving forever, I knew that Winnie was a-watching me, and that she listened, till she had to strain her ears to catch the last, faintest end of my song.

POUL ANDERSON, (b. 1926), was born of Scandinavian parents (hence the spelling of the first name) in the USA. He studied physics at the University of Minnesota, graduating with honors in 1948, but decided to become a writer instead. At most recent count, he is author of some fifty books and more than two hundred shorter pieces in magazines as diverse as *Analog, Saturday Review, Playboy, Boys' Life, National Review,* and *Ellery Queen's Mystery Magazine.* One of the half-dozen internationally most popular writers of science fiction, his awards include four Hugos (awarded annually by the World Science Fiction Convention, according to reader vote), a Nebula (awarded by the Science Fiction Writers of America), the first annual Macmillan Cock Robin Award (for mystery writers), the Morley-Montgomery Award twice, an Irregular Shilling (for Sherlock Holmes scholarship), a Knight of Mark Twain accolade, and outside of writing, a knighthood in the Society of Creative Anachronism. Married, with one daughter, he has for some years lived near San Francisco.

Journeys End

Poul Anderson

—*doctor bill & twinges in chest but must be all right maybe indigestion & dinner last night & wasn't audrey giving me the glad eye & how the hell is a guy to know*

*& maybe i can try and find out & what a fool i can look
if she doesn't—*

*—goddam idiot & they shouldn't let some people drive
& oh all right so the examiner was pretty lenient with me
i haven't had a bad accident yet & christ blood all over my
blood let's face it i'm scared to drive but the buses are no
damn good & straight up three paces & man in a green
hat & judas i ran that red light—*

In fifteen years a man got used to it, more or less. He
could walk down the street and hold his own thoughts to
himself while the surf of unvoiced voices was a nearly ig-
nored mumble in his brain. Now and then, of course, you
got something very bad, it stood up in your skull and
shrieked at you.

Norman Kane, who had come here because he was in
love with a girl he had never seen, got to the corner of
University and Shattuck just when the light turned against
him. He paused, fetched out a cigarette with nicotine-yel-
lowed fingers while traffic slithered in front of his eyes.

It was an unfavorable time, four-thirty in the afternoon,
homeward rush of nervous systems jangled with weariness
and hating everything else on feet or wheels. Maybe he
should have stayed in the bar down on San Pablo. It had
been pleasantly cool and dim, the bartender's mind an
amiable cud-chewing somnolence, and he could have suppressed awareness of the woman.

No, maybe not. When the city had scraped your nerves
raw, they didn't have much resistance to the slime in some
heads.

Odd, he reflected, how often the outwardly polite ones
were the foully twisted inside. They wouldn't dream of
misbehaving in public, but just below the surface of consciousness . . . Better not think of it, better not remember.
Berkeley was at least preferable to San Francisco or Oak-
land. The bigger the town, the more evil it seemed to

hold, three centimeters under the frontal bone. New York
was almost literally uninhabitable.

There was a young fellow waiting beside Kane. A girl
came down the sidewalk, pretty, long yellow hair and a
well-filled blouse. Kane focused idly on her: yes, she had
an apartment of her own, which she had carefully picked
for a tolerant superintendent. Lechery jumped in the
young man's nerves. His eyes followed the girl, Cobean-
style, and she walked on . . . simple harmonic motion.

Too bad. They could have enjoyed each other. Kane
chuckled to himself. He had nothing against honest lust,
anyhow not in his liberated conscious mind; he couldn't
do much about a degree of subconscious puritanism. Lord,
you can't be a telepath and remain any kind of prude.
People's lives were their own business, if they didn't hurt
anyone else too badly.

—the trouble is, he thought, *they hurt me. but i can't
tell them that. they'd rip me apart and dance on the pieces.
the government /the military/ wouldn't like a man to be
alive who could read secrets but their fear-inspired anger
would be like a baby's tantrum beside the red blind amok
of the common man (thoughtful husband considerate
father good honest worker earnest patriot) whose inward
sins were known. you can talk to a priest or a psychiatrist
because it is only talk & he does not live your failings with
you—*

The light changed and Kane started across. It was clear
fall weather, not that this area had marked seasons, a cool
sunny day with a small wind blowing up the street from
the water. A few blocks ahead of him, the University campus was a splash of manicured green under brown hills.

*—flayed & burningburningburning moldering rotted
flesh & the bones the white hard clean bones coming out
gwtjklfmx—*

Kane stopped dead. Through the vertigo he felt how
sweat was drenching into his shirt.

And it was such an ordinary-looking man!

"Hey, there, buster, wake up! Ya wanna get killed?"

Kane took a sharp hold on himself and finished the walk across the street. There was a bench at the bus stop and he sat down till the trembling was over.

Some thoughts were unendurable.

He had a trick of recovery. He went back to Father Schliemann. The priest's mind had been like a well, a deep well under sun-speckled trees, its surface brightened with a few gold-colored autumn leaves . . . but there was nothing bland about the water, it had a sharp mineral tang, a smell of the living earth. He had often fled to Father Schliemann, in those days of puberty when the telepathic power had first wakened in him. He had found good minds since then, happy minds, but never one so serene, none with so much strength under the gentleness.

"I don't want you hanging around that papist, boy, do you understand?" It was his father, the lean implacable man who always wore a black tie. "Next thing you know, you'll be worshiping graven images just like him."

"But they *aren't*—"

His ears could still ring with the cuff. "Go up to your room! I don't want to see you till tomorrow morning. And you'll have two more chapters of Deuteronomy memorized by then. Maybe that'll teach you the true Christian faith."

Kane grinned wryly and lit another cigarette from the end of the previous one. He knew he smoked too much. And drank—but not heavily. Drunk, he was defenseless before the horrible tides of thinking.

He had had to run away from home at the age of fourteen. The only other possibility was conflict ending with reform school. It had meant running away from Father Schliemann too, but how in hell's red fire could a sensitive adolescent dwell in the same house as his father's brain?

Were the psychologists now admitting the possibility of a sadistic masochist? Kane *knew* the type existed.

Give thanks for this much mercy, that the extreme telepathic range was only a few hundred yards. And a mind-reading boy was not altogether helpless; he could evade officialdom and the worst horrors of the underworld. He could find a decent elderly couple at the far end of the continent and talk himself into adoption.

Kane shook himself and got up again. He threw the cigarette to the ground and stubbed it out with his heel. A thousand examples told him what obscure sexual symbolism was involved in that act, but what the deuce . . . it was also a practical thing. Guns are phallic too, but at times you need a gun.

Weapons: he could not help wincing as he recalled dodging the draft in 1949. He'd traveled enough to know this country was worth defending. But it hadn't been any trick at all to hoodwink a psychiatrist and get himself marked hopelessly psychoneurotic—which he would be after two years penned with frustrated men. There had been no choice, but he could not escape a sense of dishonor.

—*haven't we all sinned /every one of us/ is there a single human creature on earth without his burden of shame?*—

A man was coming out of the drugstore beside him. Idly, Kane probed his mind. You could go quite deeply into anyone's self if you cared to, in fact, you couldn't help doing so. It was impossible merely to scan verbalized thinking: the organism is too closely integrated. Memory is not a passive filing cabinet, but a continuous process beneath the level of consciousness; in a way, you are always reliving your entire past. And the more emotionally charged the recollection is, the more powerfully it radiates.

The stranger's name was—no matter. His personality

was as much an unchangeable signature as his fingerprints.
Kane had gotten into the habit of thinking of people as
such-and-such a multidimensional symbolic topography;
the name was an arbitrary gabble.

The man was an assistant professor of English at the
University. Age forty-two, married, three children, making
payments on a house in Albany. Steady sober type, but
convivial, popular with his colleagues, ready to help out
most friends. He was thinking about tomorrow's lectures,
with overtones of a movie he wanted to see and an under-
current of fear that he might have cancer after all, in spite
of what the doctor said.

Below, the list of his hidden crimes. As a boy: tormenting a cat, well-buried Oedipean hungers, masturbation,
petty theft . . . the usual. Later: cheating on a few exams,
that ludicrous fumbling attempt with a girl which came to
nothing because he was too nervous, the time he crashed
a cafeteria line and had been shoved away with a cold
remark (and praises be, Jim who had seen that was now
living in Chicago) . . . still later: wincing memories of a
stomach uncontrollably rumbling at a formal dinner, that
woman in his hotel room the night he got drunk at the
convention, standing by and letting old Carver be fired
because he didn't have the courage to protest to the dean
. . . now: youngest child a nasty whining little snotnose,
but you can't show anyone what you really think, reading
Rosamond Marshall when alone in his office, disturbing
young breasts in tight sweaters, the petty spite of academic
politics, giving Simonson an undeserved good grade because the boy was so beautiful, disgraceful sweating panic
when at night he considered how death would annihilate
his ego—

And what of it? This assistant professor was a good
man, a kindly and honest man, his inwardness ought to
be between him and the Recording Angel. Few of his
thoughts had ever become deeds, or ever would. Let him

bury them himself, let him be alone with them. Kane ceased focusing on him.

The telepath had grown tolerant. He expected little of anyone; nobody matched the mask, except possibly Father Schliemann and a few others . . . and those were human too, with human failings; the difference was that they knew peace. It was the emotional overtones of guilt which made Kane wince. God knew he himself was no better. Worse, maybe, but then his life had thrust him to it. If you had an ordinary human sex drive, for instance, but could not endure to cohabit with the thoughts of a woman, your life became one of fleeting encounters; there was no help for it, even if your austere boyhood training still protested.

"Pardon me, got a match?"

—*lynn is dead/ i still can't understand it that i will never see her again & eventually you learn how to go on in a chopped-off fashion but what do you do in the meantime how do you get through the nights alone*—

"Sure." —*maybe that is the worst: sharing sorrow and unable to help & only able to give him a light for his cigarette*—

Kane put the matches back in his pocket and went on up University, pausing again at Oxford. A pair of large campus buildings jutted up to the left; others were visible ahead and to the right, through a screen of eucalyptus trees. Sunlight and shadow damascened the grass. From a passing student's mind he discovered where the library was. A good big library—perhaps it held a clue, buried somewhere in the periodical files. He had already arranged for permission to use the facilities: prominent young author doing research for his next novel.

Crossing wistfully named Oxford Street, Kane smiled to himself. Writing was really the only possible occupation: he could live in the country and be remote from the jammed urgency of his fellow men. And with such an understanding of the soul as was his, with any five minutes on a corner giving him a dozen stories, he made good money at it. The only drawback was the trouble of avoiding publicity, editorial summonses to New York, autographing parties, literary teas . . . he didn't like those. But you could remain faceless if you insisted.

They said nobody but his agent knew who B. Traven was. It had occurred, wildly, to Kane that Traven might be another like himself. He had gone on a long journey to find out. . . . No. He was alone on earth, a singular and solitary mutant, except for—

It shivered in him, again he sat on the train. It had been three years ago, he was in the club car having a nightcap while the streamliner ran eastward through the Wyoming darkness. They passed a westbound train, not so elegant a one. His drink leaped from his hand to the floor and he sat for a moment in stinging blindness. That flicker of thought, brushing his mind and coming aflame with recognition and then borne away again . . . Damn it, damn it, he should have pulled the emergency cord and so should *she*. They should have halted both trains and stumbled through cinders and sagebrush and found each other's arms.

Too late. Three years yielded only a further emptiness. Somewhere in the land there was, or there had been, a young woman, and she was a telepath and the startled touch of her mind had been gentle. There had not been time to learn anything else. Since then he had given up on private detectives. (How could you tell them: "I'm looking for a girl who was on such-and-such a train the night of—"?) Personal ads in all the major papers had brought him nothing but a few crank letters. Probably she didn't read the personals; he'd never done so till his search began, there was too much unhappiness to be found in them if you understood humankind as well as he did.

Maybe this library here, some unnoticed item . . . but

if there are two points in a finite space and one moves about so as to pass through every infinitesimal volume *dV,* it will encounter the other one in finite time *provided* that the other point is not moving too.

Kane shrugged and went along the curving way to the gatehouse. It was slightly uphill. There was a bored cop in the shelter, to make sure that only authorized cars were parked on campus. The progress paradox: a ton or so of steel, burning irreplaceable petroleum to shift one or two human bodies around, and doing the job so well that it becomes universal and chokes the cities which spawned it. A telepathic society would be more rational. When every little wound in the child's soul could be felt and healed . . . when the thick burden of guilt was laid down, because everyone knew that everyone else had done the same . . . when men could not kill, because soldier and murderer felt the victim die . . .

—adam & eve? you can't breed a healthy race out of two people. but if we had telepathic children/ & we would be bound to do so i think because the mutation is obviously recessive/ then we could study the heredity of it & the gift would be passed on to other blood-lines in logical distribution & every generation there would be more of our kind until we could come out openly & even the mindmutes could be helped by our psychiatrists & priests & earth would be fair and clean and sane—

There were students sitting on the grass, walking under the Portland Cement Romanesque of the buildings, calling and laughing and talking. The day was near an end. Now there would be dinner, a date, a show, maybe some beer at Robbie's or a drive up into the hills to neck and watch the lights below like trapped stars and the mighty constellation of the Bay Bridge . . . or perhaps, with a face-saving grumble about mid-terms, an evening of books, a world suddenly opened. It must be good to be young and mindmute. A dog trotted down the walk and Kane relaxed into the simple wordless pleasure of being a healthy and admired collie.

—so perhaps it is better to be a dog than a man? no /surely not/ for if a man knows more grief he also knows more joy & so it is to be a telepath: more easily hurt yes but/god/think of the mindmutes always locked away in aloneness and think of sharing not only a kiss but a soul with your beloved—

The uphill trend grew steeper as he approached the library, but Kane was in fair shape and rather enjoyed the extra effort. At the foot of the stairs he paused for a quick cigarette before entering. A passing woman flicked eyes across him and he learned that he could also smoke in the lobby. Mindreading had its everyday uses. But it was good to stand here in the sunlight. He stretched, reaching out physically and mentally.

—let's see now the integral of log x dx well make a substitution suppose we call y equal to log x then this is interesting i wonder who wrote that line about euclid has looked on beauty bare—

Kane's cigarette fell from his mouth.

It seemed that the wild hammering of his heart must drown out the double thought that rivered in his brain, the thought of a physics student, a very ordinary young man save that he was quite wrapped up in the primitive satisfaction of hounding down a problem, and the other thought, the one that was listening in.

—she—

He stood with closed eyes, asway on his feet, breathing as if he ran up a mountain. *—are You there? are You there?—*

—not daring to believe: what do i feel?—

—i was the man on the train—

—& i was the woman—

A shuddering togetherness.

"Hey! Hey, mister, is anything wrong?"

Almost Kane snarled. Her thought was so remote, on the very rim of indetectability, he could get nothing but subvocalized words, nothing of the self, and this busybody—"No, thanks, I'm okay, just a, a little winded."

—where are You, where can i find You o my darling—

—image of a large white building/ right over here & they call it dwinelle hall & i am sitting on the bench outside & please come quickly please be here i never thought this could become real—

Kane broke into a run. For the first time in fifteen years, he was unaware of his human surroundings. There were startled looks, he didn't see them, he was running to her and she was running too.

—my name is norman kane & i was not born to that name but took it from people who adopted me because i fled my father (how horrible mother died in darkness & he would not let her have drugs though it was cancer & he said drugs were sinful and pain was good for the soul & he really honestly believed that) & when the power first appeared i made slips and he beat me and said it was witchcraft & i have searched all my life since & i am a writer but only because i must live but it was not aliveness until this moment—

—o my poor kicked beloved/ i had it better/ in me the power grew more slowly and i learned to cover it & i am twenty years old & came here to study but what are books at this moment—

He could see her now. She was not conventionally beautiful, but neither was she ugly, and there was kindness in her eyes and on her mouth.

—what shall i call you? to me you will always be You but there must be a name for the mindmutes & i have a place in the country among old trees & such few people as live nearby are good folk/ as good as life will allow them to be—

—then let me come there with you & never leave again—

They reached each other and stood a foot apart. There was no need for a kiss or even a handclasp . . . not yet. It was the minds which leaped out and enfolded and became one.

—I REMEMBER THAT AT THE AGE OF THREE I DRANK OUT OF THE TOILET BOWL/ THERE WAS A PECULIAR FASCINATION TO IT & I USED TO STEAL LOOSE CHANGE FROM MY MOTHER THOUGH SHE HAD LITTLE ENOUGH TO CALL HER OWN SO I COULD SNEAK DOWN TO THE DRUGSTORE FOR ICE CREAM & I SQUIRMED OUT OF THE DRAFT & THESE ARE THE DIRTY EPISODES INVOLVING WOMEN—

—AS A CHILD I WAS NOT FOND OF MY GRANDMOTHER THOUGH SHE LOVED ME AND ONCE I PLAYED THE FOLLOWING FIENDISH TRICK ON HER & AT THE AGE OF SIXTEEN I MADE AN UTTER FOOL OF MYSELF IN THE FOLLOWING MANNER & I HAVE BEEN PHYSICALLY CHASTE CHIEFLY BECAUSE OF FEAR BUT MY VICARIOUS EXPERIENCES ARE NUMBERED IN THE THOUSANDS—

Eyes watched eyes with horror.

—it is not that you have sinned for i know everyone has done the same or similar things or would if they had our gift & i know too that it is nothing serious or abnormal & of course you have decent instincts & are ashamed—

—just so/ it is that you know what i have done & you know every last little wish & thought & buried uncleanness & in the top of my head i know it doesn't mean anything but down underneath is all which was drilled into me when i was just a baby & i will not admit to ANYONE *else that such things exist in* ME—

A car whispered by, homeward bound. The trees talked in the light sunny wind.

A boy and girl went hand in hand.

The thought hung cold under the sky, a single thought in two minds.

—*get out. i hate your bloody guts.*—

ROBERT HOSKINS, (b. 1933), is the author of half a dozen novels and editor of fourteen science-fiction anthologies. A native of the Adirondack region of New York State, he grew up in a very small town, where he cut his literary teeth on the fantasy pulp magazines of the 1940s. Although there have been a number of attempts in recent years to found new magazines in the tradition of *Weird Tales* and *Unknown,* none have been successful or lasted more than a few issues. The following story appeared in the first issue of the short-lived *Worlds of Fantasy.*

The Man Who Liked

Robert Hoskins

He was a little man; he bobbed and twisted down the quiet suburban street, bowing to the ladies, smiling at the children and the pets. For the storekeepers hiding from the heat of the midsummer sun in the shade of the doorways, he had a loud and cheery greeting that made them smile back and return to their work with the comfortable feeling that maybe a bit of happiness existed in the world after all.

He paused by a Good Humor wagon, choosing, after long and careful deliberation with his finger rubbing his cheek, the Cherry Nugget Delight. The unwrapping of the ice cream was a study in sheer joyfully wasted motion; the savoring of the first taste made a child laugh loudly at the silliness of it.

"What?" His eyes widened. "You laugh at me?"

The child giggled. "You're funny."

"So I am!" the little man cried. "And so are you! Everyone's funny—the whole world is nothing but one bundle of funny!"

He performed a pirouette, holding his coattails as he swirled around the street. The child clapped hands as he bowed low, then handed across another ice cream.

"For my most appreciative audience."

The child grabbed the treasure and ran quickly away. The little man beamed after the small greed in the disappearing back, then turned and crossed the street, entering a little park. A dog ran up, sniffing at the half-eaten ice cream that was suddenly thrust in its face. The pink and brown goodness dropped to the ground and was quickly followed by a scattering of peanuts that came from a bag in his pocket. Chortling lustily, he dropped to a bench and waved his hands at the surrounding legions of pigeons.

The paving of the street danced mistily in the heat. The little man studied the pigeons for a moment, head bobbing from side to side in cadence with their walking and pecking, then he turned his attention to the sailboat that was listlessly becalmed on the surface of the duckpond. Dropping to his knees, the little man eased up behind the boat's master, sucking in wind until his cheeks were red with distortion. He let the air out with a *whoosh* that sent the little boat scuttling forward, then fell on his back, rolling on the deliciously cool, green grass.

He wearied of the park, of its air of summer somnolence. Here was not enough life to suit his bursting soul. Bestowing a breezy benediction on a sleeping panhandler, he dropped a crumpled gift into the unfortunate's lap and continued down the street. Every shop window drew his momentary attention; every young mother knew the warmth of his smile.

A flower peddler hobbled down the street, the woman as aged as the blossoms were young, each approaching an end of life from opposite directions. Struck by inspiration, he swept all of her wares from under her nose, leaving in their place a hundred times their hoped-for value. The old woman gasped, as did every woman thereafter who was startled by the baby bouquets suddenly and unexpectedly in their possession.

The little man continued down the street until the flowers were gone, and then turned into the first tavern. The interior was dark after the brightness of the street, and cool under the asthmatic wheeze of an over-labored air conditioner. An out-of-register color television set over the bar held the attention of the few patrons. Stepping to the counter, he slapped down a bill.

"Innkeeper! Drinks for all!"

The acned youth behind the bar was startled into sudden awareness, the magazine in his grasp slipping to the floor. He stared at the intruder for a moment, then spotted the color of his money. He leaped into action, pulling bottles from under-bar coolers. The other patrons were soon served and attention returned to the treator.

"For you—sir?"

"A glass of water, if you please. With an ice cube in it."

The simple request was fulfilled and the magic spell that incites all human wonders quickly rung up in the cash register.

"You forget yourself," the little man said, and the bartender hurried to his bidding. The bill reduced to a meagre pile of coins intrinsically worth considerably less than their face value, he pronounced a blessing on the assemblage, and then continued once more on his way.

The city drowsed in the heat of the sun as the little man continued dispensing his good will to those fortunate enough to cross his path. Suspicious natures found themselves inexplicably charmed into agreement with the proposition that life need not be eternally gloomy. Some even found themselves believing that peace on earth among men of good will might not be eternally unattainable.

It seemed as though the gods had finally decided to bestow their blessings on the tired surface of the weary planet, even if only in this one small city on this one exhausted afternoon. Only happiness mattered as once more laughter crept from the caverns and dark corners of society, finding an unsteady way to light.

Friendships were made easily, even if of brief moment. Hatred seemed an impossible emotion. Only a few hundred of the city's citizens passed within the little man's orbit, but those few hundred helped pass the change within themselves on to others in a constantly widening circle that soon passed through almost the entire city.

And then the time came when the little man looked at his watch and gasped. "Good heavens! I'm late!"

Like the white rabbit, he scurried away, hopping aboard the first approaching bus. He stayed with it through the suburb and on to the state highway that stretched needle-sharp and straight north and south. Jumping off, he hurried along until he came to a cluster of modern adobe structures huddled behind the feeble protection of a baleful pink neon *Motel* sign.

He ran by the office door, raising his hand in brief greeting to the clerk inside the dark room. Once inside his unit, clothes were quickly stripped off and dropped onto the floor. Flesh followed as he went to the closet and drew down the long robe, adjusting the hood carefully over his shoulders.

He drew out the scythe, testing the edge against his thumb, then went over and sat down by the window.

In the middle of the hot summer afternoon, Death waited for the bombs to fall.

DEAN R. KOONTZ, (b. 1945), sold his first novel at the age of twenty-one. In the ensuing six years, there have been an additional forty-four, and by the time this anthology appears, there will undoubtedly be many more to add to the list. Initially working strictly within the science-fiction field, during the past two years he has turned his attention more and more toward the suspense novel and the general novel. His first major work in the latter area is the World War II novel, *Hanging On,* scheduled for publication this year. As with many writers of the new generation, he finds the lack of magazine markets for short stories frustrating; the problem is only partly alleviated by the recent popularity of the original book anthology. Very few of those collections publish fantasy in any form. The following story could not have been written twenty-five years ago; it is a modern look at a modern manifestation of an age-old cultural problem.

Nightmare Gang

Dean R. Koontz

Cottery was a knife man. He carried six of them laid flat and invisible against his lean body, and with these half dozen confidence-boosters giving him adequate courage, he challenged Louis to a fight, for he envisioned himself as the leader of the gang. It was over inside of two minutes. Louis moved faster than he had any right to. He avoided Cottery's blades just as if he already knew from which directions they would be swung. He delivered several punches to Cottery that looked like a small boy's blows in a playful bout with his father, but he crippled Cottery with them as surely as he would have wielding sledgehammers. The knife man went down and threw up all over his own shoes.

It was an object lesson.

One was all we needed.

Louis had many holds on us. Although he did not look it, the fight with Cottery proved that he was somehow our physical superior. Of course, there was also the fact that only Louis knew who we were; none of the gang members could remember any past, beyond joining the gang. I'm sure that all of us, at one time or another, tried to find out who we were, but beyond the moment when we were enlisted by Louis, our memories ended at a tall, obsidian wall that could not be breached. Indeed, it was mentally and physically painful to try to remember. Ask Louis? He would only smile and walk away, and that just made us twice as curious.

And only Louis knew our future.

It seemed that there was some purpose to the gang, to the slow growth of our numbers, though no one could fathom what it might be. But leave the group and make our own futures? Butch, our barbarian giant, tried that. He had driven his cycle only a hundred yards on his break for freedom when the cramps hit him and he took the spill at thirty-five miles an hour, skinning himself real bad.

Louis was our jailer; the gang was our prison; and the heavy, black cycles were the bars that contained us.

Then came the run down the Atlantic coast, the pounding of the cycles in the super-heated air, nights on the beaches buffeted by the sound of the waves as we slept, plenty of beer that Louis bought for us (he was the only one with money). On that run, I found out what I was. And what Louis was. And what was going to happen to all of us . . .

Cruising the ocean roads to take in the tourist trap towns like White City, Ankona, Palm Beach, and Boca Raton, we made a wild sight. Flowery-shirted tourists and their matronish wives always pulled off to let us go by, their faces white, the men wiping sudden perspiration from their brows. There were twelve of us in the gang, plus Louis. As in any group, there were those who stood out. Butch was six and a half feet and three hundred pounds, another twenty-five pounds for boots and chains and levis. There was Jimmy-Joe, a stiletto thin little bastard with skin like candle wax and wild, red-rimmed eyes like the eyes of a hunting hawk. He giggled and talked to himself and did not make friends. Yul was the weapons nut. His glittering head (even the eyebrows gone, yeah) distracted your attention from the bulges on his clothing: the pistol under his left arm pit, the coiled chain on his right arm.

The rest of the crew ranged along similar lines, though each seemed a weaker parody of those three. Except for me. I was a natural standout. Although I could be no more than twenty-five, my hair was pure white—eyebrows, chest, pubic, everything. They called me Old Man Toomey.

Then there was Louis.

Louis (you could not call him Lou; it would be like calling Jesus Jess) did not belong in the gang. You could see that in the fine lines of his facial bones, the aristocratic look and bearing that indicated a good private schooling in manners and carriage as well as mathematics and grammar. He didn't have the constitution for the rugged life either, for he was small—five eight, a hundred and twenty pounds, no muscle on him. Yet he was the undisputed leader, the one who had brought us together and was planning what to do with us next.

It was two o'clock on the third day of our coast run, and we were just outside of Dania, Florida, when things began to change. Ahead, a souvenir shop loomed out of the sand and scrub, announced by huge hand-painted signs decorated with pictures of alligators and parrots. Louis raised his arm and motioned us off the highway. We followed him, thumping onto the berm and crunching across the white gravel between half a dozen parked cars. When the clatter and growl of our engines died, Louis dismounted and stood before his cycle, skinny legs spread wide.

"We're casing it," he said. "Don't cause any trouble. We'll be back tonight."

We had never cased a place before. This was the changing point in our existence. Somehow, I knew it was a change for the worse.

We moved inside the shop, fingering the stuffed alligators, carved coconuts, shell jewelry, and genuine Indian thatchwork. The patrons stayed clear of us, their faces pale, their voices lower, more strained than the voices of people on vacation should be. The gang always garnered this sort of reaction from the straight citizens who came into contact with it. We all got a kick out of the sensation of power our appearance gave us, even though most of us must have sensed the basic psychological sickness in such an attitude.

Louis pushed past the sales counter at the back of the store and moved toward a thick, beaded curtain that closed off another room. The clerk, a tanned and wizened little man with gray hair and a prune's share of wrinkles, grabbed him by the arm. "Where do you think you're going?" he asked. His fear quaked down in the bottom of his throat like a wet frog.

Louis didn't answer. He turned and stared at the clerk, then down at the hand that held his arm. After a moment, the clerk let go and stood rubbing his cramped fingers. I could see dark bruises on his hand, though Louis had not touched him. His face had gone totally white, and there was a tic beginning in the corner of his left eye. His fingers seemed paralyzed; he rubbed them frantically as if to restore circulation.

Free now, Louis continued to the beaded curtain and lifted some of the strands to peer through. I was near enough that I could see what was back there: an office of some sort, small, stacked with boxes of trinkets, containing a single desk and chair. Louis seemed satisfied, dropped the beads, and came back past the clerk who made no attempt to stop him this time.

"Let's go," Louis said, walking for the door.

We went.

Two miles from the souvenir shop, we found a secluded section of beach and settled down for the evening. I was still upset about the sudden change of atmosphere, the "casing" of the store. My gut churned, and I felt cold and hollow, afraid of the future simply because I had no idea what it was going to be. Butch and a Spic cat named Ernesto went into Dania for some beer, and a celebration ensued. It was obvious that all of us shared the realization that something big was going to happen, something irreversible.

Louis stayed away from us, walking the beach, stopping now and then to watch a whitecap peel along and spill its froth onto the wet sand. Several times, he threw his head back like a wolf and laughed, high and shrill, until he made his throat hoarse. Several times, when the moonlight limed his chalky features, he looked like one of those small glass animals you can buy in old fashioned curio shops; the illusion was so real that I thought of stoning him, trying to break him. Then I thought of Cottery and the object lesson.

Half an hour after the sun had set and the first heavy

waves of mosquitoes were buzzing out of the shoreline foliage, he came up the beach, kicking sand, and stopped before us. "Let's go back," he said.

I rode up front, just behind Louis. It might have been my unreasonable terror that made me try, in desperation, what I did. I could close in on Louis, I thought, take my cycle into the back of his fast enough to leap over him before we both fell. I might be hurt and hurt badly, but Louis would get his head broken sure as hell. And then we would all be free. Whatever was about to happen would not happen.

I leaned into the bars and was about to accelerate when I felt a hand close over my nose and mouth, cutting off my air. I jerked my head about, could not shake it loose. I could see no hand, only feel it. When I was beginning to grow dizzy and the cycle was wobbling under me, the hand departed, allowing me to breathe.

Louis had won again.

We roared into the parking lot and stopped our cycles behind four cars, dismounted and stood there dumbly, waiting for Louis to tell us what to do. He climbed slowly off his Triumph Tiger and turned to face us. The large orange and green neon sign that blinked and rippled overhead cast eerie shadows on his face, illuminating a wide, toothy grin that split his face like an ax wound. Then he spoke to us. Two words. There is no way to convey the manner in which he spoke the command. He did not use his lips or tongue. Instead, the words came across the front of my mind like teletype print, burning into the softness of my brain so that I squealed. There was no denying that order. No denying it at all.

Kill them!

Almost as a single organism, we moved forward, the stones making brittle protests beneath our boots, into the flourescent brightness of the souvenir shop.

There were eleven tourists in the shop, plus the clerk,

the same little man who had tried to stop Louis from going to the beaded curtain that afternoon. They looked up as we came in, offered us the same timid reactions we were used to receiving. But that was not going to be enough to pacify us this evening. Not nearly enough.

Kill them!

Louis said it again. He stood by the door, grinning, watching, one foot crossed over the other and his hands shoved in his jean pocket.

We moved forward, taking out the hardware we carried.

Butch moved in ahead of me, surprisingly fast for the ox that he was, and swung a huge fist at a banker type in a loud yellow shirt and dark blue Bermuda shorts. He drove the man's nose back into his skull, splintering it into the fleshy gray of his warm brain. The banker did not even have time to scream.

Yul wrapped that steel chain around his fist, moving in on some of the women. His muscular arms, hanging bare from the sleeveless tee-shirt he wore, rippled and flowed like the stalking legs of a cat.

Jimmy-Joe had his hands full of knives. The one in his right was dripping something red.

Kill them!

I took my pistol out. It felt cold and unmanageable in my hand, and I wanted to drop it. I could not. It was as if my hand moved independently of the rest of my body.

A tall man with eyebrows that grew together over the bridge of his nose pushed past me, making for an open window on my right. I fired point blank into his chest. He looked startled, as if he had thought the bullets were blanks and the flowing blood was ketchup, then choked. His eyes watered, and tears ran down his cheeks. Then he fell over on the floor, pulling down a display of post cards.

I dropped my pistol and grabbed onto the sales counter for support. My stomach flopped. I gagged, bent over the counter and brought up my supper of cold chicken and beer.

The rest of that time was hazy, like a sun-ruined section of film. There were shots and screams and pleading voices, blurs of color. I heard a child crying, maybe a little girl. The crying stopped abruptly. Then we were moving out, following Louis, boarding the cycles and leaving the lot.

We went down off the shoulder of the highway, back along the sand to where we had eaten. I fell off my machine when it was parked and rolled over in the sand, face down, trying to think. Sometime later, Butch tapped me on the shoulder and offered me a beer. I declined, then rolled on my back to see what was happening among the rest of them. It was not what I had expected. Jimmy-Joe was standing in the center of the group, playing the part of a woman whose throat he had slit, alternately taking his own role in the affair. When he reached the point where he skewered her throat, the gang laughed and other stories began being exchanged.

Someone broke out several bottles of vodka when the beer ran out, and the party got noisier. I stood up and pushed my way through the gang, trying to reach Louis where he sat next to the tide line. I passed Yul who had droplets of blood spattered across his bald head like freckles. Jimmy-Joe was honing his knives on coral. Butch, his eyes very round and wild, was licking an unknown victim's blood from his hands.

When I reached Louis, he turned and shook his head to let me know he would not talk with me. I tried to say something anyway, but there was an invisible hand in my throat that stopped the words from forming, much like the hand that had almost smothered me when I had thought of killing him. I stood, watching him for some time. He was reading a newspaper, the Miami *Herald*. After a long time, he carefully tore an article from the front page, folded it, and tucked it in his shirt pocket.

Standing, he called to the gang and explained that he would be gone until morning and that we were to enjoy ourselves. Then he was on his Tiger, moving across the sand, gone.

Everyone was silent for a moment, for we all knew what this meant. The only times Louis left us was when he was going to recruit a new gang member. When the idea had sunk in, the revelry began again, slowly at first, then picking up speed and becoming boisterous and jubilant.

I went to the edge of the water and picked up the paper. There was no way to tell what the story had been about, for he had removed all of it. Then I remembered the Gulf station a quarter of a mile back the road. It was highly possible the station had a vendor for the *Herald*— or at least that the attendant had a copy of his own. Someow, the story in the paper tied in with the new recruit. I guess I had some idea that it would shed some light on my own past too. Without thinking of the cycle, I struck out along the beach, crawled up the embankment to the highway, and walked to the service station.

There were two copies of the *Herald* left. When I was about to buy one, I remembered I had no money. Luckily, a car drove up, requiring the attendant's attention, which left me free to steal. I ran all the way back to our camp, fighting the urge to look at it.

On the beach, I spread out the mutilated paper that Louis had been reading, then opened my whole copy and compared them to see what had been torn out. I read the article twice to make certain I was not wrong. Then I threw both papers into the water and went back to my cycle. I did not sleep that night.

In the morning, when Louis came back, I was awake, my eyes stinging, but my mind alert. He brought the new recruit with him, a fellow by the name of Burton Kade. He was the same Burton Kade that had been the focal point of that newspaper article. He matched the front page picture in every detail. Eleven months ago, Kade had used a shotgun on his mother and father while they had lain asleep in bed. Then he had gone on to systematically beat to death his two young brothers, one eight and one ten. He had been executed yesterday morning.

There was a very ugly thought in my mind, one that I did not want to face up to. To avoid it, I began thinking rapidly of other things, of Louis and what he might be. A demon? That seemed unlikely. Why would a demon have to summon up a dead maniac to commit violence when the demon himself could do far worse with his own powers?

No, not a demon, not a devil. I began to remember things about Louis, things that started fitting together in an unpleasant way. There had been the time he had defeated Cottery with childish blows. The time Butch had gotten cramps and wrecked because he was trying to leave the gang. The bruises on the clerk's arm, though Louis had not visibly touched him. The invisible hand smothering me when I tried to kill him. These were examples of . . . what? Mind-over-matter—one of those extrasensory perceptions you hear so much about? In that last instance, there had been a case of telepathy, for the lousy kid had known what I was thinking, had known I wanted to kill him.

This skinny little monster did not seem like the first of a new race: the first esper, the first man able to warp the realities of life and death to recover a body from the grave. Yet . . . he was. The first of a new race . . . and tainted with madness. Maybe that is the price to be paid in this new evolutionary step; maybe all espers will be monsters like Louis. Or perhaps Nature will correct this mistake and make them benevolent. I don't really care. All I know or care about is that Louis is a beast, and it is Louis who is here now, Louis who shapes my future.

And what was my past? What did I do that was so

horrible as to turn every hair on my body white, even though I am only twenty-five?

I do know what is going to happen to us. There have been two massacres since that first, there will be many more. We will never be caught, for Louis uses his psychic powers to search for clues before we leave a scene, uses them to wipe the minds clean of anyone who accidentally sees us.

I am afraid we are immortal: we will go on killing until even the sun is black and hard and dead. We have been brought back from the grave, an even baker's dozen of ghouls. We are the Nightmare Gang that sweeps, gibbering, out of the night and lays waste to whatever comes before it.

We are the Nightmare Gang. We kill while Louis watches, laughing, clutching his sides with his skinny arms.

And the worst thing, the very worst thing is that I think I am beginning to enjoy myself.

BARRY NATHANIEL MALZBERG, (b. 1939), is one of the most prominent of the new generation of science-fiction writers, the so-called New Wave. In the six short years since his first science-fiction story appeared (under the pseudonym of K. M. O'Donnell), he has established himself as one of the major figures in the field. Malzberg's view of the universe is a negative one, whether considering the ramifications of science interacting with society or taking a fresh look at mythology (as in *Cop-out,* a story often overlooked). In the following brief tale, he considers our final retreat into the nightmare world of fantasy.

Elephants

Barry N. Malzberg

It is very dark. The juggler grins, flicks the clubs from one hand to the next: orange, yellow—dim flashes of light striking out. Quick movement then: dim impact of sky to the frozen earth. The last! The last! The Last Juggler!

They watch, nine of them, ten of them, on the bare fields before the stand. Watching the juggler. What unusual intentness! But this *is* the last time. Afterward will come the trapeze, the lions, perhaps a sword eaten whole. And then, finally, the elephants.

But first the juggler. The First of the Last. He prances a little on this, the last night.

"Come," the boy says to the two who are with him. "Come closer. Watch. Maybe we can touch him."

The two say nothing, solemn little girls in pastel dresses (dreams?), lollipops dangling unheeded from their mouths. They have seen so much: fire, disease, loss. And now a juggler. The girls are Six and Eight.

The boy speaks impatiently. "We'll miss it if we don't go now!" He tugs at them, urging them on. There is always the possibility that the juggler might sign his autograph for them—perhaps on a piece of paper, perhaps in the sand. The boy is Ten: an age of significance.

The juggler speaks from his place on the parapet. "And now I will do my final trick! The end of all juggling!" He sighs, winks, tips his belled cap at the sky. "Watch closely, for it is most definitely the last!"

He hurls four, five, six—ah, a Great Man!—clubs into the air, watches them distantly, catches them, flings them one by one into the night. They fall elsewhere, and there is the sound of mud belching, absorbing the falling clubs. The juggler salutes the clubs.

"That is it," he says. "The last. There is no more."

He bows, scrapes his palms. "No applause," he reminds them. "Juggling is finished." He jumps nimbly off the parapet, runs behind the huge tent.

"We missed him," says the boy.

The girls say nothing, staring at the empty stage, hands now on their lollipops. The other watchers wink at them; they are the only children in the crowd . . . except that there are no children there at all. There is barely anybody for the final performance.

"Watch what comes next," says an old man. He nods confidently. "Lions. Trapeze nets. Elephants. Isn't that nice?"

"Very," the boy agrees, but he is thinking of other things: of the juggler who is behind the tent, never to be seen again. "Stop that," he says to Six, who is scratching her palm insistently with the fingernail of one hand. "Don't do that. You know what'll happen."

"What?" asks Six.

"Your hand will fall off."

"Oh." She is not really interested; she cannot imagine a hand falling off. She takes some gum from a pocket, slips it past the lollipop and chews.

"It turns black first," said the boy. "Then it falls off. Give me some gum."

Lights have come up on the parapet again. A man enters with a carrying case. He drops the case, opens it. Two rabbits spring out, dignified as only rabbits can be. They roll on the stage. They are the Last Rabbits, of course.

"Good evening," the man says. "Welcome."

Someone applauds, then remembers the condition. The applause trails off, as though he is ashamed to quit all at once.

"The Last Magic Show," says the man. "And I am the Last Magician."

The rabbits peer at one another. He lifts them, holds them together, touches their noses gently. The rabbits blink, touch tongues. The magician laughs.

"Vanish," he says. He does something with a hand. The

rabbits disappear; suddenly they are on the other side of the parapet.

"Watch closely," he says.

The rabbits are dancing. Their forepaws mesh, cling, they rise to a stiff posture. The magician claps his hands, softly, remembering. The rabbits lumber.

"Dancing rabbits," says the magician. "The Last Dancing Rabbits."

"I don't like this," says Six. "It isn't nice."

"Now they fly!" says the magician. The two rabbits flick out, vanish, reappear on the roof in confusion. The magician salutes them.

"Vanish!" he says.

They do.

The magician stares after them a moment, then turns to the audience. "And now, I need a volunteer."

"He was cruel to the rabbits," says Six. "He didn't have to do that. Now they're dead."

"Quiet," says the boy. He is Ten: he knows of life. Rabbits are born, rabbits die. It is the way of the universe. A condition of existence. Remember the condition. "It's only a trick."

"They're dead," said Eight, speaking for the first time, and taking Six's hand. "She's wrong about most things, but she's right about the rabbits. They're both dead."

"Quiet," says the boy again. "It doesn't make any difference."

"A volunteer!" the magician calls. "For my final trick!"

"I won't go," said Six. "He's cruel."

"Not me," says Eight.

The adults are looking at the children. "You ought to go," the old man says, but the three aren't certain which one of them he is addressing.

"They don't want to," says the boy.

"How about you?"

"Magician shows are for children," a young woman says. "One of you should volunteer—it isn't fair!"

"Not me," Eight repeats. "I ain't no rabbit."

"Volunteer?" begs the magician. He seems to be whining.

The boy shrugs, raises his hand. "I'll go. I volunteer."

The magician looks him over from the parapet. "I don't know. How about one of the girls?"

"They don't want to."

"It's only a little trick."

"Let me," the boy says.

The magician shrugs, turns his back. When he faces them again he has a different face, somewhat younger, with untrimmed mustache. "All right, little boy," he says. "Come on then."

Ten pats Six on the head, tweaks Eight by the ear, touches both for luck. He passes through the others— who, after all, are hardly a crowd—and hops on the stage. And now the boy finds that the magician is drunk. A peculiar foul smell comes from the man's clothing and his lips. He touches the boy. Up closer he is much older, which seems strange; the boy knows little of showmanship.

"Do you play well at vanishing?" the magician asks.

"Sometimes. But I don't want to vanish."

"It will just be for a while."

"They're with me." He points to Six and Eight. "They need me."

"You'll be right back. It only takes a second."

The boy sighs, argument useless. "Vanish me."

The boy hears some rustling behind him, almost applause, as people strain the condition to the limit. The magician darts to a side, brings back a large box, placing it center stage. A deep box, with the cover open.

"In," he says.

"Wait. What will you do to me?"

"Not a thing; I'll do it all. Get into the box, please."
He has adopted a professional manner, a professional
kindness.

The boy wonders if Six and Eight can see into the box.
He hopes not. It is black inside, with speckles of white
and green.

"It is very dark in there," he says.

"Of course it's dark. How did you think it would be?"

"But it's so very dark!"

"When you come out, even the night will seem bright.
Into the box, please!" Again the magician seems whining,
although he also seems much more sure of himself.

The boy shrugs, places a foot delicately inside. A
dampness comes over his foot, passes up his leg.

"I don't like it in there," he says.

"Don't be silly. You volunteered."

"I don't volunteer."

"It's too late. You already have. Get in!"

"No!"

The magician pauses, fondles his chin, considering the
audience. "He doesn't want to go in," he says. "Will anyone take his place?"

The boy hopes that even Six or Eight might volunteer,
but he hears nothing. After a moment the magician says,
"You see? You volunteered, and no one else will take
your place. You must go through with it. Now get into
the box."

The boy shrugs. He is committed to the point where
even he can recognize commitment. He gets into the box,
puts his arms at his side, looks up at the sky.

The magician leans forward, pats the boy gently on
the forehead. "Just relax." He closes the lid.

The boy tries to relax. There are stars inside the box.

"The Last Vanishing!" he hears the magician say.

Six and Eight are fascinated. Next will be the lion

tamer, and the sword swallower. And then the elephants. The elephants must always be saved for the very end.

They plan to volunteer to ride them.

Also edited by Robert Hoskins

WONDERMAKERS
An Anthology of
Classic Science Fiction

The tales included in this collection were written at a time when the technological revolution was fast becoming a reality. Man was questioning, searching beyond the boundaries of his immediate present and into the future. The answers he provided must be considered in the light of his time.

The answers these seekers suggested may now appear irrelevant. What remains important, however, are the queries themselves, universal questions that are still being asked today.

M561   95¢